T0365914

MAYHEM
and
MONKEYSHINES

GLENN CLARK

ARCHWAY
PUBLISHING

Archway Publishing books may be ordered
through booksellers or by contacting:

Archway Publishing
1663 Liberty Drive
Bloomington, IN 47403
www.archwaypublishing.com
844-669-3957

ISBN: 978-1-6657-2876-8 (sc)
ISBN: 978-1-6657-2877-5 (e)

Library of Congress Control Number: 2022915190

Print information available on the last page.

Archway Publishing rev. date: 08/23/2022

CONTENTS

MAYHEM AND MONKEYSHINES

MARY BRENT IN THE MISTY SEAS

MYSTERIES OF MACO MARU

MAYHEM AND MONKEYSHINES

1

....

Mary Lyttle's snug little room was in the attic of her parents' home, and the only thing between her and heaven was a raftered roof that had been drummed all night with a hard rain and an eager wind that had pounded the walls and rattled the windows trying to get in. Under one of these windows, Mary slept all night warm and safe.

When she woke up, it was still raining, and she rolled over in bed to steal another few winks of sleep. Then she remembered it was Saturday. The thought of no school to slow her down the rest of the day gave her the impetus to jump out of bed and go down to breakfast that her mother had waiting for her. After she was through eating, she looked out of the window again.

"Oh, dear," she said. "It's still raining."

This was a little discouraging. Mary had planned to go across town and go beach combing in search of interesting driftwood and maybe that rare sea shell that would talk to her of faraway places and adventure, but the storm had now put a stop to that. Mary, however, always had an escape. Just down the street was The Big Barn, her favorite used book store, and she could often find something fun and exciting in an old book. So, that is where we now find her: sitting on the floor going through a large pile of books that had just arrived.

She stretched out her legs and relaxed, and as she did so, the whole building jiggled slightly, and a volume from high up on a shelf fell into her lap. This small quake didn't bother Mary very much, because there had been a small one earlier, and earthquakes were not uncommon in her part of the country anyway. She set the fallen book aside. Then she picked it up again. It was a very strange looking book. On the cover were the simple words, *The Quest of Mylja*. When she opened it she was surprised to see that there was nothing written on the pages; they all seemed to be blank. She continued to examine each page more carefully and began to realize that they weren't entirely blank after all. One page was covered with something that appeared to be a picture of fog. The more she looked at it, the more she began to see something in it but she couldn't quite make out what it was. It became almost hypnotic, and the fog seemed to be actually swirling around on the page. At that moment, a huge earthquake rocked the whole building, knocking Mary over backward to the floor. Slightly dizzy, Mary sat back up. She still had the book in her hands, and it seemed to draw her into the picture. As she tried to get to her feet, she fell forward, and instead of falling on to the floor of the book store, she fell right through the picture and down an embankment. Dazed, she picked herself up dusted herself off, made sure she still had the crystal medallion that she always wore on a thin gold chain around her neck and looked around.

"Oh, dear!" she cried. "This isn't right. What happened?" She tried to climb back up the embankment, but she kept falling. "This isn't right at all," she kept saying. "Where am I anyway?" She was getting frightened and didn't know what to do. She started looking for some stairs, but there weren't any.

She then could see that she had fallen onto a long beach with a small cove by the sea and that there was an old-style ship anchored off shore. There was also what looked like a mother with two children about Mary's age picking up sea shells and examining them. Having seen Mary fall, they quickly came over.

"My, what a tumble. Are you all right?" the mother asked.

"I think so," Mary replied, examining herself. She looked up and down the beach and then up at the cliff from which she had fallen, wondering where she was and how she could get back to the book store.

"Oh, I'm sorry," the mother said. "I better introduce myself. I'm Mrs. Gimbley, but you should call me Nell. And these are my children, Willie and Nilly."

She patted the boy on the head when she said Willie and the younger girl on the head when she said Nilly.

"How do you do?" They both said together and then waited patiently while Mary gathered her wits about her.

"Well," Mary finally said, "I'm Mary Lyttle, and I wonder if you could tell me exactly where I am. I must be getting back to the book store."

"You came from a book store?" they all asked in unison, but before Mary could answer, the earth gave a big shudder which knocked them all to the ground.

"My, oh, my!" Nell exclaimed trying to rise, but the ground was shaking so much that they all had trouble getting up. "Quickly!" Nell cried. "We must get to the ship. Hold my hands, all of you, and we'll crawl to the boat."

There was a small boat bobbing about at the shoreline that was tied to an anchor buried in the sand, and they hurriedly made their way to it, hauled the anchor out of the sand, and after climbing in, they pushed off, heading for the ship that was rocking violently some way off shore. Nell pulled with a will on the oars, and they soon bumped up against the ship and were pulled aboard by some large, muscular monkeys.

"Come along now, we'll be away in a moment," one of them said.

Imagine Mary's surprise at that. She had never heard a monkey speak perfect English before, and it came as quite a shock. While this was happening, a man standing on a raised part of the stern waved his arms about and shouted orders to the crew that was made up of the same agile monkeys that had pulled them aboard.

"Avast, ye lubbers!" he cried. "Look alive now! Back the fore stay and up with the main. Down with the boom and square the yards! Clear the jib bits and walk the windless." He waved his arms and shouted as the crew went swiftly and efficiently about their business, ignoring him completely, and the ship began to move forward.

"Come along now," Nell said. "We'd best get below to the cabin before we're blown overboard." They climbed down a ladder onto a lower deck and then into a large, stern cabin where they all sat down, finally able to relax.

"That's better." Nell said as the man who had been on the quarterdeck directing the crew joined them.

"Well that's done," he said. "We'll soon be away from this accursed shore. It's not so hard to run a ship you know. And who do we have here?" he asked, looking at Mary.

Nell looked at Mary and winked, and the children sniggered. "Mary, this is my husband Elgard, but we call him El. You might want to call him Captain, but I wouldn't. He thinks he's an old salt, but the closest he ever came to that was when he recently fell overboard."

"Hey, not so loud!" Elgard whispered harshly. "The crew will hear you."

"I think they are well aware of your seamanship by now," Nell said, laughing. "And this, El, is Mary."

"How do you do Mary?" said El, looking Mary over. "And how have you come to be on my ship—oh!—look at this."

They all crowded around the large window that looked out from the stern of the ship. What they could now see was that the ship had been anchored in a small bay surrounded by an island with only a narrow passage between two high headlands. They were under way and had just negotiated the pass into the open sea when the entire island gave a great shiver and slipped below the waves, leaving only a vast empty ocean behind. They watched silently as a huge whirlpool formed where the island used to be. There was good breeze, and the ship was sailing well, but it was slowly being drawn back into the maelstrom.

"Oh, my, oh, my!" El announced and ran back on deck.

The rest of them just watched anxiously out the stern window as the ship drifted slowly toward the hole in the water. Soon the ship began to drift around and around faster and faster, and just as it began to look as if they were going to be drawn down into the whirlpool, the ship steadied and slowly began to pull away. Their eyes were glued on the spectacle when they heard a great gulp, and a large bubble rose out of the hole in the water. It got bigger and bigger until it popped, and then the sea filled in the hole and they were again sailing away on a smooth waters. They couldn't believe they were safe until El came back to the cabin and said all was well. He said that the Monkeyshines—that was the name of the crew—had thrown Dolly Fin, a dolphin that was an old friend of the Monkeyshines, a line from the bow of the ship, and she and others of her kind had been able pull the ship away from the whirlpool just in time.

All this time, Mary was pinching herself, trying to wake up from a bad dream, but all she did was make little red marks on her arm. What was happening? How would she find her way back to the book store now? Or more importantly, how would she ever get home? She was aroused from her thoughts when El spoke up.

"Well, as I was saying a moment ago, what are you doing, Mary, on my ship?"

"It's really not our ship, dear," Nell said to Mary, "it belongs to the Monkeyshines. It's just on loan to us, but we'll explain that later—"

"I would appreciate it, dear," El interrupted, "if I may find out what is going on here. Now, again, Mary, how can we help you?"

Mary was by now beginning to panic. "I don't know what's happening," she said, tears welling up. "I don't know where I am and I don't know how to get home," and she started to cry.

Nelly jumped up from where she was and went over and sat down beside Mary. "Don't cry dear, it's not as bad as you think. It's never as bad as one thinks it is. Our brains play tricks on us sometimes. You'll see. You'll be back in your own bed in no time." Nelly glanced up at El as if to reinforce what she was saying because she didn't know what was happening either.

"Mary," El said sternly, "we must get to the bottom of this. This ship is on an extremely urgent and dangerous journey and we must decide what to do with you." Something in his voice made her look up. "First of all, you must have come from the island, is that right?"

"Well, not originally."

"Where originally then?"

"I was in a book store, trying to read a strange old book, when I fell onto that island and Nelly brought me here."

"A book store," El said thoughtfully, and looked at Nelly, and Willie and Nilly looked at Mary.

"What kind of book?" asked El.

"A crazy book. I told the proprietor I wanted a silly book and he told me where one might be and sure enough I found one."

"Mary," El said exasperatedly, "What kind of book."

"I don't think I can tell you. It didn't make any sense." Mary idly put her hand in the large pocket of her dress... "oh, here it is. I still have it with me." And she handed it to El.

El looked at the book and his eyes got bigger and bigger and then he cried out, "oh, my! Oh, my oh, my!"

and dropped the book in his lap. Willie and Nilly looked at each other, and Nelly got up, walked across the cabin and took the book out of El's hand and sat down again and she too looked at the book and then across the room at El.

"What do we do now?" El finally said looking at Nelly.

Nelly looked at Mary for a long time and nobody spoke, and then she said quietly as if to herself. "Could this really be our contact?"

El heard it and blurted out. "Are you crazy? It's just a terrible mistake. My message must have been blown off course."

"El," Nelly said meaningfully. "We mustn't jump to judgment."

All this time Mary was listening and trying to figure out what they were talking about. "Does this mean that I'm never going to get home?" she finally asked.

"No, no," El said shortly, and then more softly. "No, Mary this has nothing to do with you, we'll get you home no matter what happens." They were all quiet for a long time.

"El," Nelly finally said, "I think we should consider all possibilities."

With a sigh, El agreed. "I guess we had better put all our cards on the table and see what comes of it, what do you think?"

"I think that is a good idea," said Nelly.

El turned to Mary. "It's probable Mary, that you know nothing of what I am about to tell you, but if you do, tell us immediately, otherwise please just listen." Mary sat very still and began to listen to El.

"We will want to know something more about you soon, Mary," El began. "You are undoubtedly from that other land that we've heard about. Our ancient manuscripts talk about parallel universes and mouse-holes through which a few gifted individuals might pass from one world to another and you may be one of those people, but for now we will tell you something about ourselves."

"We live far to the north of here where until recently it was peaceful and quiet. A place where everyone was friendly and considerate. But lately there has been a great change. There has been a curse put on our land. The elders of my village, of which I am one, finally determined that something must be done. As is our custom we wrote our pleas on the special parchment that is necessary, and put them all into a great fire that we built on the mound of our father's graves."

"Why did you throw them in the fire?" interrupted Mary.

"Yes, I should explain. You of course are not familiar with our customs. When it's very important to seek help in an hour of need we build a great fire on the mound where our ancestors are buried. When it is roaring we throw our pleas or requests quests into the fire and as they burn they rise as sparks into the heavens where our Great Father lives. This we did and the next day three of the elders received an answer. One of us was to make a journey far to the south, into the Sea of Ki."

"Do you mean, the Key of C" I know where the key of C is on my piano."

"No, no, Mary. Although I'm glad you are paying attention. I am referring to the Sea Of Kiwa, which we normally shorten into The Sea Of Ki. That is in fact where we are now. It's farther south than anyone in our land has ever been because it's known as a place of magic where strange things can happen at any moment. We were sent here for that very fact because it was said it is here we would find the answer to our problem. You mustn't worry though because we are heading home now. We're running low on supplies and this is as far south as we dare go. The demons dwell just a bit south of here and it seems foolhardy to go any further. Besides, if you have "The Book", Mary, we may have all ready made our contact. As unlikely as it may seem, you may be the one to help us." At that moment Monkey One, the leader of the Monkeyshines called them up on deck. As they watched fluffy clouds scud by in a brisk breeze, wondering what Monkey One wanted them on deck for, he pointed to a great flock of sea birds that were beginning to circle the ship. "That's peculiar," said El, and as they watched, the birds dove on the ship and started pecking at the monkeyshines. They were shrieking and pecking and the monkeyshines had to take cover as they were beginning to bleed from their wounds. El made it back down the ladder, but Mary tripped and one of the birds attacked her. She struggled for a minute and then drew something up that had been hanging around her neck and put it to her lips. It was a whistle and she blew into it as hard as she could, and kept on blowing. At that the birds went even crazier, flying into the masts and sails and onto the deck, finally falling overboard and into the sea, where they finally flew away.

Later, when they had found there way back into the cabin, El turned to his wife. "You see, strange things are happening even down here in this far place. The sea birds have never acted like that before. There is evil stalking about, mark my

"Yes, I know. You'd better finish what you were saying to Mary before the birds arrived," Nelly answered.

"First I want to thank Mary for her intervention in our little problem topside," El said. "That is a remarkable item you carry around your neck. What is it anyway? I heard no noise but it seemed to drive the birds crazy. Might I look at it?"

"Certainly," Mary said, and she handed it to El. "It's made of rare Crystal. My father found it years ago when he was excavating an ancient temple in Babylon. He was told it was very old, but the traders always tell you that. It's supposed to make it more valuable."

"But why did it frighten the birds. It made no noise."

"Oh, that," Mary said, and got up and went over to where El was sitting examining the item, and explained it to him. "You see, it's a whistle that's in the shape of a cross. It has three holes in the ends of the bars. You blow in the bottom end and if you cover the hole in the right cross piece it sounds like this," and she blew into the cross and sounded a shrill sound. "But if when you blow you cover the hole in the left cross piece, it sounds like this," and there was no sound.

"I didn't hear anything," said El.

Mary started giggling. "That's the trick," she said. There was a sound but you couldn't hear it."

"I don't understand," El said.

"Well, there is a sound but we can't hear it because it's so high."

"What's it good for then?"

"Dogs can hear it and it frightens them away. That's why I carry it. I thought it might work on the birds and I guess it did. My father gave it to me so I could keep from being bitten by bad dogs. And the noisy side I can use if I'm lost in the woods."

"Well it certainly worked with the birds" El said. "What does your father do?"

"He designs toys, but he's having a dry spell."

"Aren't we all." El said, giving the whistle back to Mary. "Take good care of it—and by the way, don't lose the book, either, it's priceless."

"And so Mary," El continued the earlier conversation, "you can see that we have serious trouble in our land. As I've said, we were told this is where we would find help and our neighbors the Monkeyshines who are great seamen generously offered us this ship and crew. That is why we are here. Do you know anything at all about this?" El asked.

"No," Mary said, surprised that she would be asked that. "How could I? I don't even know why I'm here—or even where I am," and her lip began to quiver.

"Now, now, Mary, it's all right. I just had to know because the title of your book, which is unusual, is the plea that I sent aloft through the great fire," and then El was silent as he looked out the window of the cabin.

Mary slowly took the book out of her pocket and examined it front and back. The children looked at each other and then at Mary. There was silence for a few moments.

"Either," El began, "there's been a mistake, or you are our contact." El didn't seem to be very happy with either deduction. "Well," he finally said, "There's nothing more that we can do here. Children, why don't you show Mary around the ship," and then he winked at Mary, "they know all the secret hiding places."

While Mary, Willie and Nilly were off exploring, El and Nelly discussed their plans.

"We're as far south as we dare go Nelly," El said. "We're running out of supplies and I don't think there's any point in staying down here any longer."

"You're right," Nelly agreed. "I think we've already made our contact, although I don't know how it can help us."

"You're right there. All right then, we'll head for home and on the way maybe we'll find out what we are to do," and El went on deck to tell the monkeyshines.

2
....

Down below, the children were checking out all the hidden nooks and crannies of the ship and out of breath, they stopped for a moment. It was a calm sea and the ship rolled lazily in a slight swell. Occasionally a larger wave lifted its bow and the ship's timbers creaked and groaned as if the ship were stretching itself in the warm sun.

"This is a pretty big ship, isn't it?" said Mary, looking down the length of the long lower deck.

"It's eighty feet long with a twenty five foot beam— that means wide, Mary, and is the newest ship of the Monkeyshines fleet. She was built as a fishing boat but, has never fished. My father hired her and the Monkeyshines right after she was launched."

"That must be why she smells so good," Mary said. "It doesn't smell of fish at all. It smells of new wood."

"Let's go to the stern," Willie said, "and watch the rudder working, that's always fun."

They made their way aft along the lower deck where bales of goods and spare sails and spars were secured.

"This is a great place to take a nap," Willie said as they passed. "You can curl up in the sails when it's stormy and you don't roll around at all." A little further on they came to the huge rudder. "These are the ropes and sheaves that come down through the deck and run back to the rudder post," said Willie, proudly showing off his knowledge of the great ship. "See how it all works the rudder, Mary? Isn't she marvelous?"

Mary had to agree that it was a most ingenious system, watching the ropes slowly pulling the rudder back and forth as the helmsman overhead steered the ship. They were so proud of their ship that she didn't want to tell them that it dated back over five hundred years in her world. "These are indeed ingenious workings," she finally admitted. "I've never seen anything quite like it. I suppose you have no auxiliary engine?"

"Our biggest engine is the one on deck. You've seen it. That circular thing that everyone walks around to work the pumps."

"No," Mary said, "I don't mean machinery," (Mary knew that in the old days any kind of machinery had been called an engine) "I mean an engine to drive the ship?"

"The wind drives the ship," Willie said patiently as if Mary didn't know a thing about ships.

"I see," said Mary, thinking it best to drop the subject.

"Let's go to the bow," Nilly said to Willie with a significant look.

"Good idea, Nilly," Willie said, and they headed off in that direction, holding onto the ship's timbers to keep their balance as the ship pitched and rolled. In the most forward part of the ship they stopped.

"Now we're going to show you, Mary, our biggest secret. This is something special. Can you keep a secret?"

"Oh yes," Mary said. "Do you want to hear all the secrets I know?"

"You're going to tell me all your secrets?"

"Just a joke," Mary laughed, and the others joined in.

"You shouldn't joke about such things, this is serious business."

"All right, Willie, I'll guard it with my life."

"Good," Willie said. "No one but Nilly and I know about this one." They were on a lower deck and when they had gone as far forward as they could Willie and Nilly stopped near the bow of the boat. "Well, do you see it?" Willie asked. Mary looked all around but could see nothing out of the ordinary.

"I told you it was secret," Willie said "follow me," and he and Nilly slipped through a space that hardly seemed possible and into a small triangular room and Mary followed "Well, what do you think?"

"Where are we?" Mary asked. "I thought I was standing at the very bow of the boat. Is this outside the ship?" Willie and Nilly burst out laughing and it took a few moments to stop.

"No, no," Willie finally said. "We're in the false bow. We call it our bow cave. You see, after they built this ship the builders decided they wanted a longer bow, to make the ship faster, so they built one right over the old one which left this area inside. This is the old bow," he said tapping a curved pointed timber behind them. "Neat isn't it?"

"It certainly is. I was standing right next to it and couldn't see it." Willie and Nilly had built a short bench along one side and a ledge for candles along the other which they now lighted and it was quite comfortable.

"I'll bet it can get bouncy when it's rough outside," Mary said, getting a little queazy as the bow went up and down in the swells.

"I did get sick once when it was really storming out but you get used to it."

"I never got sick," Nilly said.

"That's right," Willie agreed. "She's got an iron stomach."

"Tell me," Mary finally said, when her stomach settled down. "What's it like where you live?"

"Oh it's fine, Willie said, "It's way up north. We're probably heading there now. It's a wonderful place to live really—or it was until the troubles began. The water is a lot warmer than here."

"We do a lot of swimming," Nilly said, "I love to swim."

"Are you a good swimmer?" Mary asked.

"Nilly can swim like a fish," Willie answered. "She should. I taught her."

"That's right he did. He threw me in to sink or swim."

"Well you learned to swim didn't you?"

"In a hurry!"

It was a cozy place to sit and talk, but by then it was time to return to the others and they went back to the cabin not knowing how soon they were to need that very spot.

The next day they set a course for El's Island. El, Mary and the children were on deck and El asked Monkey One what progress they were making.

"Not very much," he replied. "The wind isn't cooperating. It keeps setting us to the south. It will come around though. It has to eventually," and they sailed on trying to get the ship to move north.

The next day they were all on deck again when the lookout high up in the mainmast cried out, "Ship ahoy, on the port quarter," and they all looked to see what it was.

"What ship?" called Monkey One. "Friend or foe?" There was silence for a minute and then the look out called down to the deck.

"Can't say sir. Can't make it out. She looks in distress."

"All right," Monkey One said to the helmsman, "set a course for her and we'll take a look."

El, Mary, and the others leaned their elbows on the rail with their chins in their hands and looked at the strange ship that was getting closer.

"She's in distress, all right," El said, "look at the sails," and what they saw was a derelict ship that looked as though she had just risen out of the depths from her deep sea grave. Barely afloat, she was wallowing in a mass of Sargasso Oweed, the seaweed that's sometimes found floating in the open ocean. From her two masts that must once must have carried a fine spread of sails, now only bits of canvas fluttered. And then they saw something else.

"Someone's at the wheel waving to us," Monkey One said.

"That's what it looks like," El said, but when he hailed the derelict ship through a huge brass trumpet with repeated calls, he got no response.

"What do you think?" El asked Monkey One.

"I don't like the looks of her," he replied. "She looks like a ghost ship."

"But wasn't that someone waving to us?"

"Not living."

"What do you mean?"

"An evil spirit I'd say."

"Should we board her?"

"Could be disease."

"How old does she look?"

"She's an ancient ship. I've only seen one like her in history books."

"Whomever was waving at us seems to have disappeared," said El, squinting at the other ship, "lower a boat and I'll go aboard her," but Monkey One was looking up into the rigging. "That's peculiar," he said, and they all followed his gaze up to where their own sails instead of full with wind and drawing as they had been only a minute before, were now simply hanging limp from the spars while only a few hundred yards away the sea was roiling with white caps.

"I don't like this at all," Monkey One muttered. "Something unnatural is going on here."

"It seems even more important now that I visit that ship," said El. "Maybe it can tell us something."

"I don't recommend it," said Monkey One. "I think we should get out of here and the faster the better."

Monkey One was determined to leave the area as quickly as possible, but soon realized that that wasn't going to be easy. When they had approached the derelict ship they had been caught up in a river current that was flowing in the middle of the sea and were now unable to free themselves. They were a cable's length behind the old ship and continued to hold that position no matter what they did, both being pulled along at the same rate by the river. Just a few yards on either side of them the wind was blowing spindrift off of white caps, but where they were it was dead calm and the sargasso weed that encircled the old ship was now beginning to encircle their own.

"It appears to me." El said, "that we are going to be here for awhile, and as long as we are, I think it wise for me to board the derelict and see what I can find out."

"I'll go with you," Mary said. "If there is disease aboard I don't think it will harm me."

"You may be right," El said. "You can come along, but just the two of us," and the boat was lowered. They struggled through the weed that was getting thicker and thicker, over to the hulk, and climbed up some of the old rigging that was hanging over the side that was not too rotten to break.

On deck they viewed disaster. There was no one about, not even a skeleton, only the broken remains of a once fine ship. Shrouds, the ropes, that were holding up the mast were being pulled out of the rotten hull and bits of sail and tarred hemp littered the deck. The ships wheel where they thought they had seen someone earlier now stood alone and where the pilot should have been standing there was only a bit of magnetic iron floating on a piece of wood, once an ancient compass.

They made their way, carefully avoiding holes in the crumbling deck, over to a ladder that led below where they searched for the captain's cabin. In the dim light they thought they had also found the captain resting his head on his desk, but closer inspection found only the white bones of his skeleton clothed in animal skins.

El fingered the clothing that fell apart in his hands. Then they gently pulled a large ledger part way out from under the arm that had been resting on it and they read a terrible tale. It was the log book of the "Threwn" the unlucky ship they were standing on and it chronicled the last year of its voyage.

"On the thrice of Yen, we slipped Old Jephne over the side." the captain had noted and continued to chronicle the loss of his shipmates.

Later he wrote, "Only Cooker and me left. It looks like the end is near."

And then, "Food gone. This accursed stream has had us in its claws for two years and I know now I'll never be free. Cooker went today." That was why there were no skeletons on board. They hadn't died of disease, but of starvation and had been buried at sea. And then the final page read:

"Today, the Belf of Gander, I make my last entry. They've all been laid to rest and may our God be gentle with them. I alone remain to close out the log this Midland day in the reign of Gondorf the Third—". With no writing material left he had been writing with his own blood and at that point there was a long smear across the page where his life had run out.

El stood staring at the last page for quite a long time and then muttered to himself. "That's not possible."

"What's not possible?" Mary asked.

"Gondorf reigned a thousand years ago." Mary looked at the ledger again.

"The Flying Dutchman," she said to herself.

"The what?" El asked.

"The Flying Dutchman," Mary repeated. "It's a myth about a tattered old sailing ship that is cursed to sail the seas forever. It can sometimes be seen on stormy nights. Maybe it's not a myth at all."

"Maybe not," El mused. He started to pick up the log book but it was too rotten to stay to together and he put it back down. "We'd better leave things as they are for now," he said and they made there way back to their own ship.

Back on board they related to the others what they had found.

"But what about the man we saw at the wheel waving to us?" asked Nelly.

"There was no one on board," El replied.

"I told you what it was," Monkey One reminded them.

"Well whatever it was," El said, "we had better see if we can get out of this stream. Do you notice how cold it's getting? And look how much farther north the sun has become. We're drifting south and will soon be in the ice fields if we're not careful" and they all got out their heavy coats finding one for Mary in Willie's things.

For the next several days they tried everything to break out of the grip of the stream. The sails were useless and trying to whistle up wind didn't work. They even lowered one of the ships boats trying to tow the great ship out of the stream without success. Gloomily day after day they followed the derelict ship across leagues of open sea.

Monkey One had been strangely thoughtful since El and Mary had gotten back from the derelict ship and he suddenly said, "I've been trying to recollect something I read long ago and now I remember where it was. Come with me to my cabin. I want to show you something."

Monkey One, being the Captain of the ship, had his own small cabin and Mary and El followed him down to it. From a small book case on one wall he took a book., "This" he said, "is a book of runes—ancient songs handed down from our ancestors that record important happenings in our distant past. Some of them go back thousands of years. This is not an original but a recent translation from the old runic tongue." All the time he had been talking he had been going through the book's pages and finally said, "Ah—here it is. Read this." Mary and El took the book from Monkey One and read the following.

> Sailing alone in the southern sea
> In a tempest's eye, trying to flee
> I saw a vision drop from sight
> Then rise again in the dawns cold light
>
> From out of the deep on crested wave
> Where spindrift flies o'r deep sea grave
> A ship in distress I see just now
> Deep in the stern and down at the bow
>
> With tattered rag sails she struggles by
> A little ship that's about to die
> I hail her then a fathom broad
> But on she sails with nary a nod
>
> From a specter gaunt with lifeless stare
> And bits of seaweed wrapped in his hair
> Tied to the wheel with rotting slime
> The Captain stands gaunt with little time

And on the ships stern I barely read
Through barnacle old encrusted weed
My own ships's name, frightening to see
For here I sail and here I will be

A wandering soul for ever more
Never again to reach a shore.
When in a trough it disappears
To slip away as a new night nears

Leaving a wild and wandering wake
Where now I sit and shiver and shake
Fearful of what I next will see
Sailing alone in the southern sea

"What do you think of that?" Monkey One said, when they had finished reading.

"When was that written, do you think?" asked El.

"These were from—" Monkey One looked in the back of the book—"in the reign of Gondorf II."

"Gondorf II," El mused. "That would be a thousand years ago."

"That's right, a thousand years," said Monkey One.

"Well," El said, "only we three have seen this so far and we want to keep it that way. I suggest we now forget it. We don't want to spook the crew. No one must mention it again."

"That will be easy for me to do," said Monkey One with a shiver, and put the book away. Mary heartily agreed.

Back on deck they noticed patches of ice beginning to form around the ship, and then the small patches of ice began to grow into icebergs. Soon they were surrounded completely by the ice that was getting thicker and their ship began to slow as it ground against the frozen snow and then suddenly stopped. The derelict ahead stopped for just a moment and then it broke free from the ice and they watched as the ghost ship that had so long been their companion began to move away. With great relief they saw it sail away over the horizon still in the grip of its tenacious stream while they stayed locked in the ice.

Although they wondered about the fate of the other ship they were happy to see it disappear and celebrated with the last of their hot tea The party was short lived however when the realization set in that they were then locked in ice that was slowly carrying them south into the unknown where few had ever been and from where no one ever returned. They each went to bed that night with their own thoughts and dreams.

The next day they took stock of their situation. They had been six months out from their last landfall and although there was plenty of water in the form of ice and snow, there was little food left and El summoned everyone on deck.

"People," he said, "I must be honest with you. I don't know how much longer we can hold out. If the worst should happen I want you to know how sorry I am to have subjected you to this ordeal. However I have not given up and hope that you haven't either. I have confidence that we'll make it through all this after all—" At that moment Nilly happened to look out over the vast ice sheet.

"Daddy," she said, "What's that way over there?"

"Where, Nilly?"

"That dark spot, over there."

"Well, let's see—" El said picking up his telescope. After a few moments he called Monkey One over. "Look at this," he said, and Monkey One took the glass.

"Well, I'll be," Monkey One said. "If it's not a mirage I'd say it's an island sticking out of solid ice. It seems to have green trees and growing things on it."

"If we can make it over there," El said, "maybe we're saved. At least for awhile."

It must be several miles across the ice and I don't know how firm it is," Monkey One mused. "Through the glass it appears to get thinner as you reach the island—or whatever it may be."

"This ice sheet that we're in seems to be drifting in that direction," El said. "I suggest we do nothing until tomorrow and then see what it looks like. Keep a good watch on tonight, Monkey One, and the rest of us had better get some sleep. We'll need our strength tomorrow." They all went to bed with new hope that their situation would look better in the morning.

At first light the next day they all rushed on deck wondering what they would see and were overjoyed to find themselves in a bay just off shore of the land that they had seen the night before. They were in clear water and the ice that they had been locked in for several days was now about a half mile away. It still encircled the bay they were in and stretched out as far as the eye could see, but at least for now they were free of it. The ice must have been thinner toward the island and had moved the ship in the direction of least resistance. It seemed that this part of the world was warmer than its surroundings and had thawed a hole in the ice. Only a few hundred yards to the south lay the land that had seemed so far away and now here it was almost tropical with its green foliage and tall trees. After they had quickly anchored their ship they observed figures standing on the beach waving to them.

"Whoever they are they look friendly," El said.

"Yes," Monkey One said, "but you can never tell. It may be a trap."

"Well, we need to find out and in a hurry. We can't hold out much longer. Put a boat down and Mary and I will go ashore."

"You'd better take some armed men with you," Monkey One said.

"No, we'll go unarmed. We don't want them to think we're hostile"

And so El and Mary put out to shore. As they approached the figures on the beach El exclaimed, "They're the Elves! Well I'll be!" and he ran the boat onto the sand where he and Mary got out. Mary was now only a little surprised at anything in this new world and saw that they were indeed Elves who rushed up to cordially greet them both.

"Welcome to our home strangers," the leader of them said, "It's not often that we have guests."

"Thank you indeed," El replied, "You have no idea how glad we are to see friendly faces. You are northern Elves I believe. What are you doing way down here? My people haven't heard of you in years."

"Ah, I thought you looked familiar," said the elves leader "You are our northern friends. Well, even though we no longer are neighbors we are still friends and I speak for all of us. I am Trando and you are?"

"This is Mary and I am called El."

"Well, El and Mary, you are a long way from home. Why so?

"I'm afraid that's a long story that we'll tell you later, but why do we find you down here encircled by ice."

"First come to our lodge," Trando said, "we must have a little celebration of your visit—and by the way—you can take off your coats now. You may not have noticed, but we live here in a temperate zone. You will need no wraps as long as you're here with us."

It was true. El and Mary had been so involved in talking with the Elves they hadn't noticed how warm the air had gotten. "How is this possible," El observed, "you're surrounded by ice."

"Come along and we'll explain everything. Is there anything your crew can use. We can send a boat out to them."

"I'm afraid they need just about everything. We've had a hard trip and had just used up all our food when we spotted your island. This has been a miracle."

"Well, I'll have you resupplied in no time," and he called to some of his people who rushed off into the jungle. "By the end of the day you will have enough supplies to last a year. You see we have an abundance of natural resources here. We are never in need."

While the ship was being supplied Mary, El, and Trando and some of the elf elders retired to the lodge and feasted and when they were done, Trando told El and Mary the Elve's story.

"You are in the southern ice fields. From here south there is only ice, thousands of miles of ice. There is land beneath the ice, but it lies one mile below and does not surface—except for this bit that you are now sitting on."

"Then this is not an island."

"No, it's just a point of the land that from here sinks below the ice. It's a vast land that surfaces only at this point."

"Why does it surface here do you think?"

"You've noticed how warm it is here? There's a great fire beneath us that has pushed up the land and brought it to the surface. Those fires bubble to the surface creating warn pools of water in which we swim and bathe, and in the hotter ones we cook our food. It creates conditions ideal for crops and the lush growth that you see all around you."

"That's what keeps the ice melted in the bay and the temperature so mild," El added.

"Exactly."

"But how did you find this place and how long have you been here?" El asked.

"We found this place much as you did, being shipwrecked on its shores roughly seven hundred years ago."

"Seven hundred years!" El exclaimed. "I knew from our histories it had been a long time since any of you had been seen, but had no idea it had been so long. Do any of you go back up north?"

"Oh, no. We have peace here. We have everything we need. We don't miss the 'Out Side' at all."

"But if your ancestors came here seven hundred years ago, aren't you who have never been 'Out Side' curious as to what it might be like."

"We are our ancestors. We've been here from the start."

"What do you mean?"

"We are the same people that were originally shipwrecked here. I remember it as if it were yesterday. I also remember what it was like on 'The 'Outside. You see here we live forever. Even if we wanted to leave, which I assure you we don't, we wouldn't last a week. Away from these life giving waters we'd die."

"So that's why we've missed you up north," El said.

"I'm afraid that's it. Now you must tell us about yourselves."

"It's a rather long story and just now I must get back to my ship to see that everything is well. If we may, we'd like to come back tomorrow and then we'll have time to tell you all about it."

"You are welcome anytime," Trandy said. "I look forward to your return." El was inclined to believe Trando's fantastic story, but even though Mary had experienced other strange things in this land, she wasn't so sure about this one.

3

On the way back to the ship Mary asked El something that had been bothering her.

"Tell me El," she asked, "How is it that we—specifically I—can understand what all these people are saying to me. For instance, the monkeyshines, the Elves and even you. I have the feeling that you're speaking different languages, but I understand you completely."

"I've wondered about that myself," El said. "I know these languages because I've studied them, but with you it's different. There is a theory brought forth by some of our brightest that in some cases thought alone can be transferred from one person to another. In these cases language is only important to form the ideas in the senders mind and then the thought itself is transferred to the receiver—mind to mind. It has never been proved, but in your case it seems to be possible."

"Wow, I've got to ask my father about this—that is if I ever get back," she added wistfully.

"You'll get back all right. You needn't worry about that."

Back on board there was rejoicing. A banquet had been laid out and all the monkeyshines were making the best of it devouring food they hadn't seen in a year.

"What kind of place is this?" called Monkey One. "Look at this food. Are you sure your friends are not just fattening us up for their kettle?"

"No, no," El laughed, "I'll tell you all about it later. Continue your feast."

They all celebrated most of the night, and the next day El told Monkey One, Nelly Willie and Nilly, all about the previous day and when he had finished he and Mary, and this time Nelly Willie and Nilly, went ashore again.

"I can see why the Elves might be reluctant to leave this place," El said to the others, as they approached the beach, "it's a paradise."

"It seems creepy to me," Willie said.

"Oh?" El said, "what bothers you?"

"That food I had last night. It was too good. It must have been enchanted."

"It tasted a little like mango to me—with a bit of banana, said Mary. "We have something like it back home. You may not have it up north."

"That's probably it," El said and when they reached shore the Elves were there to help pull the boat up on the beach.

"Come along now," Trandy said as he escorted them up to the roundhouse where, after the new members Nelly Willie and Nilly were introduced to Trandy, they all sat down.

"Now, El." Trandy said, last night we never got to talk about you. What brings you to our fair land?"

"Fair enough, I'll try to explain, El said. "You are pretty well insulated down here from what's going on up north so you may not be aware that recently there's been an increase in trouble in our land."

"Things don't change much, do they?" Trando said.

"Well, for quite some time we had a reasonable peace with only the occasional upheaval, but two years ago things got so bad that we elders decided that something extraordinary had occurred. We decided we must do something about it and to make a long story short, I was voted to look into it. The Monkeyshines were nice enough to put their ship at my disposal, but along the way we have had some set backs," and El went on to tell Trandy their story up to the present.

"Well," Trandy said when El had finished, "You have had an eventful journey. As you suggested, we here have no knowledge of your problems up north, but I can tell you something about the mystery of your phantom ship. You see we encountered one and the same. It was he that brought us here—against our will. We also saw a ship in distress and when we went to help were caught up as you were. It worked out well for us however. That was seven hundred years ago. And once every few hundred years we see the same ship again sail by on it's endless journey."

"Do you mean to tell me it's that old?"

"Oh, much older probably.—It's history has been lost in antiquity. You are fortunate that you could free yourself from her. It's said that she sails the seas setting traps for unwary mariners that are never seen again. Did you see her captain waving for you?"

"We saw something that seemed to be waving, but it may have been a bit of rag."

"Yes, possibly."

"Mary here tells me of a ship that in her land too is cursed to sail forever."

"That brings up a question that I have, Mary. If I understood El correctly, you are from that other world that sometimes bumps into us?"

"I don't know about bumping, but I am definitely from another world."

"Well we welcome you. I am in accordance with El in thinking that you must be here for an important reason. Such things have only been hinted at in our histories and I for one have never known one of you. I hope you'll take back to your world good memories of ours."

"Oh, I will. You've all been so kind."

"We may be, but keep your wits about you. It appears that you are here for some serious business and that could mean something more than sight seeing. But enough of the gloom, I believe I see our food arriving."

After dinner they discussed the possibilities of El getting their ship through two or three miles of ice and back to open water.

"Well," Trandy said, "there's a good possibility of that—eventually anyway."

"What do you mean, eventually?" El wanted to know.

"It depends on the spring thaw. Up north right now it's your summer, and here it is our winter. We are right now in the dead of winter, that's why you see so much ice. If we have an early thaw, by mid summer the ice may be thin enough for you to break out. There's about a two week window. If it's a late thaw—well, there's always next year."

"What do you think? I mean what are the chances? Next year is out of the question."

"There's no way to tell at this time. Maybe we'll get a better idea in about six weeks. Anyway, you have about a month to wait so relax and enjoy our hospitality. We'll take good care of you. Come back tomorrow. I might have another idea for you." It was by then time to go and after thanks all around for the dinner they went back to the ship.

"What's the news?" was the first thing Monkey One wanted to know.

"No chance until next spring and we won't know about that for several weeks. Do you have any ideas?" El replied.

"None at all. We'd better listen to the Elves. They know best what the conditions here are."

The next day Nelly had chores to do and stayed on board while El, Mary, Willie and Nilly went back to visit the Elves.

Trandy was waiting for them on the beach when they arrived and escorted them to the meeting house. Have you had breakfast?" Trandy asked.

"Oh yes, we are all well fed."

"Good," Trandy said, "Then we can get right down to business. I've been thinking about your problem and there may be a way to help you. There's a wise man that lives far to the south of us that on rare occasions we consult. The journey is long and dangerous and we rarely attempt it unless our need is desperate—one of our expeditions was lost and never found—but on other occasions when we were able to reach him he has helped us. I want to warn you again it's a treacherous trip, but it might be worth seeing him. Although he's a very strange character he seems to be of good heart."

"Why do you think this wise man could possibly help us?" El asked.

"You seem to have doubts, but I'll explain. We are very resourceful and need little help but a few things have occurred in the past that were out of our control and that is when we have searched him out. On these occasions Cesibourne—that's his name—has performed miracles. He's more than a wise man, he also has powers that are not of this ground."

"How far south is this Cesibourne?"

"As far south as you can go. With only the normal difficulties of the trip it takes about a week, but if you encounter the unforeseen it can take months. It has been said that on one of our trips it was so cold that when a fierce gale blew the coat right off of one of our people he froze solid in mid stride. He was still standing there on the return trip and had to be chopped down as you would a tree to get him buried. If that story is true his death was not in vain for that trip saved our village."

"How does he live in such a climate?"

"Cesibourne lives in a castle made entirely of ice crystals. It is perched on top of a mountain that is the only other bit of rock that is above the ice besides the one you're standing on. However it's not warm there as it is here. It's a cold mountain that he heats with a magic stone that warms his castle without melting it. I've seen it only once and hope never to see it again."

"What do you really think our chances are in getting away this spring?" El asked.

"I didn't want to tell you, but it's about one chance in ten. You washed up here in one of the rare thaws that occur every ten years. It usually means we're in for several years of hard ice. Sorry."

"Thank you for being honest with me. You see it has baring on whether we need to see your Cesibourne or not. We'll have to think it over carefully. We can let you know tomorrow."

"One other thing," Trandy said, we have to notify Cesibourne that your coming. He's a recluse, very private, and must always be notified. It's not a problem. A message is sent by Stormy—he's our resident petrol sea bird—that takes two days round trip to be affirmed by Cesibourne on Stormy's flight back. This only affects you in that you must be ready to go on the arrival of Stormy. You must be ready around noon the day after you decide to go. That is enough time for the two messages to be sent."

"That's satisfactory. Noon the day after we make the decision to go. Whatever that day is."

"That's correct."

"Well, I guess that's all we can do today. We'd better get back to the ship. We have a lot of thinking to do."

"That you do," Trandy agreed. "We'll be hearing from you tomorrow then," he said, and escorted them down to their boat.

All that night they discussed the pros and cons of taking such a journey. Monkey One said no way should they make that journey. It was better to wait out a thaw even if it took years than to stake one's life on a trip like that. El thought they should look into it further. If this were such a wise man, it might be smart to communicate with him if that was possible. So they decided to talk it over with Trandy again.

The next day they asked Trandy if he thought they could ask the wise man what to do and it was agreed that Trandy would send a note to him outlining the request. It had been decided that in the event that they attempted the journey, only El, Mary, one of the monkeyshines and one elf would go, and they spent the two days waiting for the reply to their message in outfitting themselves.

They were ready when Stormy returned with the reply from the wise one and it wasn't what they had expected.

"Under no circumstances attempt your trip. There is no possibility of success. Conditions are unusually bad with mountains of ice a thousand feet high and crevasses a thousand feet deep. Anyway it's too cold. You seem to be in desperate straights and so I offer you an alternative. Misty— my eagle—can easily make the trip in a day and can carry one person. That person will be the girl Mary. That is my offer. Make no amendments to it. You have three days to reply."

When they had read the note they sat around looking at each other. Finally, El asked Trandy what he thought of the note.

"Cesibourne is never wrong. If he says it's too dangerous it certainly must be. The trip cannot be made as far as I can see." They sat silently for a minute and then El looked at Mary studying her.

"Why do you think Cesibourne wants Mary, Trandy," he asked.

"I have no idea. He's never made this offer before. I did mention in my note to him that there was a girl called

Mary possibly from that other world that would like to talk to him. I thought it might help him make up his mind."

"I think it did," El said. "But I wonder why he wants to speak only to the girl. He could have picked any one of us that might better understand what we are to do."

"As I said before," said monkey One, "I'm for forgetting the whole thing. We can get out of here eventually and besides this place isn't so bad."

"He may be right," said Trandy. "I doubt if you'd be here more that several years. It has always thawed—in time."

"I don't mind going," Mary spoke up, "if you want me to."

"El turned to Trandy, "How safe do you think Mary would be. Do you know Cesibourne that well?"

"I can't say that I would stake my life on her safety—let me put it this way. All our dealings with him have been straight up. I believe him to be good and honorable. If it were I that he requested I wouldn't hesitate to go."

Finally El stood up. "I have a headache, and we have at least one day to make up our minds so I suggest we go back to the ship, get a little rest, and continue this later. We'll see you, Trandy, tomorrow, and let you know our decision."

"I suggest you think it over well, El and particularly you, Mary."

"That we will, Trandy and thank you," said El. "We'll see you in the morning," and they went back to the ship.

4

Back on the ship they discussed their problem. "All we have to go on is what the Elves have told us about this Cesibourne fellow," said El. "They seem to know him pretty well, but I'm not at all at ease in trusting Mary's life with him."

"He seems creepy to me," said Willie.

"I tend to agree with you, Willie.

"I tend to agree with you, Willie. On the surface, even though we don't know him personally, he seems strange, but that's not always bad. Conclusions jumped to can get one in a lot of trouble."

For hours the banter went on and with seemingly no answer until Mary finally put it to rest. "I'm going," she finally said with finality.

"I'm not sure we're ready to make a decision, Mary," El said.

"I know, we've been at this for hours and nobody can make a decision, that's why I'm making mine. I'm going. Now lets go to bed, I'm tired," and that is how it was decided.

In the morning there was little discussion about the night before. All were pretty quiet. "Are you sure Mary?" El finally asked and Mary assured him she was.

"You are not in my shoes, El," she said. "Look at it from my point of view. How can this stunt be any more crazy than what I've already been through?"

"Strange as it seems," said El, "I've come to the conclusion that if anyone should make this decision it should be you." Ell knew that every week they spent where they were would be a week spent in not doing what they had been sent out to do and another week that his people would be suffering. Maybe Mary knew best anyway. "All right everyone let's go ashore."

When they had made the arrangements Trandy sent "Stormy" off to deliver the message that Mary would go and that Cesibourne should send "Misty" for her as soon as it was convenient. By then Mary was having second thoughts about her decision, wondering what she was getting herself into, but it was done and she always kept her promises and she waited patiently with the others for "Misty".

"Misty" was not expected until the next day so while El talked over old times with Trandy, Mary, Willie and Nilly explored the forest that surrounded Trandy's home.

The clearing that held Trandy's settlement was surrounded by a forest that seemed to go on forever and they set off to see what they could see.

"I've never seen a forest like this before," Willie said, looking up at the trees that towered over their heads.

"We have trees like these where I come from only they're smaller. We call them palm trees. They only grow in the tropics so you probably wouldn't have seen them—well look at this!" Mary exclaimed as they came into a clearing. Before their eyes was a large pool of crystal clear water. Around the edge were benches with towels draped over the backs. "This must be the pool they talked about. The one they swim in." Mary leaned down and touched the water, that was not hot, not cold, but just right. "What do you say we go for a swim," she said.

"I don't know if that's a good idea," Willie said. Maybe we should ask Trandy first. Besides we don't have bathing suits."

"Oh it will be all right." Mary said, "and don't be so modest. You go undress behind those trees over there and swim in that end of the pool, and I'll swim here," and so that's what they did and had a wonderful time.

When they got back to the others Mary told them about their swim and Trandy's eyes got very large.

"Oh you shodden't have done that," he said very seriously.

"I told you so!" Willie blurted out. "I told you so!"

"Why is that?" Mary asked getting a little worried. "There were towels and everything."

"Oh you just shouldn't have done it. Oh my, Oh my, you've done it now," and Trandy rolled his eyes.

"Mary's heart had moved up into her throat at those words. "But why?"

"Well I guess there's no point in not telling you now that it's done," Trandy said tragically. "Now you'll never be able to leave our village. You're here forever I'm afraid."

"I knew it! I knew it!" Willie blurted.

"What are you talking about?" Mary wanted to know. She wasn't quite sure about Trandy.

"That's the pool that we bathe in. It is why we live for ever. But it also makes us vulnerable to the 'outside.' Once we have bathed in the pool of perpetual life we may never leave this area or we will die."

"Mary looked over at El who was stone faced. She looked back at Trandy while Willie kept repeating "I knew it, I knew it." As she stared at Trandy trying to see if he was serious she saw a little twitch in the corner of his mouth and then he burst out laughing.

"All right, you have me," he said still laughing. "Just a little joke of mine. You're all right. It didn't hurt you to swim in our pool, but after this, ask first. There are situations here that could be dangerous for you."

"We'll be all right, then?" Willie wanted to be assured.

"You'll be fine Willie."

"Don't do that again, Mary," Willie scolded. "It could have been serious."

"All right, Willie," Mary said, and she was laughing too. By then it was time to go back to the ship and there they went to bed early so as to get a good rest. Tomorrow was to be a big day.

El, Mary, Nelly, Willie and Nilly, and Monkey One were sitting in the patio of Trandy's house at ten as they said they would be and they made small talk between the silences as they waited for Misty to fly in. Mary had made many friends in her short stay with the Elves and they were all there to see her off and it being so quiet was making Mary nervous. It was more like a funeral than she would have liked. It was just to be a simple trip after all she kept telling herself. Soon they saw a speck in the distant sky that kept getting larger and larger until it loomed into view. It was the biggest eagle Mary had ever seen. It glided in and looked as though it were going to make perfect landing, but as it touched down its little legs gave way and it did a perfect somersault. Misty got up quickly looking unconcerned, brushed himself off with his wings and said "Please don't applaud good people, just one of my many tricks. I'm afraid I won't be able to attend my arrival party. We must go immediately if you're ready. There's a storm on the way and it looks like a big one. Just jump on my back, Mary, and hang on. You'll be all right." By now Mary was getting used to talking animals so was not very surprised at his announcement.

El and Trandy hoisted her up onto Misty's back and El whispered in Mary's ear, "Are you sure?" and as Mary said "I guess soooo"—'Misty' took off with a great swoosh. Mary had just enough time to look back and see her friends waving from Trandy's patio before they were out of sight.

Mary had been fitted out with the warmest clothes available to her, but she was beginning feel as though she were freezing and she buried her face deeper into "Misty's" feathers where it was warm.

"Hang on Mary," 'Misty' called back to her, "we're in for it now I'm afraid. I told Cesibourne it would be bad, but he insisted I go for you immediately. He seems very anxious to see you—Oh, Oh, hang on—" and they were immediately shot skyward in a blast of frigid air. For the next fifteen minutes they were thrown about like a cork in the gale, right side up and wrong side down, sideways and backwards until they were finally out of the worst of it and when they had leveled out, Misty asked, "Are we all here?"

"I think so," Mary replied. "Are you all right?"

"I'm all right, but a little tired. I'm going to put us down behind that big ice bank. We can get a little rest there."

When they had landed Mary asked with a little concern, "Is this wise? shouldn't we continue on. Mightn't this storm get worse."

"Oh, it probably will." But instead he sat down.

"Well then shouldn't we go."

"We probably should," Misty said, "but I've lost my way."

"You don't know where we are!" Mary said incredulously.

"Oh, I know where we are," he said, but made no move to get up.

"Well then, shouldn't we be on our way?"

"Yes we should. You're entirely right. You see I know where we are, we are behind this large block of ice—the problem is I don't know in what direction to go."

"I thought you made these trips often. Aren't you Cesibourne's best?"

"Oh, my, no—I once was—but that was long ago. The other eagles are on patrol so here I am."

Mary considered this bad news. "But you must know the way to your home."

"I do, I do. Have no fear. When the sky clears I'll be able to navigate by the sun—or the stars. I used to fly by the stars a lot. It's beautiful flying by the stars I don't do it much anymore. It's my eyesight you see—not what it used to be."

"Are you being serious," Mary asked beginning to panic.

"Oh yes, I wish I weren't, but I am. Besides being almost blind I tire easily. I'm very old. I don't know why Cesibourne hasn't retired me, but we go back a long way."

"May I ask you a simple question?" Mary asked.

"By all means, Mary, I am your servant."

"Are we ever going to get out from behind this big block of ice?"

"That is an excellent question, Mary. I commend you on your simplicity." And then there was silence.

"Well?" said Mary losing patience.

"I beg your pardon," said 'Misty'.

"Are we ever going to get out of here?"

"Oh, I'm sorry. You'd like an answer. Well,"—and after thinking it over for a few moments, "I'd say we will. In fact right now. Get on and we'll be away."

With the rest, 'Misty seemed to be strong again and they soared into the air.

"Tell me Mary, now that we are removed from that bit of berg, I must ask you, do you know this area well?"

"I don't know it at all. Are you lost again."

"Still, I'm afraid," he said and began circling. "Let's see," he began mumbling to himself, "If the wind is still blowing from the south as it was when I came out of the south and I fly into it now, it stands to reason that I should eventually get back to the south—yes I'll try that. Hang on Mary, I think I have it now," and off they went straight into a howling gale.

Mary buried her head in Misty's feathers and held on, and just when she was losing all hope of ever seeing her friends again, not to mention home, they broke out into clear air. It was dusk with just a few clouds in the sky, but Misty seemed to have found what he needed.

"That's better," he said. "Now I've got my bearings. Do you see the South star over there, Mary?"

Mary looked in the direction Misty indicated and saw what looked like a star brighter that the rest. "If you mean that bright dot dead ahead, I guess so, but I've never heard of a South star, only a North star."

"Is that so?" Misty said as he stroked his huge wings toward the dot in the distance. "Have you ever considered the possibility that there may be many things that you've never heard of?"

Mary knew by then that Misty was right. In fact she had never known there were so many things she didn't know, but still it made her a little mad to hear it from Misty. "What makes you so wise, Misty?" Mary said with just a bit of sarcasm.

"Why, thank you my dear," Misty replied, taking her seriously. "I'm not often told that and I appreciate it. I have had a lot of experience, I guess."

Mary felt a little guilty that she'd not been totally serious with him and decided to be nicer. "That's probably what it is. Wisdom comes with age they say." At that point she noticed that Misty was beginning to circle. "What are you doing now, are we lost again?"

"I hope not, Mary, but I think it's time to descend and find out where we are. I have a very good sense of smell and I seem to detect Cabbage frying."

"Fried cabbage?" Mary asked. She didn't smell anything and was thankful that she didn't.

"Oh, yes, Mary, it's my favorite food after a long flight. If you like it too, you're in luck."

With the luck Mary had had so far, this bit of 'luck' was probably to be expected.

5

They circled lower and lower and sure enough, Misty was right. There, below them was a crystal castle casting rainbow colors of light on the surrounding snow. They glided through an open door and landed in a large room where a man was sitting on a stone throne fingering his long white beard.

"Well, here you are. I was beginning to worry about you. Did you have some trouble. You've been getting a little absent minded lately, Misty."

"Oh, no," Misty said, confidently." Nothing to it. You can always count on me you know. Had a late start is all."

"Glad to hear it. You may go now, your favorite dinner awaits you. Had a devil of a time keeping it warm though. The worms kept jumping out of the pan."

"Cabbage and worms, "Misty said rolling his eyes in anticipation. "You're too good to me, Cesibourne," and he rushed to his dinner.

"Well," Cesibourne said, "and you are Mary. Come with me, you must be hungry too." Seeing Mary turn a little green at the thought of cabbage and worms, he added, "it's all right, Mary, I have prepared something for us that you might enjoy," and he led Mary into a small dining room with a table filled with food. When they were seated Cesibourne served Mary a plate covered with something that she didn't recognize and she looked up at Cesibourne.

"Try it and tell me what you think," he said.

Tentatively she took a bite. And then she took another. "This is delicious," she said. "It tastes like roast beef, but it isn't is it?"

Cesibourne broke out in satisfied laughter. "Wonderful, wonderful," he said. "I wasn't sure I could get it right. No, it's not exactly roast beef because as you probably have guessed we have no beef down here, but it's identical to the real thing. I grow in my garden all the chemicals and ingredients that make up organic substances. With the right combination I can duplicate every known food. I'm just now coming up with some successes and I just had to try my roast beef on you."

"Well, you got it just right," Mary said. "My father's a scientist too. I'll have to tell him all about what you're doing here. How did you know I liked roast beef?" she asked, daintily putting away the last of her dinner.

"Oh—well—" he hesitated, "I know more about you than you think, but we'll get into that later. So, your father is a scientist. What branch?"

"He's really retired now. He invents things."

"All right, but what about you? I want to know your story. I understand you are from another land?" he asked.

"Yes, I'm afraid so," said Mary.

"Why afraid?"

"Because for one thing I don't know if I'll ever get home," and she told Cesibourne everything that had happened to her.

When it was all said, Cesibourne leaned back in his chair and looked up at the crystal ceiling. Finally he spoke. "You've had quite a journey and I can understand why you have so many questions. I'm afraid most of them I'll be unable to answer. There are things in life that have to play out for themselves. Answers will come only when the time is right. That's what makes life so fascinating, don't you think?"

"I guess so," Mary answered, skeptically, "but as to my last question about the ice? can you help us with that?"

"That's an easy one. I'm not sure. We'll get to that later. What I want to know now are things about your world."

"I don't know if you'll understand, it's so different from yours."

"Can you keep a secret?" Cesibourne almost whispered.

Here we go again, Mary thought, more secrets. "I know many secrets and I've never told anyone any of them," Mary said emphatically.

"Good. I will then tell you mine. No one knows what I'm about to tell you and it must go no further than you."

"I promise," she said patiently.

"Wonderful—I've been to your land," he said and waited for her reaction.

"You have?" Mary said. She hadn't expected that.

"It was many years ago, but when I heard about you, I had to assume that you were probably from the same place. That's why I demanded that you alone come here."

Mary was beginning to wonder if Cesibourne was serious or maybe a little balmy. "If, as you say, long ago you visited my land, where exactly was it?"

"I was actually on the island for several years. We, the priests, were copying treasured volumes that contained their history. Those were the beautiful times. I remember it as if it were yesterday. And then the bad ones from the north came in their long boats. There were hundreds of them. We were not ready for that. The priests were peace loving, doing their Gods work and they were overwhelmed and routed from their island to the last man by those barbarians—excuse me, I still get worked up over it."

Mary suddenly realized what had caught her eye when she had first seen Cesibourne. It was his clothing. And now she recognized it as the robe of a ninth century Irish Monk that she'd seen in a history book. "And you were one of those who got away?" she asked.

"That's right, they were monks," Cesibourne exclaimed. "You were there then or at least in the vicinity when all this occurred. What good fortune for me now!"

"How did you get away?" Mary repeated.

"That's a mystery," Cesibourne said. "I was knocked down and the next minute I woke up here. Have the north people left? Have monks returned?"

"That all happened a thousand years ago. I only read it in history books."

"A thousand years ago! I can't believe it! It seems only yesterday."

Mary studied Cesibourne. "You don't look like the people of this land," she said. "You look like me. And you have an Irish accent. You didn't visit our island did you? You are actually one of us—my people, aren't you? and got here long ago, maybe as I did?"

"That's a possibility, isn't it. I've thought of that myself. You see I really don't know. I have strange dreams sometimes of rocky cliffs and wild waves smashing on a desolate beach—which does not happen around here—and look at this," he said pulling some old parchment papers from a niche in the wall. "Other than the clothes I'm wearing, these were all I had with me when I woke up here."

Mary looked at the ancient writing, but it was in a strange language and she could only make out a word here and there. "Can you read this?" she asked.

"That's the strange thing, I sometimes think I can, but then frightening scenes from a distant past overwhelm me and immediately it all becomes lost to me—anyway" he suddenly said, putting the papers away, "that's neither here nor there," and he quickly changed the subject. "Let's get to your problem. You should listen to the Elves. They know all about the ice sheet. If they say it could take years to thaw, it probably could. Now, I said I might be able to help. This is no guarantee, mind you, but it's your best chance as I see it. Follow me." And he led Mary down through the crystal floor to where he entered a small tunnel. At the end of it was a shelf with several boxes of various sizes on it. He selected one about a foot long and looked inside "This should do," he said, looking it over as they would ??? brought with him from the tunnel. The rock inside didn't look like much to Mary, just a common rock. The only thing strange about it was its smooth surface that seemed to be giving off a green glow.

"Keep this rock in its box until you need it. Don't touch it unless you're wearing gloves, it can get very hot. I know it doesn't look like much, but it may be just what you need.

Under certain circumstances it can give off quite a lot of heat. Hang this rock from the bow of your ship about a foot off the surface of the water as you approach the ice. It may not help if the ice is very thick, but if it has thawed at least a little, it might help melt it. Now I imagine you are anxious to get back to your people. I'll call misty and you can be on your way."

Mary had noticed during this conversation that the storm she could clearly see through the crystal walls of the castle hadn't eased up a bit and even looked worse. Before Cesibourne could call Misty she asked him about it. "The storm looks pretty bad, don't you think Cesibourne?" Cesibourne peered out into the storm.

"No worse than it was. If Misty had no trouble getting you here, I'm sure he can get you back."

Mary didn't want to tell Cesibourne the truth, that Misty wasn't what he used to be—and that they almost hadn't made it— but at the same time she wasn't sure she wanted to go out in that storm again. "How long will it last do you think?" she asked.

"Oh, a day or two," he replied. "It's just about blown itself out," and he started to call Misty.

"Wait!" Mary said a little too desperately. "A day or two more won't hurt, and besides it will give me more time to hear your fabulous stories."

"Well, Mary, I do have some good stories, don't I?" Cesibourne said a little puffed up. "If you think it will be all right with your friends?"

"Oh yes. It will be fine," Mary said, thinking that it might be the only way they would ever see her again.

There was plenty to talk about and Mary kept Cesibourne busy with her questions. "You've lived here a long time, then. And you spoke of the Irish monks?"

"A long, long time ago to your first question," Cesibourne said, "and yes to your second question. You see the monks had set themselves the task of recording all our—their scriptures which were getting lost or destroyed. They had been working on this for a hundred years when the North people came and destroyed it all."

"By the way," Mary said, "to answer your earlier question, yes the monks did return and many of your—their manuscripts were saved."

"Well thank God for that. You have just made me very happy."

"And this is where you ended up. Why, here, do you suppose—and by the way, where exactly is here?"

"Why I am here and not someplace else, I have no idea, but I make the best of it. And as to where you are now exactly, is easy. You are at the end of the road.

"What do you mean by that?" It sounded ominous.

"I mean, you've gone as far as you can. You're are at the nadir of our world. The bottom. From here you can only go back from whence you came. This is the most southern point of our land. Every foot, every inch you move from this point will take you north. You can go no further south. Isn't that interesting?"

"Fascinating," Mary said dully. What was even more interesting was her conclusion that Cesibourne was stark raving mad.

"Now, Mary, before you go," Cesibourne said seriously. "I want you to consider why you are here in our land. It wasn't by accident that you fell down that cliff. You are here for a reason. So far you say you've met mostly nice people, but believe me there are others not so cordial. Your Mr. El appears to be on a crusade for a peace that has for some unknown reason left his land and presumably you are here to help. Take what he says seriously and be careful what you do. Your returning to our—your own land may also depend on it." Mary certainly didn't want was getting late and after some more small talk, they retired.

On the morning she was to leave, the sky was clear and it was time to say goodbye.

"Thank you for everything, Cesibourne. I haven't seen another one of 'us' down here—"

"Now Mary, our little secret don't you know," Cesibourne interrupted.

"I know, it's safe with me, and thanks again for the stone. I think we'll be all right now," and Mary climbed onto the back of Misty, holding tight to the stone.

"I hope so. I've enjoyed talking with you, Mary. It sometimes gets lonely down here. If you're ever in the vicinity again, look me up. Just ask anyone. And good luck. All right, Misty, away you go."

As they climbed up into a clear blue sky, Misty called over his shoulder to Mary. "Thanks for the respite, Mary. I overheard you asking for another day. I owe you one for that. I don't think I could have made another storm flight to save my soul." I wonder where he got that phrase, Mary thought, as they made good time to the north.

It wasn't long until Mary saw the Elves settlement and they glided down to perfect three point landing. Eagles of course don't have three points so it wasn't exactly a perfect landing, but as Mary knew, any landing that you can walk away from is not bad.

Mary had grown fond of Misty and bid him goodbye with a lump in her throat. "Good luck" she called after him.

"Skill needs no luck!" he called back with a little waggle of his tail.

6

By then El, Trandy, Nelly, Willie and Nilly and the others had rushed up to greet her and giving thanks for her safe return, they retired into the long house where Mary told them her story—all but what she promised to keep a secret. And then she explained to them the stone that Cesibourne had given her.

"Well, you've had quite a trip,' El said. "It's a wonder you're still alive."

"What about getting my ship out of here," Monkey One wanted to know, examining the stone in its box.

"According to Mary," Trandy said, "you should wait until the ice is at it's thinnest and then try the stone. It will be as thin as it gets in about two weeks. You might as well get the ship ready and try it then. You've nothing to lose."

For the next two weeks they fitted out the ship. They careened it on the beach to clean its bottom so that it would slide through the water as easily as possible, and attached a metal strip to the bow so that it wouldn't be damaged by the ice. And then they waited.

Trandy tested the ice daily until he felt it was ready, and then rounded everyone up. "The ice," he said, "hasn't thinned anymore for three days and that means it will soon begin to thicken again. It's as thin as it will get. You had better set sail first thing tomorrow morning."

The next day they were ready, and even though it might be bad luck, they hugged each other and said their goodbye's as if this were to be just another cruise. After the Elves had all left the ship, they pulled up anchor and with silent prayers and crossed fingers, they knocked on wood and headed for the huge ice sheet that stretched out before them as far as the eye could see. Fortunately the wind was from the south and they were making good speed when, hanging tightly onto the rail, they hit the ice and stopped dead in the water.

"So much for your rock," Monkey One said overlooking the bow.

"I guess I forgot to tell you" Mary said. "The rock should have been taken out of the box." Skeptically, Monkey One pulled up the chain that held it and set the box on deck. He took the rock out and immediately dropped it. "Ow," he cried. "That's hot!"

"Better wear gloves", Ell said. "And by the way, you had better not hang that rock near the ship. If it gets that hot it could cause damage. Why not take it forward about thirty feet, set it out directly on the ice and see what happens". And that is what they did.

It took about four hours for someone to call out, "It sank, sir. It sank through the ice". Sure enough, the rock was now hanging straight up and down on its chain from the bow of the ship and fifty feet of ice in front of the ship had been melted away, and they were able with the small boat, to tow the ship up to the remining ice.

For three days they melted what ice they could and were able to tow the ship three hundred more feet before Ell called everyone back to the rear of the ship. "Look what's happening behind us. The ice is filling in as fast as we move forward. If that rock ever quits working we'll be locked in the ice. Well, we're committed so carry on" for another five days they moved the ship forward until they heard a cry from the small boat. "The stone is gone sir. The stone is gone." The rock had slipped off its chain and was missing.

"Oh, oh!" Ell said "If we don't find that rock we're in bad trouble" and he called over to "DEEP SEA" his best diver to dive down and look for it. Soon "DEEP SEA" came up from the bottom. "I've got good news for you and bad. The good news is the depth is fairly shallow here and the bad news is it's deep mud and it will be difficult to find anything in it."

"Well, do what you can" Ell said. 'If we can't find it we're doomed.'

It took three more dives before the diver came up triumphantly with the rock in his hand. "I've found it sir, I've found it."

"Where did you find it?" Ell asked.

"It was giving off bubbles. Must have been the heat."

"All right, carry on, but make sure that chain is tight this time."

By now it was apparent that the ice was getting thinner and Ell decided to try something else. They pulled the ship back as far as they could in the clear water, put the rock back into its box, dropped anchor and set all the sails that they had. Then they waited for a strong wind. The idea was to sail up into the ice at full speed and try to crack the ice that way. In two days a strong sowester blew up from the south and they were ready for it. With all sails set and the ship straining at its anchor. They had quarter of a mile to get up speed and when they hit the ice the ship stopped dead again.

"Put that rock down," Ell said, "And take it out of the box."

Finally they got it back over the bow again and down to where it rested a few inches off the ice. Nothing happened. The Monkeyshines were frantically trying to keep the ship from slewing around sideways against the ice—and they waited what seemed like an eternity.

As they watched the stone slowly swinging below them, it began to give off a green glow that spread out further and further across the ice. Then there was a loud crack and the ice began to separate before them. The ship with its bow edging into the crack helped to break the ice and as it began to pick up speed the crack got wider and wider. Pretty soon they were sailing at hull speed, racing through open water. They all ran to the stern and waved to the tiny figures on the beach that were waving madly back at them and getting smaller by the minute;

"Hooray, for Mary!" hailed the Monkeyshines led by Monkey One, and the others joined in.

"No, no!" said Mary. "Hooray for Cesibourne!" and they all hooray'd for Cesibourne too.

It took three days sailing to get completely free of the ice and then they were once again in warm water. With a fair south wind they were making good time, but within a week, conditions had changed. One morning the wind began to die and when it did blow it came in fits and starts and then it would stop before another puff would come. Monkey One was looking at the sky and he looked worried.

"Is there anything wrong?" Mary asked.

"I'm afraid we're in for a blow, Mary," he said. "Do you feel how the air seems dead, with no life. We sailors have an old saying, 'Red sky at night, sailors delight; Red sky in the morning, sailor take warning'. Look at the sky." Mary looked at the sky and sure enough it had a red glow. "And," Monkey One continued, "do you feel these huge swells that are lifting the ship? Well, they're being formed by a great storm far to the north and I'm afraid we are directly in its path. You had better go below and make everything secure. I'm afraid we're in for it."

By the time Mary, El, and the others had tied everything down the best they could the storm hit. The wind came on howling, knocking the ship down on its side and then began tossing it around like a cork and when it tried to right itself it was knocked down again. The monkeyshines finally got all the sails down and the ship back up on its feet, but even under bare poles and the wind screaming in the rigging the ship still tore on through the storm, flying off the tops of waves and then to crash down into the trough.

Down below the others had tied themselves to their hammocks and were hanging on for dear life as occasionally they would do a complete loop before getting right side up again.

"Borol's certainly in a rage, Nelly," El yelled, to be heard over the crashing waves and breaking spars and rigging on deck. "We got in his way and he's mad."

"Who's Borol?" called Mary cupping her hands to her ears so that she could hear the others.

"Borol," El explained, "is the Storm God, Mary. When a great wind blows it's Borol rushing across the sky leading the hunt for the great stag. Can you hear the hounds baying? Borol can never quite catch the stag and it makes him angry. We have unfortunately found ourselves in his path and he's furious with us for interfering with his hunt. Hear how he claps his hands in rage while he hurls fire balls at us," and at that moment lightning began striking the sea all around them as thunder rent the heavens.

All day and night the little ship raced on, and then in a particularly fierce gust of wind it was thrown completely down on its side and just lay there not responding to anything that the crew could do.

"If you ever prayed to your God you had better do it now," called El. "If we don't get righted we're doomed." And they all prayed that they would see the sun come up again and waited. On deck the monkeyshines were desperately throwing nonessential objects overboard to lighten the ship and several, shines were crawling, with waves breaking over them, out onto the masts that were lying flat in the water. Two topsails were still attached to these masts helping to hold the ship down and the shines were now able to cut these loose and crawl back on board before the ship was struck by a huge wave.

Those below were praying and as Mary prayed she unconsciously stroked the medalian she wore around her kneck.

Whether it was caused by the huge wave, the shines getting the sails cut away, or Mary stroking her medal as she prayed, we'll never know, but at that moment the ship gave a great shudder and slowly rolled back upright. El rushed over to the ladder and called to Monkey One who had been on deck through it all trying to save the ship. "What shape are we in?" he called.

"We're all right now," Monkey One called back. "We took on a lot of water but the pumps are handling it now. I believe the worst is over."

By morning the sky had cleared and the sun shone through wispy clouds that were all that was left of the storm and they all went on deck. It was a wreck. Both masts were standing but the yards that held the sails had been torn away, some gone entirely and some hanging over the side held only by the rigging.

"What do you think?" El asked Monkey One.

"Well, it's not as bad as it looks. It could have been a lot worse. We still have our masts and most of the rigging. We have plenty of spares and if we can find some quiet water we can have her sailing again in a couple of days. For now we'll get up what sail we can. We should be able to make a few knots for now." Mary knew that would be very slow, but at least they would be moving.

The Monkeyshines got right to work. They hauled one of the yards back up the main mast and were able to jury rig a patched sail. That was all they could do until they found some quiet water where they could do the major repairs.

For two days they sailed slowly on, making discouragingly slow progress to the north until on the third day their luck changed when the lookout called, "Land ho! Two points off the port bow."

"How does it look,? called Monkey One.

"Pretty barren, sir," the lookout called back, "but it seems to have a lagoon that will serve our purpose."

The island was down wind from them and they easily reached it by sundown. What they had discovered was a small mountainous island encircled completely by a rocky reef that enclosed a small lagoon. They sailed back and forth until they finally found a break in the reef and sailed carefully through it and anchored.

As Monkey One had said, in two days they had brought up from below the spare timbers, sail and rigging they would need and had the ship back in shape and ready to sail. They then needed only supplies. Their food was low and the water casks frightfully light so Monkey One sent a party ashore to look for supplies and Mary and Willie and Nilly went along.

On shore the party of Monkeyshines spread out across a rocky, barren looking land landscape lying below a central mountain that Mary, Willie and Nilly climbed. Until near the very top they sat down to rest.

"We're not going to find any food on this island," Mary said, "it's all volcanic rock."

"That's what it looks like all right," Willie agreed. "There's not a tree on the whole island that I can see." They were leaning up against a large rock when suddenly it swung away and they fell back into an opening in the mountain. It appeared to be a long cave and there was a dim light at the far end.

"What do you think that is?" Mary asked.

"I don't know," said Willie, "but I don't like it. I think we had better get back to the ship."

Mary decided that as she was already on a great adventure she would follow it to the end—'In for a penny, in for a pound'—was her father's old saying. "I'm going in," she said. "You can follow me if you want or you can go back to the ship."

"I'll come," Nilly said with a slight quaver in her voice.

"Oh, all right," Willie conceded, "let's go in."

They were careful where they put their feet as everyone should that go in caves and as they got deeper into the cave the light got brighter and brighter until they saw it was a shimmering glow surrounding the figure of a lady all dressed in white with a green coronet atop her head.

"Welcome," the figure said, "I was wondering whether you would come in for a visit."

"I'm afraid we were a little startled," Mary answered. "It's not often that we are greeted in this manner."

"No, I suppose not," she said, "I'm not too familiar with your world. We Gods however find little that surprises us."

"You're a God?" Willie blurted out.

"Of course. Let me introduce myself. I am Grinda, Queen of new life. That is why I am here on this rock. I will soon be bringing it to life with all the new growth that it will need to support fruits and vegetables that will feed the animals that will arrive."

"That's why this island is so barren then." said Mary. It's brand new."

"That's quite correct, it's been but three weeks since it rose from the sea. And who might you all be?"

"I'm Mary," she introduced herself, "and this is Willie and Nilly."

"Willie and Nilly," Grinda mused. "You are from the ship that is anchored in my bay, the ship from the northern climbs. You see I know of all the people that inhabit this land, but you, Mary, you are a mystery to me. You I believe are not from here?"

"No," Mary replied, "it's a long story, but simply put I'm from a very long way away—

"We found her falling down a cliff on an island that sank into the sea," Nilly interrupted, "she said she fell out of a book."

"Oh yes," Grinda recalled. "You are the little girl from the other world. I've heard about you. You must be here for a good reason and so I welcome you. By the way, as I am Grinda, I am also the wife of Borol the storm God who gave you some trouble the other night. I apologize for his rude behavior, but he gets carried away when he's on the hunt. I'll give him a good scolding, and you'll have nothing but good sailing from now on. I'll see to that! For now I want to give you each a little memento of our meeting. For you Nilly, I give a locket to hang around your neck on a golden chain. As long as you wear it you will tell only the truth. You will not be able to tell a lie. As you grow older you will realize that it may be the most valuable thing you own. Don't lose it. Willie, I give you this amulet. It's not just any trinket. At times in your life you will not know how to proceed or which way to go. Two paths may look the same, but one may lead you to disaster. At these times examine this amulet very carefully and you may find the answer. But don't abuse it's power. Now Mary, I'm at a loss as to what to give you. What could you possibly take back to your world commemorating this day that would be of use to you? Do you have any suggestions?"

"I have no suggestions your highness. Having met you and all the wonderful people already on my journey is enough."

"Well said, my dear, although I must warn you. Not everyone you meet in our land will be as congenial as those you've recently met—In any event I must give you something. If you still have the book, could I see it?" Mary gave Grinda the book, and she wrote something on the flyleaf and handed it back to Mary. "If you are ever in our land again, that will introduce you. Just show anyone the book. They'll know what it means. Now I must go," and in the next instant she and the tunnel were gone and they were once again leaning against the large stone.

7

The first thing they all did was to look for their mementos and sure enough they were in their pockets. "Well," Mary said, "I guess it wasn't a dream," as she looked at what Grinda had written in her book. "Wishing you sunlit days and cool nights." And it was signed, "Queen Grindatalis and her friends."

"It may not have been a dream," Willie said truculently, "but it was some kind of magic and I don't like magic. I'm going back to the ship."

"Where's your sense of adventure, Willie," Mary chided, as they made their way back to the ship. "Besides, she seemed very nice to me."

"I like adventure as much as anyone," Willie replied, "only maybe not as much as you. You're going to get us in trouble one of these days."

Half way down the mountain they joined the others and went back to the ship.

"I'm sorry El," Monkey One said, when they were back in the cabin, "but I've bad news. There isn't a blade of grass on this island and it's dry as a bone. No water at all. It's a dead island. I've never seen one like it. I think we had better leave this place. I have a bad feeling about it.

Mary, Willie and Nilly looked at each other, but didn't say anything. It was their little secret, and besides there was nothing that they could do that would help their situation.

"How about our own supplies?" El asked.

"We're low on water and the food's going bad, but we'll be all right for about a month."

"Well, as soon as the wind shifts we'd better be off then."

"Yes sir," said Monkey one," and he left the cabin.

Mary, El, and Willie and Nilly went on deck where El checked the direction of the wind. "That is strange," El mused.

"What's strange?" Mary wanted to know.

"The wind. It should have swung around to the south by now. This time of year it always shifts to the south."

"Is that important?" Mary asked.

El looked at Mary as if he couldn't believe what he'd heard. "Important?" he said. "Of course it's important. But then you probably aren't familiar with how ships sail. You see it's the wind that propels a ship. In the winter the wind blows from the north and we sail south. In the summer it blows from the south and we can sail back north. We plan all our shipping this way. It's important that the wind follows it's natural path. Until it shifts back to the south we're stuck here."

Mary had spent much of her time on deck with Willie and Nilly watching the Monkeyshines swinging the huge yards back and forth that carried the sails, trying to get the ship to point north with little success and Mary could see by the way the ship was rigged why it was so. It was an ancient system probably five hundred years old in Mary's world.

"You mean you can't go upwind in this ship?" Mary asked.

???ell Mary, no ship can sail against the wind,"

??? Mary said tentatively, "my father and I do a lot of sailing and we sail ??? time. "Mary." El said condescendingly, "you may have thought you were sailing upwind, but believe me it's not possible, now run along, I have some work to do."

Mary realized that in El's world they hadn't discovered the fore and aft sail yet and that it would take a demonstration to prove it to El.

The next day she had the ships carpenter make an exact model of the ship she was on. She had it rigged the same with square sails on the foremast, but instead of square sails on the mainmast, she had the carpenter fit a boom and a gaff that would carry a for and aft sail. This she knew from experience was a brigantine rig. Now she had to convince El and the crew that it would work.

El was busy trying to determine what to do when Mary approached him.

"Can I borrow one of the shore boats?" Mary asked him. "I'd like to row around the lagoon."

"Sure" he said absentmindedly, deep in thought. "Just check with one of the Monkeyshines."

"I'd like you to take me, I want to show you something," Mary said.

"I'm too busy for that, Mary. I've got some important thinking to do."

"Will you please, El," Mary said, and there was something in her voice that made El sit up. He looked at her for a moment and got up. "O K." he said. "If it's that important. I could use some fresh air anyway."

They lowered one of the boats and El took the oars and pulled away from the ship. It was only then that El noticed the model boat that Mary had in her lap.

"That's a fine model you have there, but the rigging is all wrong. I'll have to get after who ever made it for you. He should know better."

"It's my own design," Mary said. "I had him build it that way."

"Whatever for?" El said.

"Stop here and I'll show you." El stopped rowing and the boat came to a halt gently rocking in the quiet lagoon. Mary splashed a little water high up in the air and the spray drifted off to the south. "The wind is coming from there," pointing north, Mary said, "is it not?"

"Yes, yes, what are you up to, Mary"

"Watch closely and you'll see," Mary said, and making some adjustments to the sails on her model, she put it in the water and gave it a gentle push to the north and away it went, healing over as it sailed into the wind at about a forty five degree angle.

"Very nice little sailor, Mary, but what's your point."

"Don't you see where it's sailing? El," Mary asked and she threw some more water up in the air. El watched it for a minute and then threw some water up in the air himself.

"It's sailing north, but it's not possible, it's a trick. It's not possible."

"Take a bearing on that rock over there," Mary said "and El took a bearing on the rock and then rowed over to the model boat where Mary made a few adjustments and then set it off on the opposite tack. "You see," she said, "By tacking back and forth you can make good headway into the wind.

All after noon they sailed the model boat back and forth. El thought it was magic until he finally accepted the new design as real.

It took two days to re-rig the ship to the new design and by then the wind had swung around to the south and was blowing exactly in the direction they wanted to go.

"Well, look at that," El remarked, "The wind has finally shifted to the south. My prayers have been answered." Mary smiled to herself. Grinda had kept her promise. She wondered how Borol had taken her ultimatum.

They were soon underway and sailing north again and El turned to Mary. "I guess we didn't need your sail plan just now after all, but we will one day, and when we do we'll be able to out sail anything on the water. There has never been a rig like this before. This will revolutionize our shipping. How did you come up with it?"

"It's very common where I come from. It's all we use these days."

"Well you must come from a very advanced world, that's all I can say."

"In some ways, yes, but we're having our problems too just as you are."

"Yes, we can't always get it right can we?"

They went below and El said to Mary, "I want to explain our situation to you. You're a bright young girl and I think you will better understand it if I begin from the beginning. What do you think, Nelly?"

"Yes." Nelly said, "I think it's a good idea. Mary is wise beyond her years and may have some ideas of her own."

"In the beginning, Mary," El began, "long, long ago before anything here existed and there was nothing but nothing, the Great Father we now call Oldmeister, decided to build another world. He is the great architect and builder of the various universes and had made many worlds and was ready to build another one. He took some dust from his last job and created our world as you see it now with all its living forms and all the stars that you see in the sky. He was enjoying himself so much that he wanted to share his joy and selected out of the night sky some of the brightest stars making them lesser gods. These lesser gods were to manage all the necessary day to day jobs that running a world requires. Gemini would keep the sun in orbit and the moon from falling out of the sky. Boron would control the wind and respite the sea—

"And Grinda would bring forth new life!" Mary said excitedly.

"Well, well, you are more informed than I thought."

"I—well—stammered Mary, afraid she'd given herself away. "I keep my eyes and ears open."

"I can see you do," El said, surprised at Mary's knowledge. "Anyway, all these lessor gods were happy and enjoyed their duties immensely, much preferring to be useful than just to hang out and shine. That is, all were happy except the one called Grumbles who was assigned to manage the tides. From the beginning he was discontent. He was lazy and didn't want to be a worker, he wanted to be a supervisor. In fact he wanted to be a great god. He even wanted to share equal power with Oldmeister himself. When he wasn't allowed that, he began to cause trouble. Tides were reversed and rivers overflowed their banks and there were great floods that spoiled the other's works while Grumbles walked about talking to himself. He caused so much disruption that Oldmeister finally had to banish him from his domain forever. Terrified at Oldmeister's anger, Grumbles removed himself to the under life where he stayed for a long time.

Grumbles however was not subdued. He sulked and brooded resenting all the others and planned revenge and retaining still some of the power granted to him by Oldmeister, he formed a realm of his own far beneath Oldmeister's realm. There he assembled creatures who were also unhappy, mainly snakes, and sent them out into our world to cause trouble. Snakes are not all bad, being created by Oldmeister, but some were unhappy to be snakes having preferred to soar in the sky rather than to crawl around on their stomachs and, disgruntled, they joined Grumbles, and these malcontents he endowed with the ability to look like us when in our world. Grumbles mistake was to build them too big and so if we should see one we would recognize it at once because in human form they would seem giants.

"Where is this Grumbles?" Mary asked.

"Grumbles lives in the realm he created, a dark fiery place that he reserves for those he can trick into joining him. But soon his guests discover that there is no way out and must forever dwell in the fire themselves. But Grumbles himself is not our worry. Only Oldmeister can destroy

Grumbles. The ones we are after are the wayward snakes, the third level power that has taken the form of giants."

"Where are they?"

"They live in Fire Mountain. It's a Peak that forms the very top of Grumbles lair. It is supposed to be somewhere north of here but is difficult to find because it's always moving. It never stays in one place for long. The secret is to look for a column of smoke that rises from ts fiery peak and the mountain should be beneath it blowing smoke and fire. It's said to be where Grumble derives his strength and woks his magic, forging new giants in its flames. Few have seen it and those who search for it have never been heard from again."

"But Grumbles now has found a new venue for his wrath," El continued, "Man. Man now inhabits Oldheimer's world and in the beginning was happy and content, loving and working together to improve their new place. Oldmeister had given them wisdom so as to be able to discern between good and evil but also gave them the freedom to make their own choice. Grumbles saw opportunity here and studied this new man until he had found a way to wriggle himself into man's brain and here he began to plant discontent, mistrust and hate."

"Now Oldmeister does his best to keep Grumbles under control, but occasionally he breaks out. As I have said we've had peace for many years but recently Grumbles has again come to the surface and is again causing trouble over a wide area of our land."

At that point Monkey One came into the cabin. "You had better come topside, El, we've spotted a small boat adrift. It may have someone in it." When they all got on deck the crew was just pulling the life boat aboard. The body that lay in the bottom moved.

"He's alive," El said, and they took him below. After he had been fed and revived he had a tragic tale to tell. He was the first mate of a fishing boat that had been caught in a severe storm and he thought that he was probably the only survivor. "What day is it," he asked. El told him and the seaman exclaimed. "I've been adrift then for a week."

"That corresponds with the storm that we've just been through. It was a bad one all right. What's your name and where do you come from?" El asked.

"My name is Ben Lindle and I come from Southland which is two days North by east from here." he said.

"Why is it called Southland?"

"I suppose it's because it's south of Northland."

"Yes, that's where I'm from," El said. "Well that's not far out of our way, we'll drop you off before we head home— that is if our wind holds out."

"You don't have to worry about that," Mary said without thinking.

"How would you know that, Mary?" El asked, beginning to wonder about her.

"Oh well," Mary stammered, It's just a hunch."

8

·····················

They sailed north by east and reached the sailor's home island in two days. As they pulled up to the dock Ben, spoke up. "There's something wrong here."

"What do you mean," said El.

"There's no one on the embarkadero. It's deserted." It's normally teeming with fishermen." There was only an old man sitting on a barrel tying fancy knots in a rope. "Old man," Ben called, "Why is there no one about? You remember me? I am Ben off the ship The Hooker. I've been three years out and have returned. What have you to say?" El, Mary and the others were standing on the rail listening to all this wondering what the trouble was. The old man slowly looked up still knotting the rope. "I've not forgotten ye. Ye' be son of Yon and Menthe, brother of—

"Yes, yes, but what has happened since I left?" Ben interrupted. Is there something wrong?"

"Aye, that there be," the old man replied "Ye'll soon be finding out," and he went back to knotting his rope as a crowd of ruffians armed with clubs approached the dock.

"You can't tie up here," demanded it's leader. "Shove off. At that moment another group equally armed marched up.

"You've no jurisdiction here, Charlie," demanded the second group's leader. "Leave this area or you'll taste a bit of lumber in your mouth." The two groups stood eyeing each other, sizing the other up and as the second group seemed the stronger, the first group began to leave the dock. It's leader was the last to leave with a few parting words. "You win this one, Hermi, but you know we'll be back, and he left wearing a sinister smile.

When all was quiet, Hermi, called up to the ship. "It's all right now. Come ashore. You're a stranger's ship but you're welcome—Isn't that Ben on the rail. What are you doing on this ship—never mind, you can tell us later. Come along all of you and we'll fix up some food for you," and he marched them all up town to the main hall where they all sat down around a huge banquet table. There, Ben told the town of the loss of the ship with all hands except him who he feared was the sole survivor.

"No, no," the town cried. "The ship did not founder. It's at this very minute in the yard being repaired. You were the only one washed overboard and now you're here. It's a miracle," and they all cheered The village bell was rung to celebrate the news and Ben was overjoyed to see all his shipmates again.

After they had had their meal, Ben spoke up. "I've been gone only three years and now I see many of my friends are missing. What's happened?"

"Much has happened," replied Hermi, who seemed to be their leader, "and it's not good. Those who greeted you first at the embarkadero were our friendly neighbors until they turned on us. They call themselves 'The Forum For

Freedom' Hermi said with a wry smile, but I fear their real goal is to take away all of ours."

"Typical course of action of tyrants," replied El. Make people think they are protecting their rights and then slowly take them away. When did all this happen?"

"It all began when a stranger landed on our shores—I hear he's a giant of a man. On top of our highest mountain he set up shop. He pawned himself off as a profit, teaching the unwitted. He played to the weak and hopeless at first and as his following grew, the curious and gullible joined him, and now he's recruited a large part of our population."

"What specifically does he preach. Are the people so lost as to follow a pied piper of evil?"

"He has a golden tongue, I'll give him that. He's selling a new utopia. It's the age old saw of new enlightenment. Out with the old, (which in this case are the freedoms of our people) clear out the junk (the monuments that express our creeds and beliefs we've worked and died for over the centuries) and in with immortality and corruption. They've infiltrated our schools and universities and even our courts with this new philosophy."

"What's this giants name." El asked.

"He calls himself 'Enlightenment," but we call him "The Enforcer."

"Giant, you say. I wonder if it could be one of Grumbles giants?"

"It could be. He proclaims himself to be the only true god."

"Well," said El., "we are all tired out and I suggest that we get some rest. We can think about this in the morning," and as by then it was getting late they went back to the ship and retired for the night.

The next day was spent in forming a plan. Hermi suggested, and it seemed wise, for the new comers to attend one of the enforcer's meetings which were scheduled monthly and open to the public. Ostensibly a forum for local news, but in reality a recruitment device. One was due to convene in two days and they all attended.

The meeting place was held in a valley surrounded by high cliffs and was conducted by one of the giant's helpers who called himself 'Smiles' but was refereed to by El's new friends as 'Mr. Slick.' In the center of a clearing, cut out of a dense forest, a huge bonfire roared and on a wooden platform a man stood preaching to a crowd, some of whom Mary recognized as the ruffians that had met them at the dock.

"—and so you can see," he was saying, "the progress being made in the social and economic conditions of our fare village. We will continue to make further improvements in the future, but it will only be possible if we don't waver. Keep doing your duty to the cause and we will triumph! Are there any questions before we adjourn?"

El put up his hand. "We in our group are new to your land and need further guidance. How do we learn more about your movement?"

Mr. Slick peered intently through the smoke. "Who is speaking please?"

"Over here," replied El, "by the large stone."

"Oh yes, I see you now—ah, I see, you are from the strangers ship, we meet again. What is it you want with us?"

"Well, to tell you the truth, we are unhappy with the conditions in our part of the land. That's why we have traveled so far from home. We are looking for a new beginning—a new way of living—and we'd like to know more about your program. Maybe we could start a branch of it in our own land." This was how El and the others planned to learn more about this man—or whatever he was.

"Well, if you're truly interested, attend our next meeting. It will be in thirty days, and now the meeting is over. Thank you for your attendance and we'll see you next time," and he picked up his notes waiting for the others to leave. El, Nellie and the children slipped through the crowd and approached Mr. Slick.

"We would like just a moment of your time now that the meeting is over if it's not too much trouble."

"I can give you a minute or two of my time, but no more." the enforcer said impatiently. "I'm a busy man."

"I can see that and so are we, that's why I must talk to you now. We must be leaving in a day or two and won't be here for the next meeting. We are very much interested in your program. I am the elder of my community and I think I could easily begin an outreach branch of your beliefs—program. If you could send me off with some kind of authority, I believe we could do business—to your advantage of course."

"You are an elder."

"Yes, I lead our council."

"If what you say is true?" the enforcer said scratching his head as he thought. We might indeed do business. When exactly do you plan to leave?"

"No more than two or three days."

"Well, I don't give out this kind of authority, you understand, it has to come from the High Mucky Muck, but I'll talk to him and get back to you," and he started to leave.

"Wait a moment please. Who is this High Mucky Muck, I thought you were the leader of this movement?"

"No, I'm not, although I am second in command and am responsible for all the day to day work. The High Mucky Muck is the supreme ruler of this island and I carry out all of his orders."

"If I agree to this, on my island who do I take orders from?"

"At first you will take orders from the High Mucky Muck of this island until a superior of your own is sent to your land."

"Then if I am to take orders from your High Mucky Muck, he will probably want to speak to me personally. When can I meet him?"

"That's impossible," Mr. Slick said emphatically. "No one sees him but me," and he began to move away.

"I'm sorry about that," El called after the enforcer, "but it's a requirement of mine. It might have been a lucrative relationship. Mine is a wealthy island. I'll be in town until Tuesday if you change your mind," and El led their group away. Glancing back once just before leaving the canyon, he noticed the enforcer watching them go.

When they got back to their ship they sat down to go over the day's activity.

"What now?" Mary asked.

"That's a good question." said Ben. "What do we do now?"

"We wait," said El. "All we can do now is wait. I have a hunch that we may be hearing from the enforcer before we leave. He sees a possible valuable connection here and I can't believe he'd let it slip through his fingers without looking into it further."

"You think he'll arrange a meeting between you and this High Mucky Muck?"

"I think it's a good possibility. He knows I won't do business with him. I do think we should have a plan in the works, however, if we are to be successful. We'll be able to do something about that as soon as we get more information."

Just as El had suspected, the next day the enforcer hailed them from the dock. "May I come aboard," he called.

"Come aboard Mr. Slick—that is, Mr. Smiles." El called, kicking himself in the shins for making such a blunder.

Mr. Slick stiffened for a minute and El thought he was going to leave, but then relented and came aboard. "What was that you called me?" he asked?"

El knew very well that Mr. Slick had understood what he'd said, and so tried to make a joke out of it. "Mr. Slick. I heard someone last night call you that, and I thought it funny. I didn't mean to insult you."

"I've been called that, but don't ever use that term again with me. It is not funny at all. If you wish, we can talk in your cabin," at which they all went below.

"What is your news, then?" El asked.

"I'll get right to the point," Mr. Slick said. You have an appointment." He sat for a moment possibly waiting for some kind of reaction, but El and the others sat motionless waiting to hear more. "I must tell you, this has been very difficult for me," he continued. "The High Mucky Muck has never granted an interview before, but under these unusual circumstances, with much persuasion from me you are to meet him at midnight on the 7th, that I believe is in three days. Only the four of you. No one else or there will be dire consequences. Now I'll give you a little advice. The High Mucky Muck is a dangerous man. Do nothing to arouse him. Follow these instructions to the letter, and mind what I say," and he handed El a piece of paper with the instructions.

"Three days," mused El, "I had hoped to be on my way by then. I'm not sure this is possible," he said blankly.

"You—you don't know? You have no idea what a commitment this is for the High Mucky Muck. You've been granted what no other ever has. You are a fool. I'll tell him then that you aren't interested."

El realized that Mr. Slick had called his bluff and that he had better not play the game any longer.

"All right, if it's that important I'll be there. I'll just do my laundry another day. On the 8th you say?"

"On the 7th," fumed the enforcer and steamed off the ship.

9

When he was gone, El spoke to the group. "Did I over do it a bit, do you think?"

"You were right on the edge," Ben replied. "When you called him Mr. Slick—"

"Yes that was a mistake."

"—and then when you feigned little interest. You should be a little more careful."

"Yes, I suppose so. Well, let's look at our instructions," and they all sat around the table and read the sheet of paper. Finally El straightened up. "Not much to that. In any event we will make our own rules. Essentially this tells us to come alone, tell no one and bring no one. Now, I don't want to take this lightly. I am fully aware that we will be in a delicate and dangerous situation. That is why we will have to be prepared for anything. The High Mucky Muck will certainly not come alone, he will have guards all over the place, probably hidden ahead of time in the forest. What we must do is beat him to the punch, so to speak. We'll get there first."

And so they made their plans and to make sure the crew of monkeyshines, would be at the rendezvous first, they were sent ahead the night before. They waited half a day for the High Mucky Mucks goons to arrive, and when they did about noon, one by one they were subdued by the Monkeyshines who gagged each one tying it to a tree. Meanwhile, El and the others rounded up ten of the most influential of the F.F.F. followers, telling them that they were all invited to a secret meeting at the clearing at midnight. The only rule was that they would be hidden in the trees where they must stay making no sound. The rest of the Monkeyshines were supposedly on hand to escort them to the arena. In truth they were there to enforce the rules with a bump on the head if one should forget.

"The plan," explained El, "is for us to get the High Mucky Muck to divulge his real plan to subjugate everyone on the island and to make them slaves. We want those hidden in the woods to hear all this so that they will rebel and overturn his power."

"What if he doesn't reveal himself." Mary asked.

"A good question," and the answer is that I don't know exactly. It's important that we get it out of him. If not we will have to modify our plan to fit the circumstances."

They left for the meeting place a little early to see that everything was as it should be and concluding that it was they sat themselves down on a stone bench. It was an hour before midnight and they waited for the High Mucky Muck to show up. Exactly at midnight he appeared as if by magic. He was huge, standing nine feet tall. He was partly in shadow with Mr. Slick to his right and another to his left. He pointed to the fire pit that was stacked with wood, and the Mr. Slick stepped forward and lit it. It went up with a roar and then settled down. The giant stepped forward into the light from the fire. They all noticed immediately his enormous ears, but the most important feature was his eyes. When the firelight reflected off them they shone like white hot embers, but when, because of the flickering flames or a momentary shift in his position, the light was not in his eyes, they were a flat sleight gray resembling snake's. And then he spoke.

"Well, I see you're here as requested. That's good. I understand you are from the strange ship that now lies in our harbor. Is that true."

"Yes it is," said El standing up address the High One. "We are travelers who are on a voyage in search of the truth and have traveled far."

"A search for the truth," the High One mused, "and in your 'far' travels have you found it?"

"We are still searching."

"What if you find your 'truth', what then?"

"Why, I'll take back to my people the news, and share it with them so that we will be free of the strife that has been on our land."

"Yours is then an unhappy land?"

"I'm afraid so, sir. We seem to have lost our way."

"You have some influence then in your community?"

"I am the senior elder and have complete trust of my people."

"Why did you want to see me?"

"Since we've been on your island we have heard rumors of a wonderful new way of life, and understand that you can enlighten us."

The high and mighty was thoughtful for a minute or two before he spoke. "It's true what you've heard. From our gods we have received on this island a new beginning. Maybe it's the truth you've been looking for. However it is a long process and takes absolute dedication. If you were to accept it and take it back to your people what would be your reward?"

"Why, the love and respect of the people."

"You are not interested in a monetary compensation for your troubles?"

"Well I would expect a salary and what gifts I might receive. You see I'm a relatively poor man and have some ambition to improve my standing."

"Excellent! We are now understanding one another. You truly are simply an adventurer, searching for treasure. Am I not right?"

"No, not entirely but if I should come across a few baubles, I dare say I might be tempted."

"I dare say. I suggest that you are an adventurer entirely. And now the evening is getting late. I suggest that you attend our next meeting in twenty days and see if you're still interested."

"That's impossible," El said, we must be at sea in two days. I was in hope you could fill us in on enough details get us started and then you could send an envoy to instruct us later."

"You have no idea what you're asking."

"I know, that's why I want some instruction tonight. Mine is a wealthy island. If treasure is the issue, it could be very lucrative for both of us."

"I'll make a deal with you," said the high one. "There are secrets here that must never be disclosed. I must warn you that our journey to the high places is not easy. It requires sacrifices you may not be prepared to carry out, but the rewards are beyond measure. If you were to become my representative on your island you would be entitled to everything on that island. Everything. Further than that I cannot go without your total commitment."

"It seems to me the rewards would be worth it."

"There is one other thing. If I tell you the mysteries of our world you are committed. Do you understand me?"

"I think so."

"No you don't. You are not thinking. You may leave this valley safely now and sail safely back to your island brooding on what might have been. Or—you can stay and discover a world only dreamed of. The only catch—a minor one—is that in knowing the truth, you are committed. You are forever committed to our way. If you decide to refuse our offer—well, you will not be allowed to leave this valley."

"You would keep us in this valley?"

"No, worse than that." At this there was silence.

Finally El answered. "Give me five minutes if you will, to discuss it with my people."

"Five minutes, no more, I'm a busy man."

El Nellie Mary and Ben put there heads together for three minutes and then replied to the high one. "We want to be part of something bigger than that that we have yet known. We agree to your terms."

"I do hope you have considered your decision well. I am at heart a good and loving person and it would truly distress me to find you later change your mind. You then are sure?"

"Yes we're sure," El replied confidently.

"All right then let's begin. The ultimate goal is the complete subjugation of your people. All the wealth and the services will belong to you. Everyone will be your servant. You will be a demigod on your island. You will be soul owner of the people and what they produce—except for a small remuneration to me for my services—"

"How much remuneration?"

"A small fifty percent—please don't interrupt me. You may do with the people as you like. I have found that a plump child at dinner parties goes over well with the guests. That might not be to your taste but to each his own. You are now probably getting the idea why you won't leave here alive without complete adherence to the rules?"

"Oh yes," El said, "I do indeed."

"Excellent! cried the high one who was getting excited. As you've seen we are not quite to our goal on this island yet—there are still hold outs that prefer their old god, a week and forgiving god that rarely punishes—but we are getting new recruits daily and as soon as we are strong enough we will prevail!" And the high one spread his arms reverently to the sky. At that moment, Mary, who had been sitting in the shadows away from the others stepped forward.

"Are we on our own to rule or will you send someone to advise us?"

"Well, little girl, your parents will control all the—" the high and mighty started and then stopped. He stepped back one step out of the fire light as if he had been pushed and his eyes turned a flat steel gray, and a thin long tongue shot out of his mouth. It had a small fork on the end and it darted around as if trying to detect something, and then it disappeared. He stepped forward and his eyes reflected fire. "You!"—he cried. "Who are you? You are not from this land. I know everything and everyone on this globe and you are not from here. Why are you here?"

"As El told you we are here to learn," Mary said, frightened, realizing that she had somehow been discovered as not one of their world.

The giant took a step forward peering at them closely, and then emitted a piercing scream. "You have tricked me!" He howled. "You have come to harm me! You fools, you could have had it all, instead you defy me. Did you really think you could interrupt my plans! You fools. Now you will die." He let out a wail just as a long flame shot out of the giants mouth causing Mary and the others to jump back. It was fortunate that they did because the tongue of fire split in two the stone they were sitting on. They jumped behind a huge boulder as the giant spat out fire, splitting rock wherever it hit. Soon the boulder itself began to crack. "Quick! Mary, the whistle!—the whistle!" El screamed. Mary who had been too terrified to think grabbed the whistle and blew through the loud end. She blew and blew and blew until they heard a chilling sound coming from the giant. They peaked over the top of what was left of the boulder and saw the giant holding his ears and making that awful sound. He was swaying back and forth in front of the fire with his eyes closed, covering his ears and Ben, who had been concealed in the trees, stealthily circled back around the giant until he was directly behind him. Ben was strong from all his fishing and was able to lift a large stone over his head and reaching as high as he could, he struck the giant's head with it. It was a formidable blow able to kill most people but the giant still holding his ears staggered forward and stepping off the platform where he had been standing he tripped on a fire brand that had rolled out of the fire. With one frantic effort to right himself he slipped and fell headfirst into the fire. Mary and the others watched as a white sheet of flame shot into the air and the giant was gone, only a few scales resembling a serpent's remained.

10

Mary and the others came out from behind the rock where they had been hiding and over to the bonfire that was then burning down to its embers.

"You won't need that," El said, pointing at another rock that Ben was holding and he slowly put it down. All those who had been in the forest watching slowly began to come into the clearing.

"What have you done?" one said. Where is the great one?"

"You won't have to worry about him anymore," El said, pointing at what remained of the High Mucky Muck. "You are now free. You are all free from the tyranny of evil—." At that point Mr. Slick who had been standing in the shadows interrupted frantically.

"But he was the great one. He was going to lead us to the heaven that is on earth."

"Listen to me, friends. Did you not hear him? From his own mouth this charlatan revealed his true nature and what was finally in store for you all. Did you not hear him?"

The crowd shuffled it's feet mumbling to one another. And then the leader of the ten former followers of the F.F.F. stepped forward. "Yes we heard it all," he said. "We have been foolish children to be so gullible. But now we see our true God. The child has come to us to lead us into a new beginning. Hurrah for the god child!" and they all cheered.

"No, no," El said, stepping up to the platform where the high and mighty had stood. "No, this child is not your savior. She has only come to free you of your bondage. No, your true savior is the one you abandoned when you went off to chase whirlwinds. Go back to your homes, rest, and remember what went on here this night, and in the morning go to places where as a child you worshipped the only true God. Go to your priests and ask forgiveness and then tell all of your friends what transpired here tonight and you will be placing your foot on the long path that will take you to where you want to be."

"Where is it we want to be?" asked one.

"Yes that is the problem," El mused, "but do as I have instructed. Return to the old ways. Spend time with your priests and listen to them and you will find what you are seeking. Go now, it's getting late."

Mary El and the Monkeyshines stayed behind as the former followers of F.F.F. filed out of the valley.

"Have I been of some help," Mary asked.

"Oh yes, Mary. A great deal of help."

"Then I am happy. Have you finished what you set out to do?"

"Peace will be on this land for now. Evil has many tentacles and what we have destroyed here is only one of them, But with informed and faithful people to carry on the fight, this island should be all right for a long time. For us however the journey is not yet over."

On the following day as they were getting ready to sail for home, crowds of villagers covered the dock carrying enough supplies to last two voyages. After sorting it all out Mary, El, Nelly and the children said a tearful good by and sailed out of the harbor. As evening drew on, under a canopy of flickering stars, Mary and the others looked out on an azure blue sea and watched streaks of phosphorous flow off the backs of dolphins as they played in the bow wave. Then, tired and content, they went to bed.

11

That night, they were all startled out of a sound sleep by something bumping up against the side of the ship and before they could get on deck four giants stepped into the cabin. They were at least eight feet tall and resembled the one they had just subdued on the island.

"What's going on!" cried El, jumping out of bed, but one of the giants scooped him up like a grocery bag and tucked him under one arm. As they were tying up El and Nelly, Mary Willie and Nilly shot between their legs and down into the ship.

"Catch those kids!" screamed one of the giants, but Mary, Willie, and Nilly were on their way.

"Hurry" Mary cried, "back to the hide out." The giants were fast, but lost sight of the children momentarily and when they rushed up to the bow there was no one in sight.

"Where the devil did they go?" Mary and the others could hear the giants talking from where they were huddled together inside their bow cave.

They heard some scuffling around and then one of the giants angrily said, "I don't know how they did it, but they slipped us. There's no point chasing 'em any further, they could be anywhere on the ship."

"Hardscum aint goin to like this!"

"Aw shut up. We'll just have to face it. Anyway, what can those kids do. Come on, let's go." Mary, Willie, and Nilly listened to their footsteps going away.

"Willie," Mary quickly said. "You stay here. I'll be back as soon as I can. If anything happens to me maybe you can do something. I've got to find out what's going on." The other children at first wouldn't hear of it but soon realized it was the best plan and Mary slipped out of their hiding place, looking carefully one way and then the other to make sure no one was still around, and made her way back to a food locker that was next to the main cabin where she could hear what was going on.

One of the giants was screaming insults at what Mary thought must be the two who chased her.

"You hopeless dunderheads, you're worthless. Do you know what the others have done while you were being outwitted by dwarfs?—They've got the whole crew of this ship locked up and under key—"

"Wait, what are you're doing?" Mary heard El, speak up. "What do you want with us?"

"Want with you?" the giant said. If I had my way I'd throw you overboard, but the great one insists I bring you to him. You are foolish people. You could be enjoying a beautiful sea voyage now if you had interfered with our plans. Now you idiot," speaking to one of the other giants, "you take these two topside and put 'em on our ship—think you can do that without falling overboard?"

"Yes sir," glumly answered one of them.

Mary heard all this as she peaked through a crack and saw one of the giants with El and Nelly under each arm crawl over to another ship that was now tied up to their's. Mary listened again to the two remaining giants talking in the cabin.

"You gonna burn this scow—Sir." one of them asked. There was a short silence, and Mary imagined that somebody was going to get it, but it wasn't so bad.

"You are stupider than my goldfish and I've gotta feed him by hand. Of course I'm not going to burn her. What if there's another ship in the area?"

"There's nobody anywhere that you can't handle—Sir," the other said, and Mary smiled to herself at the wheedling tone.

"That's not the point, idiot," the other said. "I just don't want be bothered or waste any time. What we will do is scuttle her. I'm going back on to our ship and you come on up when you're through."

"Through?" the other asked.

"Yea, through. You are going to scuttle this ship. Do I have to explain everything? Get an ax, go down below and chop a hole in her. Think you can do that?"

"Yes Sir." the other said, "but what about the kids and their crew?"

"The crew is locked up in a small room forward of the main hold, the kids would have no reason to look there. The place is almost hidden. No, it's a package deal. Straight to the bottom with all hands lost I'm afraid—ha, ha, ha! now get below and start chopping—a nice big hole now."

After hearing this, it took about a minute and a half for Mary to get back to the bow cave where she told Willie and Nilly what was going on. "Do you know where the room is that they were talking about? Where they locked up the Monkeyshines?" she asked them.

"Oh sure," Willie said "it's —

"Never mind, you can show us," Mary said. "Come on." As they quietly sneaked down to where the locked room was, they discussed what had to be done. "First we'll free the monkeyshines and then wait till the giants are gone or they'll just catch us again."

"The Monkeyshines will know what to do. They're the best seamen afloat," said Nilly."

"I'm counting on them," Mary said, "but first we have to get them out—and in a hurry! By then they were at the door to the locked room and on examining the door they could see that it wasn't really locked. It just had a long steel rod jammed into the hasp so it couldn't be opened from the inside and the children soon had the rod out and the door opened.

"Mary, thank goodness. We thought we were lost. What's happening?"

They could hear the giant chopping in the bilge's as Mary explained the whole situation to the Monkeyshines.

"Yes," Monkey one agreed. We'll have to wait until they're gone to try and fix the damage he does, but it's obvious we can't wait too long. I hope it's not a very big hole the giant is chopping."

All this time they were sneaking along the keel until they could see the giant whacking not very enthusiastically at the planking, but even with his inadequate strokes he finally broke through the hull and a great stream of water shot, as if from a fire hose, into the ship knocking the ax back into the giants head and sending him flying into the scummy bilge water in the bottom of the boat. Mary and the rest almost gave themselves away trying to cover their laughs as the giant staggered to his feet wiping blood from his eyes. "I guess that'll do," he yelled between curses that are better off not repeated here as he climbed up the ladder and disappeared above.

"Follow him and see that he doesn't return." Monkey One said to one of the others, "we'll get to work on the hole. Thank goodness he didn't care much about his work, that's a pathetic hole. We'll have it plugged in no time," and they went to work.

12

Old sailing ships always carried spare parts. There were extra sails to stuff into the hole and plenty of timbers to make a temporary patch, and by sunrise they had the hole permanently repaired. All the time they worked one of the Monkeyshines was on deck watching the other ship until it was well out of sight, and then they all went on deck.

"What course did she sail?" asked Monkey One, referring to the other ship.

"North by east," said the Monkeyshine.

"All right, bear away North by East, helmsman, and follow them, but stay out of sight, we don't want them to know we're still afloat. We'll need Dolly Fin to help us. She can follow them and come back and tell us of any course change she might make." Monkey One then made the sounds of a dolphin, loudly squeaking and clicking until Dolly shot to the surface next to the boat. They clicked at each other for a few moments and Dolly shot off after the other ship.

"Now," Monkey One said to Mary, "Dolly will keep us informed of all their movements and we'll follow and keep out of sight. They must be going to land somewhere and then well decide what to do."

"Couldn't we catch up to them or something?" Willie asked, "they might kill my parents."

"There's nothing we could do if we caught them. They're too strong for us and would probably kill us all. I don't think they intend to kill your parents though. Those pirates have orders to take your parents to someone else and they'll be well taken care of until they've been delivered you can be sure of that. We'll be there by then and we'll find out just how tough they really are."

"But why would anyone want them," asked Mary.

"I think it has to do with this trip of ours. You see, Willie and Nilly, your parents were sent down here to get help to solve the problems that are troubling this world of ours. I wouldn't be surprised if the kidnappers weren't sent by Grumbles himself or one of his followers." At that announcement there was complete silence and everyone looked at one another with dread.

"If that's so," said one of the Monkeyshines, "there's no hope. I've heard that no one ever caught by Grumbles is ever heard from again. We can't fight him."

"Not quite correct. Anyone can fight Grumbles, the secret is to win. Anyway, Grumbles is not our immediate problem. He never does his own dirty work. We'll have to deal with one of his subordinates and although they are always dangerous, they are not indestructible." At that there was a groan by everyone except Mary.

"I've heard of Grumbles," Mary said. "El told me something about him.

"Well Mary, the giant we just slew on South Island was one of these subordinates. Grumbles himself is always looking for places where he can cause trouble. Our world was reasonably peaceful for a long time, but recently there has been much trouble. People are fighting each other, birds are squabbling, animals are restless, even sea creatures are unhappy. El and Elli were sent on a secret mission to find help and thought that it would be found down here. Grumbles must have known about this trip. I think the plan I just laid out is our only hope."

"It sounds like a good plan," Mary said to Willie and Nilly, "under the circumstances the only plan."

For two days they followed the other ship staying out of sight easily following the other ship by all the trash and garbage that it tossed overboard. When Dolly returned, she and Monkey One chattered for a few minutes and then Dolly waited, treading her tail while Monkey One spoke to those on the ship.

"I'm afraid I was right. That ship is sailing for Fire Mountain." At that they all moaned. "Fire Mountain, explained Monkey One to Mary, "is the island home of the followers of Grumbles. It appears to Dolly that they are heading for a lagoon on the east side of the island. Now, Dolly knows of a river on the west side of the island that is navigable where we can hide among the trees and not be seen. That seems like the best place to stay while we plan our next move, what do you think?" They all reluctantly agreed to what was becoming a scary business, and followed Dolly as she led them toward their new destination.

For two days they sailed north west until they saw on the horizon a wisp of smoke. It wasn't long until a large island came into view with what Mary determined to be a volcano as its main feature. Dolly headed up the west coast of the island and then turned toward shore, and it looked as if she were going to run right up on the sand. Monkey one had the crew back the sails so as to slow the ship down. He didn't want to run up on the beach.

"What's she doing now," Monkey One wondered allowed. As they all watched Dolly disappeared, but soon came back into sight flipping her tail. "We're supposed to follow. All right, take the ship in slowly now and take soundings of the bottom. We don't want to run around." They slowly headed in and after a few nervous minutes a hidden bay opened up before them and a river that they hadn't been able to see from further out wound up into a forest.

"Well, well!" Monkey One exclaimed. "Dolly was right. This certainly is a wonderfully hidden spot." As the wind had by then died down, they dropped a boat into the water and some of the Monkeyshines towed the ship the last mile to where they could anchor behind some trees. Dolly, who had been leading them in came over to the ship and chattered with Monkey One for a minute and then scooted away back down the river.

"Dolly is going to keep watch at the entrance to the bay. This is a fine spot to hide, but we don't want to be caught in here without warning."

They all pitched in to get the sails down and to clean up the ship. When that was done they gathered tree branches and brush and camouflaged the ship until it was completely hidden. By then it was getting dark and after a fine meal they went to bed to tired to worry about what might await them the following day.

They were up at daybreak and after a hearty breakfast they all sat around the large round table in the main salon. "Here we are," Monkey One began, "but what do we do now is the question. Dolly tells me that the other ship is anchored on the far side of the island. She saw them going ashore taking El and Nellie with them. They were being led by a rope, but, otherwise looked fine, so I wouldn't worry about them for now, but we need to decide what to do—and soon. Anyone have any ideas?" There was silence around the table and then Willie spoke up.

"We have to find my parents."

"Yes, I know Willie and Nilly, that's why we're here. That must be the first thing we do. But we need a plan. We can't just blunder into their camp. We wouldn't last five minutes."

"Well, I'm going to go then," Willie said angrily. "Nilly and I will go."

"No, Willie," Mary spoke up. "We'll all go. That's what we're here for, but Monkey One's right. We have to have a plan or we'll never get your parents back alive. It's important to have patience until we know exactly what we're going to do. This won't be easy so it better be well thought out. What do you think Monkey One?"

"The only thing I know for sure is we haven't much time. Let's put our heads together and see if we can come up with something." So that's what they did, finally realizing that without more information on the giants they were wasting their time.

"The village that we saw when we were approaching the island is where we have to start, but it's obvious that we can't all go up there." Mary had been thinking it over by herself and knew what she had to do. "I'll go up to the village by myself and get as much information as I can about this bunch. I'll leave early in the morning and be back before dark."

"I'm coming too," Willie said emphatically.

"No, it's better that I go alone."

"No it's not," Willie argued. You don't know anything about our world. You probably don't even know the language, and I do." That made sense to Mary.

"Your right, Willie. All right you can go with me."

"And me too," cried Nilly."

"That's out of the question, Nilly. That would be too many—besides," Mary added to clinch the argument, "If something should happen to Willie and me, you must stay here to carry on."

"Well, O.K., but nothing better happen to you."

"We'll be all right," Mary assured Nilly.

And so before the sun was fully up the following morning, Monkey One, Nilly and the crew stood on deck wishing them good luck as Mary and Willie, with some food and a ship's lantern in hand in case it was dark before they got back, set off for the village.

Because the forest at that point was impenetrable, they followed an old path that meandered along the shoreline of the river. They could tell it was a very old path and hadn't been used in years because it was overgrown with brush and new trees and it was difficult going. After about an hour Willie stopped.

"Are you sure this is the best way? I sure wouldn't want to have to go back and start over."

"This is the right way," Mary replied. "I watched the village as we were coming in on the ship and I know it's up here some place. We'll have to head inland pretty quick though. You might start looking for a path that will take us into the woods."

Shortly after their talk Willie, who was leading, stopped again. "The main path looks like it goes on by the river," he said, but there's a branch of it over there that takes off through the trees."

Mary looked where he was pointing. "We'd better take it. I think the village must be up there some place." It was tough going and soon Willie stopped again.

"I think this is a waste of time," he said sitting down. "We should just head for the top of the mountain. That's where we have to go eventually anyway."

Mary sat down beside him. "And what would you do when you got there? Unless we know some secret about them, or someway to out smart them we would have no chance. You've seen how big they are. There is an old saying, 'know thine enemy', or something like that. It means, find out what you can about your enemy, their weaknesses for instance. We'll probably need everything there is to know about these fellows and then some."

"You're full of old sayings aren't you?" Willie said wearily. "O.K., as long as we've come this far," and he got back to his feet and started off again. "Something is funny though," he said. Why aren't there any animals. I haven't seen as much as a rabbit so far."

"Maybe there aren't any on this island," Mary said skeptically.

"Very unlikely, Mary. These islands are usually covered with them."

In another fifteen minutes they stepped out of the forest into a clearing.

"Look at that," Mary said. "There it is."

"Why the big fence around it?" Willie asked.

"I don't know, it's a stockade. They must have built it to protect themselves from something." What they were looking at was a solidly built fence of eight foot high timbers that seemed to enclose the whole village. "Let's see if we can find a gate."

13

They began walking, but could find no opening until, as they turned a corner, Mary suddenly stopped and grabbed Willie by the shirt and put her hand over his mouth.

"Shh," she said, and whispered into Willie's ear. "Over there, on the ground." A few feet away from a large gate in the fence was a giant, lying on his side with his head resting on one arm. They stood very still and watched him for a minute. Even from where they stood they could hear him snoring.

"He's asleep," Mary said.

"He's drunk, is what he is, Willie said, and there was the strong smell of alcohol in the air.

"You're right, Willie," Mary said. They stepped carefully back into the woods and around to where they could see him better. "Look there, on the gate, it's a padlock. It's on the outside of the stockade."

"That fence is made to keep the people in not to keep anything out. That giant must be there to guard the gate," Willie said.

"You're right. What are we to do?"

"We'll find out just how drunk he his first," Willie said and picked up a tiny rock.

"What are you going to do?"

"This will seem no more than a gnat to him. I'm going to bounce it off his head and see what happens."

"O.K., but we had better be ready to run if he wakes up." They made a plan as to where they would run so as to make a clean getaway and Willie tossed the stone. It made a perfect landing right on top of the giant's head and he didn't make a move. Willie then found a bigger stone and tossed it onto the giant's back. Still no move.

"He's really out," Willie said. "I'm going to get me one big giant. He picked up the biggest rock that he could find and approached the giant from behind. Mary was skeptical of this idea, but Willie was determined and so Mary approached the giant from the front holding in her hands a large limb broken from a tree, just in case Willie's rock didn't do the trick. Willie raised the rock over his head as high as he could and then brought it down on the giant's head. Quick as a flash a huge hand darted out and grabbed Mary by the ankle and with the other the giant quickly took the branch out of Mary's hand.

"Well, well,!" the giant exclaimed, "what have we here? What a dainty morsel! This is my lucky day," and he tied Mary up with twine around her feet and with her arms at her side. "What are you doing up here all by yourself?" He said looking around. The minute the giant had moved, Willie had jumped back into the forest and disappeared.

"Ow, you're hurting me." Mary cried out. "What are you going to do?"

"Oh, that's a shame, little girl. You won't hurt for long. And what am I going to do with you? I'm going to eat you. I haven't eaten in two days. Those oafs at the top of the mountain leave me down here to starve. They bring me no food and expect me to guard the beasts. It aint fair, I tell you. Ah, but this'll get em. You see, your kind are a big treat to us and the big shots usually get the likes o' you. When they find only your bones, it'll drive em crazy. Mmmm—" he yawned, "but first I'll just have a little nip outa my bag and finish my nap," and he took a bag from his belt and took a long swig. "Don't you worry," he said, "I'll be with you soon enough," and he lay back down as he had been before. Except that when he had grabbed Mary, a long sharp knife had slipped from its sheath that was around his belt, and it now rested on the ground next to the giant.

Mary looked around for Willie and saw him hiding in the trees. She was tied and couldn't move and only her eyes followed Willie as he slipped quietly into the open where he stood for a moment not moving. And then he crept closer to the giant a step at a time until he could reach the knife. It was a small knife for he giant, but a huge sword for Willie. He could barely pick it up, but finally had it wavering over the giants neck and then he brought it down as hard as he could. It went clear through the giants's neck and came out the other side. The giant with a bellowing scream that must have been heard for miles, leaped to his feet and with blood spurting out both sides of his neck, he grabbed Willie by the throat. Willie's eyes began to bulge, and as he was beginning to turn blue, the giant staggered and fell to his knees and as he relaxed his grip Willie popped out. The giant then rolled over and was dead.

"Willie! Willie!" Mary cried. "Are you all right?"

Willie was sitting on the ground getting his wits together and finally croaked a feeble "Yes".

"Willie, you are my hero! You saved my life!"

Willie got unsteadily to his feet and went over to Mary and untied her and trying to hide his pride, he sauntered nonchalantly around the dead giant, occasionally kicking him as if he did this sort of thing every day. There was a set of keys hanging from the giant's belt and Willie grabbed them.

"These may be the keys to the gate," he mused.

"All right," Mary said, "but what are we to do with him?" pointing at the giant.

As they were wondering what to do with the body they were startled to hear a voice. "Have you killed the giant?" it said, and they turned around to see a giraffe looking over the fence.

"He's dead all right," replied Willie. "Who are you?"

"I am Raffia, and who are you. Are you here to let us out?"

"Well, I don't know. I had better find more about—" but Mary grabbed the keys and had the gate open in seconds.

"You're now free. How did you get caught up in there, anyway?"

"It was trickery, of course," and what looked like an entire village of animals one by one peeked out through the gate, but went no further. "You see we are reluctant to leave our prison. We fear it's a trap."

"It's no trap," Mary assured them. "There is the giant, your recent guardian, and you can see he won't hurt you anymore." Tentatively the animals began to leave, occasionally kicking the giant's body to make sure he was dead.

"I speak for all of us," a leopard said. "We are indebted to you. We are at your service."

"I don't want you to be indebted to us, but you might be able to help us," and Mary told him why they were on the island and that they could use all the information about the giants that they could get. Could they help?

"Oh, I'm sorry to hear your story," the leopard replied. "We know little about the giants, only that they have probably killed all of your kind. This village used to be full of you, but one by one they disappeared and we—all of the animals were tricked into bondage. I hate to run, but we must get back into the jungle before more giants arrive. That roar he made must have been heard on top of the mountain. You had better be careful too."

"Will you be all right now?" You won't be tricked back into this cage?"

"Never! We are much wiser now. We must go. Good luck and if you ever need us we'll be here for you," and he followed the other animals who were now leaving the compound in large numbers to disappear into the trees.

"They're right," Mary said. "More giants are bound to show up soon. They must have heard his scream. We had better get out of here."

They called a large bear over to help them drag the giant's body into the woods where they buried it and then they began the long trudge back the way they had come.

Back on the ship the Monkeyshines were told all that had transpired.

"You have done a great deed to have released all the animals. If you do nothing else you will be remembered on this island. Unfortunately we have learned little about the giants. What do you intend to do now?"

"We talked it over on the way back to the ship and we've decided that we must act. There is no more time. First thing in the morning we will leave for the top of the mountain. If you haven't heard from us in three days, or if you are in danger, you should leave. If we are lost you must save yourselves. If we need you again we will signal you somehow. This is our fight, and we'll come up with something. We'll be leaving at day break."

Before the sun was completely up the next day they were on their way. It was hard going struggling through the dense forest and underbrush and before they had gone far, Mary heard a little cry from Willie and he disappeared right before her eyes.

"Willie!" she cried, where are you?"

"I'm down here!" Willie called. I fell down this hole. Can you see me?" Mary peered down a hole that had opened up in front of her and there was Willie about six feet below her. "I see you. Can you get out?"

"Does it look like I can get out?" he called peevishly.

"O.K., hold your horses, I'll get a vine and you can climb up that." and she got a long strong vine, and tied it to a tree and dangled it down into the hole. "O.K., you can climb up that."

"You know something Mary? I think you should come and look at this."

"Oh no you don't, you just want me to get stuck down there too."

"No, I'm serious. There seems to be a cave down here that goes up the mountain, like a big tunnel." Willie seemed serious and so Mary lowered herself into the hole and sure enough there was a tunnel that seemed to head up the mountain.

"You're right, Willie. Do you know what this is?"

"No, I don't, but I suppose you do?" Mary ignored his sarcasm.

"I believe this is what's left from a lava flow."

"A what?"

"A lava flow. When a volcano erupts its lava sometimes flows underground leaving these tunnels when it stops and cools. This could go clear to the top of the mountain."

"It could also start flowing again. Let's get out of here." But Mary was thinking.

"If there's an opening at the top, we could get up there this way. It would be much easier."

"You're out of your mind. You saw the smoke when we came in. It could blow at any time."

"I don't think so. Volcanoes can smoke like that for years without erupting. Anyway I'm going to go up a little way." And she started up a modest incline after lighting the ships lantern that she held.

"O.K., O.K., wait for me, I'll go up a little way with you," and they started climbing. It wasn't steep at all and the roof of the tunnel was well over their head so they could stand straight up and they made good time.

"I think this is far enough, I think I hear the lava coming," said Willie, stopping.

"Nonsense, there's no Lava coming. In fact there must be some opening someplace because the air is so good. You can even feel the air moving like it's flowing down the tunnel."

"Right. In front of the lava. Let's get out of here."

"Will you stop it. There is no lava. You can tell that there hasn't been any lava down here in years."

"That's all the more reason it's probably due any minute," Willie grumbled. Mary just ignored Willie and kept moving up the tunnel and Willie followed reluctantly. It was getting steeper and they began to huff and puff when suddenly a voice came out of the darkness that just about scared them out of their wits.

"Halt! Who goes there?"

"Who asks?" Mary answered, peering into the darkness beyond the reach of her lantern.

"Well, that's the correct password, but you don't look like one of us. How do you know our password?"

"It seemed like the logical answer. Who are you? Come forward so that we can see you."

"I'll ask the questions in here. Now, who are you?" and the biggest rabbit that Mary and Willie had ever seen stepped out of the shadows. "Oh, I see now," the rabbit continued. "You're people children, but there are no people on this island now. Where did you come from?"

"Well, that's a long story, and if we had a lot of time we could tell you about it, but we don't—although" Mary decided at that moment not to be so impatient. Although," she continued, "you might be able to help us. We're looking for some giants. Do you know anything about giants here on this island.

"Why do you want to know about the giants?"

"You do know about them?"

"Of course I know about them—you must be from very far away. I can tell you all about them, but come along with me where we can be more comfortable and out of the draft," and he led them down a hall and into a cave fitted with comfortable chairs, a table in the middle of the room and pictures of other rabbits and carrots on the wall. "Now you had better explain yourself. What are you after, and what's your name?"

"My name is Mary and this Willie," Mary told him. "What's yours."

"My name is Cabot and I am an elder of our clan."

"Cabot the rabbit. All right. Are they your friends, the giants?" Mary wanted to know who she was dealing with.

"You don't know a thing, do you. Do you think we are friends when we have to be cooped up in this dark cavern all the time, fearing for our lives? Why are you looking for them? Do you have business with them?"

"Something like that," Mary replied. "I'll tell you the whole story if you promise to help us. We need help badly."

"If you have a grievance with the monsters, I'll help. If you are their friends you have come to the wrong place."

"Oh, we have a grievance all right. A serious one." And Mary told Cabot all about Willie's parents being abducted and that they were there to save them. Cabot listened carefully to the whole story and when she was through, he sat for a moment on his hind legs staring at the ceiling, and then he spoke.

14

"You've come a long way on a dangerous mission. You can't know how dangerous. You see, the giants are the arms and legs of Grumbles—"

"Yes, we've heard of him. Is he on this island?"

"Patience, child, and I'll explain everything to you," Cabot continued. "His Evilness—that's what we call him down here—is Grumbles 1st lieutenant and he not only lives on this island but is right now within a half mile of you." "Oh!" Mary and Willie both exclaimed at the same time, but Cabot shushed them and continued. "It's all right, you're safe in here, but all of this island is now under his cruel rule. It wasn't always this way. For as long as anyone can remember the fire on the mountain was quiet, only now and then spouting a serious flame, but then more and more of your kind came seeking His Evilness—no offense please— and as they were fed to the flames, his strength grew until he controlled the whole island. When all your kind were in the flames His Evilness began to devour all the animals, and the only ones who survived went underground like us or otherwise hid themselves away."

"Yes, we saw a village containing animals."

"That's where His Evilness Keeps what animals he finds, penned up until he needs them for the fire. It's well that you ended up here."

"What about the giants? Where do they fit into the picture?"

"The giants are part of His Evilness. They are extensions of his being and can't be destroyed—that is unless His evilness is."

"Oh, My," Mary said to Willie. "This is what your parents were talking about. The trouble in your own land—"

"Do you mean," Cabot interrupted, "that it's gone beyond our own little island?"

"Oh, yes," Mary continued. "Trouble seems to be all over your land far and wide."

"You say your land. Where do you come from?"

"Well, you see I come from another world," Mary said, and told Cabot of her own story.

"And so that is how you ended up on Monkeyshines boat. Well, well," Cabot mused. "You seem to be here for a reason. I don't think it could be an accident." After a minute or two of silence, Cabot jumped up out of his chair and declared, "All right, come along with me. The first thing to do is find out if His Evilness has your parents, Willie, and if they're still alive." At that Willie gave a little cry of distress. "Well, Willie, we have to face the fact that maybe they've already been sacrificed, but my thinking is that they are somehow important to His Evilness and are being kept alive. In fact he may be using them as bait to lure the rest of you into his grasp so we must be careful. Anyway I have a way of finding out what is going on. Follow me," and he led them back into the main tunnel.

"They continued going in the direction that Mary and Willie were going before their encounter with Cabot. "You see," He explained, "this tunnel runs right up against the wall of His Evilness' chambers. I keep track of what they're up to and we'll be able to see if he's holding Willie's parents there. We'll have to keep quiet from now on. The giants have big ears." That, Mary and Wily knew and so they kept very still as they crept forward. After about fifteen minutes they saw a tiny light in the distance. As they approached it they came upon a pile of rocks that appeared to have fallen in from the roof of the tunnel. It reached almost to the ceiling blocking entirely the tunnel and the light was coming from a small opening at the very top. Cabot put his finger to his lips telling them to be very quiet and then motioned them to crawl up some steps that were cut in the rubble to where the they could peak through into another chamber where the light was coming from. It was a large room that the giants had carved out of the original tunnel and it had cages lining the wall and a table and chairs where two giants were playing some kind of game. As they peered into the room Willie suddenly drew in his breath and pointed to one of the cages against the wall that was in the shadows. There were his parents sitting on the ground leaning up against the walls of the cage. It was a very small sound that had come from Willie, but loud enough for one of the giants to sit up and look around.

"Did you hear that?" he said.

"Hear what?" the other said, also looking around.

"I thought I heard a noise," the first one said, "I'd better go outside and check," and he got up and went out through a door at the side of the room. Cabot again put his finger to his lips and shook his head vigorously meaning, you've done it now. But soon the first giant came back in the room. "I guess it was only the wind," and he sat back down at the table. "I'll be glad when this duty's over. I'm going out of my mind with boredom."

At that moment another giant came into the room and Mary recognized him as the leader of the ship that carried off Willie's parents.

"Complaining again, eh," the new one said.

"No, sir," the first one stammered, caught off guard. "It's just that I could use a break."

"Hold on for now," the new one said. "We're just holding these fellows for bait. To draw the others in. They thought they were so smart to follow us, but we knew it all along. We'll catch em soon enough. They're here somewhere. Just then El spoke up from the shadows.

"You'll never catch them." At this the captain went over to the cage and kicked it,

"You're lucky we're holding you alive for bait, old man! If I ever have you to myself you'll be screaming for mercy," and he limped back to the table and sat down. "We've got the whole crew searching the island so it won't be long now."

Cabot motioned for Mary and Willie to leave and they went back down the tunnel to Cabot's home. When it was safe for them to talk again, Willie spoke up.

"We've got to get them out of there. They're in a cage!"

"Patience," Mary said. "First we've got to warn the ship. If the giants find it we're lost."

"Well," said Cabot, "Now you know what you're up against. This won't be easy. Do you bring great magic with you, Mary?"

"I don't have any magic at all. I don't think I even belong here. It's all a mistake."

"Oh, dear. After hearing your story I was hoping you had come with magic powers to save us."

"I'm afraid not, but as long as I'm here I'll help out in any way I can."

"That's the spirit!" Cabot exclaimed, then added under his breath, "but it looks hopeless to me."

"Nonsense!" replied Mary. "We just need to get to work, and the first thing to do is to get back to the ship and tell them what we've learned, and then we can make a plan. We now have an advantage because we know that they know we're on the island."

"I'll stay here With Cabot," Willie said. "Maybe we can come up with some ideas too." Mary looked at Willie for a moment not saying anything. She didn't like that idea. Willie might just be staying behind to do something stupid on his own. Finally she agreed. Cabot might have knowledge that could be useful and anyway Mary would travel faster by herself.

"All right, Willie, but don't do anything crazy. Think first about everything you do. It could mean your parent's life. Keep an eye on him will you, Cabot. Willie can be a little reckless."

"I'll watch him Mary, and now you'd better be on your way. It's getting dark outside."

"Oh, my, I didn't know it was so late. I'll be back as soon as I can." She lit her lantern and left Wily and Cabot in the door of his home as she ran down the tunnel as fast as she could, careful, as she had been taught, not to trip, because the floor was a little rough.

When Mary reached the hole where Willie had fallen into the tunnel, she climbed carefully up the rope to the surface and looked carefully around to see if she were alone. All was quiet, and she was glad Cabot had warned her of the time because it was getting quite dark and she could just make her way back to the ship.

A look out was watching for her return and pulled her on board.

"Thank goodness!" he said. "We were getting worried about you—but where is Willie?" he asked worriedly when he saw that he was not with her.

"It's all right. It' a long story. Take me to the others and I'll explain it all to you."

Everyone was just sitting down to dinner and jumped back up to greet her and after a few words she sat down with them and ate a hearty meal because they would be up all night working out a plan.

Mary explained what she had learned and that it was known that they were somewhere on the island and that it was just a matter of time before they would be found.

"We haven't much time. Does anyone have any ideas?" Mary asked.

"Is Willie really O.K.?" Nilly wanted to know.

"He's fine. He's trying to get more information from Cabot the rabbit. We'll see him shortly," she said, hoping that that would be the case.

"I don't know exactly what we can do," said Monkey One. They have so much more power than we do. It seems a hopeless situation. If they know we're here, we're in great danger. Maybe we should leave the island for awhile and try again later."

"Now is our only chance," said Mary, "but I agree. We are in a tight spot and I don't want to endanger you and you're crew. It's true we can't over power them, it will have to be by stealth, by trickery. I'm going back up there by myself first thing in the morning. I can't leave Willie there and I'll be safe with Cabot until I decide what to do. What will you do?"

"If there is anything that we can possibly do to help you we will, but I think your right. We would just get in the way. You must do it on your own. In the meantime we'll stay right here as long as we can. If we're found out we'll fight our way out to the open sea and try to help you later."

15

The next morning Mary was very careful not to be seen as she made the uneventful trip back to Cabot's cave where she unfortunately heard the bad news that Willie had as Mary suspected been captured by the giants.

"I urged you," Mary pleaded, "to keep an eye on him."

"I know it's all my fault. It was late and I was so tired I fell asleep just for a moment—well maybe fifteen minutes—and when I awoke he was gone."

"No, it's not your fault. You couldn't have watched him every minute. Do you know what happened to him?"

"He's with the others. The minute I saw he was missing I went back to the peep hole and it wasn't long that I saw Willie sneaking into the giants room. I had shown him a way to leave this tunnel—I thought it would help later—and he'd gone out that way and around to the giant's room."

"How was he caught?"

"He couldn't get the cage open and the giants snatched him. It was pretty easy. I think maybe the giants saw him coming from the start."

"So now there's only you and me."

"You recruited no others?" Mary told him what they had decided, that they would only get in the way.

"What do you intend to do?"

"I don't know, but I've got to do something. Do you know anything that might help me?"

"I don't like to say this, but I see little hope for success."

"Well, I can't do anything from in here. Can I get outside without going all the way back?"

"I showed Willie an opening just down a little way from here, but I think the giants spotted him when he came out so you had better not try that. I know another spot in another tunnel that you might try, follow me, and Cabot led Mary into another part of the cave until they came to a raised spot in the floor. "Many years ago the ceiling fell in here and left that small opening in the roof. You can probably get out there."

Mary stepped up onto the pile of rubble on the floor and could just reach the ceiling where she pulled herself up until she could see through the hole. She peered carefully around to see if it was safe. "I think it's O.K.," she told Cabot.

"Be very careful, the giants are all over the place," Cabot said.

"I will, and if I don't see you again, thanks for everything."

"I wish you lots of luck, and I'll keep an eye on things from down here."

Mary carefully pulled herself up onto the level ground where she lay on the ground in some trees making sure there was no one around and then got to her feet and carefully headed in the direction that she thought might be the entrance to the giants room. Soon she saw two squirrels eating nuts and she thought they might be able to give her some directions. "Pardon me, but can you understand me?" she said. The squirrels spit out their seeds and seemed a little startled.

"Oh, yes indeed. We've been waiting for you. Follow us," and they started off in the direction that Mary had been headed. Mary followed and suddenly the two squirrels turned into two giants who grabbed her by her arms. "Come along little girl, we knew you'ld show up," they said as they dragged her along.

"You weren't squirrels at all were you," she said struggling to get away. You tricked me."

"Of course. You're as stupid as your little brother," one of the giants said. Mary almost told them that Willie was not her brother, but decided she had better not tell them anything. They soon reached the giants main room where they dragged her inside.

"Well, well," their captain said. "We finally have the whole family. That is nice. Families should stick together don't you think? Of course you do because here you all are." Turning to one of the other giants, he said, "Let the others out of their cages but see that they're tied up tight, we don't want any more delays, the Great King wants to see us at the blood stone now that they're all here." and he laughed wickedly. When they were all secured they marched away.

It wasn't long until they came out of the trees onto a cleared area, and Mary saw that they were on the very rim of the volcano. She could feel the heat as the smoke and flames lazily rose up from the depths. El, Nellie Mary and Willie were pushed to the ground where they huddled together.

"I'm sorry Mary. I didn't mean to get you into this."

"It's not your fault El, I just don't know why I'm here in the first place."

"Quiet! boomed a voice from out of the shadows and a giant bigger than any they had yet seen stepped forth. All the other giants including their captain stepped back one step and bowed their heads. Even Mary and the rest were impressed. There was power in this giant that they could feel it. The very earth shook with every step it took and even the slight breeze that had been blowing was stilled as this huge presence stood in front of them all.

"How dare you enter my realm!" it roared, looking at Mary and the others. "Don't you know the price you must pay? Who is your spokesman? Speak up!"

"I speak for us all." said El, "I alone am responsible for all of us being here, and I earnestly request that I alone be held accountable for our actions. Hold me, but let the others go and I will submit to what ever you have in store for me without complaint."

The giant listened to this, glaring down on them and then burst out laughing.

"You will will you? If I let the others go?"

"Yes, that is what I said," said El.

"Why do you insist on this perilous venture, anyway?"

"It's because of all the trouble that has been occurring in our world. For many years we've had peace and contentment in the land but recently there has been nothing but misery. We could put up with your occasional curses, but lately it has become untenable. And that is why I came on this journey to ask you to give us back our peace." The giant listened to all this intently.

"You say you previously put up with my little curses until they became unbearable?"

"Untenable."

"Put up with them!" roared the giant. "Of coarse you put up with them. Did you think you had a choice? You should have thanked me for the little peace that you did have. Put up with them? Put up with them? You either have a sense of humor or you are fool." The giant shook his head in disbelief. "Oh, and you—" he said as an afterthought— want me to restore your peace?"

"Why?" Well, let's see—" and he thought for a moment— "Oh, yes," he finally said. "Because that is what I do!" and he roared with laughter. And then with his red eyes shining he told one of the others to bring Mary to the blood stone, that Mary realized was a large rock covered with dried blood that sat close to the edge of the crater.

"Wait!" cried El. "At least take me first. The girl isn't even one of us. She comes from far away and was only on my ship by accident. At least spare her."

"Is that so?" said the giant, who seemed interested. "From far away, eh?" and he thought about that for a few seconds. "This is something I'll have to look into," he said almost to himself, but Mary heard it and groaned to herself. "All right, old one," the giant finally said, "I'll take you first. Bring him here," and El was dragged to the stone.

As El was placed before the stone the giant began sharpening with a whetstone a huge double bladed ax that was propped up beside the rock and he began to talk quietly to El. "Now, sir," he began. "I know you mean well, and that is why I am going to be lenient with you. I usually just throw malcontents into the fires, but because I like your spunk I will behead you first. You may thank me now if you wish". There was silence. "Ah, well then, we'll just get on with it, the giant said, and took a hair from his head and dropped it onto the sharpened blade, where it fell into two pieces. "You see how nice I am? I've even sharpened the blade for you, I usually leave it dull—sometimes takes three or four whacks."

El's head was placed on the stone and the giant lifted the blade high into the air. All this time Mary was trying to free herself but with no luck. The twine that held her wrists was too strong. She began to lean back, farther and farther until she was looking up at the sky, her head lower than her body.

"Ah," the giant said, looking at her, putting the blade down for a moment "You don't wish to witness the moment, very wise, it can be quite bloody." and he again raised the blade, but Mary wasn't listening. She was shaking her body and finally shook her whistle that had bean hanging from her neck into her mouth and she blew it harder than she had blown it in her entire life. There was no way to cover either end so that she was blowing through both sides at once so that both the dog side and the shrill side sounded. It was a sound even she had never heard, and it even hurt her own ears, but she just kept blowing as hard as she could, and she began to hear another scream. It was the giant screaming. He dropped the blade so that he could cover his gigantic ears to keep out the sound of the whistle, but Mary just kept on blowing. The giant was writhing in pain as blood began to seep through his fingers because the giants huge ears magnified the noise and the whistle's sound broke the giants eardrums and began to penetrate further into his head. He dropped to his knees still screaming and began to bang his head on the ground.

The minute El saw the ax drop beside him he crawled over to where one of its blades was sticking out of the ground and started furiously to cut his hands free of the twine that bound them. The blade was very sharp and it only took a moment to be free. He quickly grabbed the ax that was so heavy he at first couldn't lift it but with super human effort he finally got it up in the air and down on the giants neck where it easily severed his head from his body. The head slowly rolled to the edge of the crater and then over the side. As it reached the bottom of the chasm there was a sudden roar and a ball of fire burst out of the volcano. At the same time the giant's body was writhing on the ground and strange things were happening to it. Its arms began to change shape until they had formed wings, and its legs fused together forming a tail, and its entire body became covered with scales. You could still hear its head screaming for its body from the bottom of the crater. When the body had completely turned into some kind of a dragon like creature it began to lift off the ground. It was flying but with no head it didn't know where to go and it flew over the volcano where a huge ball of flame roared up out of crater. The dragon was consumed with only bits of scales left to fall into the depths of the inferno.

Mary stopped blowing the whistle and sat up. All the other giants were also changing form. They were squealing and shrinking smaller and smaller until they had turned into snakes, but tiny harmless things that slithered into the forest where they made tasty meals for the hungry animals that Mary and Willie had set free.

Cabot, who had been hiding behind a tree watching it all happen, came rushing out cheering and waving his arms but no one heard him, in fact no one could hear anything for several minutes because they had been deafened by the sound of the whistle, but then they slowly began to hear each other again. "Wonderful, wonderful, magnificent!" Cabot was calling. "You've destroyed the Evil One! Hooray! We're free! We are all free!" and with a sweeping gesture he surveyed hundreds of animals of all kinds who had come to the edge of the clearing and were now standing in reverence to Mary and El, Nilly and Willie.

"It's true, Mary," said El. "We have finally accomplished what we came for, the destruction of Evil in our land, and we owe it all to you. You, indeed, were sent to us by our savior. Look around you. These are the creatures of the forest, of the air, and of the sea. They were forced to hide wherever they could—for years—to escape the wrath of The Evil One. Am I not right?" El asked the forest people.

"You are right," answered a great stag with magnificent antlers who stepped forward. "We have been in fear of our lives—for generations. Once humans also peopled this land, but they were lured to this place with offers of all kinds of pleasures and foolishly, one by one, they followed the evil one. In the end however, instead of riches they were fed to the flames until they were all consumed. We of the forest were not so easily fooled, but many of us were caught also and so we were forced to hide where we could. Thank you humans, we are indebted to you. What ever you need, wherever you are, we are here for you," and he bowed his head, and the other animals followed.

El turned to Mary. "You've made some friends, Mary."

"I am only happy to have been able to help," she said. I had no idea why I was here, but now I know and I'm glad I made the trip," To this a great cheer came from the animals. "Does this mean," she continued, "that you are now free from this evil forever."

"For a long time I hope, but it's not over. I'll explain the whole situation to you later on the ship. I presume the ship is near?"

"Oh yes," Mary replied, "It's hidden in the trees—on the river."

"All right then, lead on," El said. "We should be going."

"We'll show you the way," came a cry from the animals, and with Cabot leading, they escorted Mary, El, Nilly and Willie down to where the ship was waiting for them.

There was much rejoicing from the ship's crew who of course wanted to know all about their adventures and after she had bid her animal friends good night, Mary told them the whole story. Everyone was excited, but they soon calmed down and were able to take to their beds.

16

The next day they prepared the ship for the trip that would take them back to El's family home and as they were about to hoist the anchor, a huge crowd of the forest people came to the edge of the clearing laden down with gifts of food. They had fruits and vegetables of all sorts, mangoes, watermelons, coconuts, berries of all kinds, breadfruit and special dishes of prepared food to take on the journey. With some tears and lumpy throats farewells were said and the ship was underway, navigating the winding river to the open sea. It was wonderful to see the ocean again and soon the ship was under full sail, racing at hull speed for home throwing spray at Dolly Fin and her friends who joyfully gamboled in the aquamarine blue bow wave.

Later, El, Mary and the others watched as the sun in fiery splendor slipped into a violet sea and then they went below to the cabin and as Mary, El, Nilly, Willie and Nilly sat around the table El explained to Mary what had been going on in his world.

"Yes. He's the helper that went bad."

"Originally he was a helper, but now he causes as much damage in the world as he can. These beasts that we've just destroyed were some of Grumbles followers, his snakes that I told you about. They were Grumble's second in command and were very dangerous. Grumbles will eventually recruit more discontents and we will again have to defend ourselves, but with your marvelous help, our recent victory has caused him a grievous defeat at his mountain and it will take time for him to recover. One day Olldmeister will destroy Grumbles for good and we will have peace for ever, but for reasons entirely his own, for now, he allows Grumbles a little room to do his dirty work. It's possible we've not worked out our own problems, and he's giving us time to do that—who knows. In any event we must continue to be vigilant."

"Yes, I see," said Mary. "You might need me again."

"Well, we don't know do we?"

Mary didn't mind so much because of her marvelous adventure, but she didn't know if she wanted to repeat it.

"You of course had no idea why you were here, Mary," said El, "but it's obvious it was meant to be. Without your help I fear to think where we in this land might be today. That is a magic whistle indeed. Take very good care of it—and for that matter don't let anything happen to your book. You still have it I hope?"

"Oh, yes," Mary said. I have it right here," and she took it from her pocket. She glanced inside it and exclaimed, "oh, my, this is strange, It now makes sense. I can read it." El got up and went over to where he could look over her shoulder while she read a perfectly normal story. But what soon became evident was that it related exactly everything that had transpired from the moment she fell through that first page, up to the present the moment.

"That is strange," El said. "It appears to me that the story as it is written down only becomes clear as it is lived."

"Why would that be?" Mary wondered.

"It makes perfectly good sense in a way. We can never know how life turns out until it has been lived, can we? Well a story is only a life in a book. I guess you have to live it before you can understand it. Does that make sense, Mary?"

"Yes it does. I think that is what my father was trying to tell me about reading. You've got to really experience it."

"Your father must be a wise man," said El. "It would be nice, however, to know how your story ends."

Mary looked up at El.

"I know," he said with a sigh, "what are we now to do with you?"

"Mary looked as if she were about to cry. She had been so busy with her adventure she had no time to think of home, but now she suddenly realized she was no closer to it that when we started this journey, and she wanted to be there very much.

"Now wait a minute, Mary," El said comfortingly, because he could well believe just how she felt, "we haven't forgotten that there may be a little problem now. "It's obvious that there is no way for you to get back home the same way that you arrived, but I don't think that was ever the plan. I have no doubt in my mind—not a bit—that you'll soon be home with your loved ones, it's just that we—or maybe you—have to discover how it is meant to be. I know that you were not sent to us without a way of getting home. Our God would not do that, nor yours I would think. In the meantime, it seems prudent to get back to dry land as soon as possible."

After a delightful two days of sailing, right on time, they stepped ashore into the arms of a welcoming party. There was much cheering and tears shed for the safe return of the ship that had been so long at sea it had been thought lost. Nothing was yet known as to what had transpired on it's voyage and when the entire story had been told and the people had been informed that there would again be peace in their land there was great rejoicing. Mary was feasted as a hero and made an honorary elder even though she was only twelve. Eventually things settled down and Mary had time to think about going home and how she would go about it, and one day discussed it with El.

"I want to thank you for taking care of me these last months," Mary told El. "I've had a great adventure that I will never forget, and I will always remember all the new friends that I've made, but now it's time for me to go home. Do you know how I can do that?"

"Mary," El said, "it is we who will forever be indebted to you. If it were not for you, I'm not sure our adventure would have been successful, but as to your immediate, question: I have no specific information that will help you. All I can do is to reassure you that you will be going home soon. I know in my heart this is true. My suggestion is for you to enjoy the next few days that you have with us, don't worry or even think about how you will get home. We believe here on this island that our god takes care of us and I know that when the time is right you will be returned to your loved ones.

Now that your work here is done, I think you will be leaving us soon, no matter how much we would like you to stay."

Mary had been taught that no matter how discouraging things are, no help ever came from worry, and no salvation from tears, so she proceeded to make the best of her situation and spent the next few days exploring the island with Willie and Nilly who wanted to show her their island home.

One day the three of them climbed the hill behind their house to show Mary their hideout that was situated in a cave. Mary was a little startled when a wolf stepped away from the entrance, but when it bowed and said, "Enter, Mary, you are always welcome," she got over her fright and followed the others inside.

"Sorry about that, Mary," Willie said. "I keep forgetting you are not at ease with the animals."

"I love animals, Willie. It's just that where I come from we have not yet become this friendly."

"That's a shame, we've learned a lot from them."

In the cave streaks of yellow lined the walls. "Is this gold?" Mary asked, running her fingers along the vein.

"I've heard it called that. This is my father's hobby mine."

"Some hobby. No wonder you have a wolf guarding it. This is worth a fortune."

"The wolf is only here to keep the kids out. They come in and hurt themselves. As for this stuff, it's worthless. My father makes trinkets out of it because it's easy to work. He tried to make useful things out of it like knives and spoons but it's too soft. They just folded up."

"This looks like real gold to me. In my world there's enough here to make you rich."

"Is that so? What do you do with it?"

"Melt it into blocks that we keep in vaults."

Willie looked at Mary skeptically. "And then what do you do with them?"

"That's it."

"You're kidding me."

"Yes, I guess it does sound a little strange to you."

Nilly looked like she was getting bored and spoke up. "Let's go to the beach, she said. "Can you swim, Mary"

"of course," Mary replied, "I was practically born in the ocean. My father taught me to swim when I was about three. He had a boat and didn't want me to drown if I fell over board."

"Great," Willie said gleefully. "We'll show you a surprise." They stopped by their house to put on their bathing suits and Willie and Nilly ran ahead while Mary followed a trail that wound down to a rocky inlet and a small sandy beach. "Last one in is a fraidy cat," cried Willie and he and Nilly jumped in. Mary was not to be intimidated and first stuck her toe in the water to make sure it wasn't freezing and that they weren't playing a joke on her and then she slipped into the water. "I guess You're the fraidy cat, Mary," Willie said.

"You cheated, Willie, You were almost in the water before you told me."

"Yea," Willie admitted, "I cheat a lot," and laughed happily as he splashed around. They swam out to a semi-submerged reef where they could stand up and look around.

"What's that over there?" Mary asked, pointing to a crumbling stone building far away on the point of the island. It had partly fallen down and looked ancient.

"Oh, that's an old monastery," said Willie, "It's haunted, You'd better stay away from there. People go there and never come back. It's creepy. Come on I'll show you something that's fun, and he dove into the water and didn't come up. Nelly watched Mary to see her reaction and when after five minutes Willie still hadn't surfaced, Mary looked at Nilly. "Where's Willie?" Mary said, a little concerned. Is he all right?"

"I don't know," Nilly replied. "Maybe he got caught in a rock."

"Mary didn't hesitate, and dived in after Willie, but when her air ran out and she had again surfaced, there he was beside her.

"Where have you been?" said Willie nonchalantly treading water.

"Where have you been!" cried Mary angrily, "you scared me half to death!"

"Sorry about that," Willie apologized, realizing he'd over played his little joke. "Come on I'll show you, follow me," and he dove down gain. This time Nilly dove in too and swam like a fish down to where Willie had disappeared. Then Mary watched as Nilly swam under an overhanging ledge and also disappeared, so Mary followed with just a little concern. She was beginning to worry about her air when her head popped out of the water and she was in a large under water cave. Willie was sitting on a rock under a small opening in the ceiling where a shaft of sunlight shone down on him. Nilly was just crawling up to join him. Mary looked around.

"Well, what do you think?"

"You knew about this all along, didn't you and didn't tell me?" Mary said, sternly looking at Nilly.

"Yes, I admit it. It was our little joke."

Then Mary laughed. "Well, I can take a joke, and it was a pretty good joke."

"How did you ever find this place?"

"I can't take credit for that. It's not our secret place, it's been well known for many years, but few people come here. We like it though."

"You have to be good swimmers don't you? I was almost out of breath."

"Yes, that's probably why it's not used. Like you, Nilly and I have been swimming since we were very young. The beach is where we spend most of our time."

"Do you do any surfing?"

"What's that?"

"I guess you people haven't discovered it yet. If I'm around here long enough I'll show you some real fun."

The three of them spent the whole day on the beach only going home when the sun went down. Mary went to bed early that night. She had important things to do in the morning.

Mary got up with the sun, made a lunch that she packed in a paper bag and set off across the island. She didn't know exactly how far it was to the old monastery, but she thought it was probably a long walk. She had known the moment she saw it that she would have to explore it. It fascinated her. She left a note for El telling her where she would be before she left in case they worried bout her.

Sometimes what looks to be not so far away proves to be very far away indeed and this was one of those cases. She stopped for lunch around noon thinking that she wouldn't have much farther to go, but the sun was well down in the west before she arrived at the stone walls of the old building.

She stood in the middle of what must have once been a courtyard and marveled at its size. From a distance the building hadn't looked so big. It was huge. What little roof there was still standing soared forty feet over her head and foundation stones covered acres of ground. Half of the massive stone structure was still standing and she walked on intricately fitted mosaic stones over to a ten foot high opening that had once held a huge wooden gate that, having fallen, was now turning to dust. Inside, the walls were covered with barely discernible ornate paintings and in the center of the room was the remains of a stone altar, inlaid at one time with gold, where now there were only bits of color.

It was difficult walking because of all the rocks and rubble as she made her way to a raised stone platform with a crumbling wooden structure. She climbed up it and stood on the platform and looked out across the room that would have held a thousand people and wondered what it would have been used for. It certainly had been important at one time.

She hadn't been watching the time and noticed that it was getting dark. She realized with a little concern that she could never make it back to El's that night. There had been no trail. She had simply kept the monastery in sight as she walked through the brambles and brush, taking bearings off an occasional tree until she had arrived at the old building. She remembered gaping holes in the ground that had to be avoided and knew it would be far to dangerous to attempt the return journey until morning. There was no moon and it was getting pitch black. Fortunately it was a warm night and she was reasonably comfortable, having dressed well covered to avoid being scratched.

In the last of the light she made out a large ornate wooden door in the wall and she went over to it and twisted the large iron handle. To her surprise the door creaked open and she found herself in a small room that was off the main hall. As her eyes got accustomed to the gloom she saw that it had been a library of some kind with old manuscripts falling out of cubicles in the wall. Before the light failed completely, she saw a bundle lying on the floor at the end of the room and she walked toward it. She remembered what Willie had said about this old place being haunted, and although it hadn't bothered her at the time, being here was another story, and she wanted to run, but something seemed to pull her along. Suddenly she realized the bundle was a body, or maybe someone sitting reading a book. Whatever it was it had it's back to her and Mary couldn't see a face. She approached it as if she were propelled and fell forward onto the bundle. Sitting up, she looked around and found herself sitting alone on the floor holding a book in her hands. She looked at the book and it was the one she had been carrying with her for her whole adventure.

"Ah, there you are," a voice said behind her. "I guess you were wondering what happened. Well we've had a power failure. It will be back on in a minute. It looks like you've found a book—ah there the lights are now—well good reading.

Mary was stunned and speechless through all this. It was the owner of The Big Barn that had been speaking to her and she was again sitting among its stacks. She opened her book and read the last pages. It was now complete and she could read it easily. She had had to complete the adventure to have the book complete she thought. But what am I talking about. What adventure. Had it all been real. How is that possible. She looked at the fly leaf of the book and there were the words:

'To Queen Quemonialy. With all our love, her friends.'

She snapped the book shut and sat silently for several minutes thinking. Then she got up and went up to the front desk. Mr. Quigly was reading a book.

"Mr. Quigly,"

"Ah, professor," he said turning around. "You've procured a valuable book from my collection" he said with a twinkle in his eye.

"Well sir." Mary said worriedly, "I hope it's not too valuable, because I'd like to buy it. I really like it."

"Well, let' me see it," Mr. Quigly said importantly. "I'll have to charge you what it's worth you understand. Strictly business you know," and he began to study the book. "Very interesting"—he'd mutter, or —"fascinating binding," or— "very unusual." Finally he turned to Mary. "This is a very valuable book. I've never seen anything like it. What do you think it's worth?"

"I don't know, Mr. Quigly," Mary said dejectedly.

"Well how much do you have to spend on a book today."

Mary dug around in her purse. "Only three dollars and—thirty nine cents, sir."

"Oh my, this book is worth far more than that," Mr. Quickly said.—Now let me see. If we start with three hundred dollars—not counting the binding—," Mr. Quigly said, absently twiddling his fingers—"and subtracted the good will of my best customer—how does thirty nine cents sound?"

"Are you joking Mr. Quigly?" Mary blurted.

"I beg your pardon!" Mr. Quigly snorted, "I never joke about business. Do you accept my offer or not, as you can see I'm a busy man," and he put his feet up on his desk, leaned back in his chair and closed his eyes.

"Yes sir, yes sir, I do. Here's the thirty nine cents," and Mary plunked the change on his desk next to his feet.

"Excellent!" Mr. Quigly said, sitting up and counting every cent. "You have dealt me a hard bargain, but business is business you know. Come back soon, I've enjoyed the challenge."

"Yes sir, I will and thank you Mr. Quigly." Mary started to open the door as Mr. Quigly called after her with a big smile, "Don't forget your umbrella."

"Yes, yes, thank you Mr. Quigly," Mary cried as she grabbed her umbrella and rushed out the door.

Running home Mary didn't care if she missed a puddle or two, she was so excited. She ran in the front door and up to her room with only a quick 'Hi' for her mother. Mary lay back on her bed and thought about all that had happened. She occasionally opened the book to a particular chapter that she wanted to remember and then closed the book and closed her eyes again. "I wonder if they'll miss me," she thought. "They knew where I went because I left them a note. It will only prove to them what they already think, that the monastery is haunted and that it swallowed me up—and it did in a way. El and Nellie will know though, I'm sure of that. I'll miss them. I'll miss all of them," she was thinking as she went to sleep.

THE END

MARY BRENT IN
THE MISTY SEAS

1

If you should one day paddle your canoe far north to where tall cliffs rise straight up out of the ocean your gase might follow the weathered rock all the way to the very top to where, in a forest clearing, a small house stands. In this little house Mary Brent has spent most of her 13 years growing up with her grandmother and because they have few neighbors they have learned to create their own fun. One thing they enjoy doing is to sit on a wooden bench positioned at the edge of the cliff over looking a vast sea, watch seabirds soaring, and tell each other stories of their own creation. Having now finished their stories they walk back to the house while Mary ponders a strange story of the sea that her eighty seven year old grandmother has just told her. She wonders how in the world she ever comes up with such exciting tales.

Wanting something to read, Mary is now looking over books in their small library. She selects one that looks interesting, but as she removes it from the stack, a book that had been hidden behind the others falls to her feet and she picks it up off the floor. It's a strange looking book and obviously very old. She takes it into the living room where her grandmother is sitting in a bow window watching some soaring birds.

"Gram," she said sitting down across from her grandmother. "Do you know anything about this book? It's very strange. I can't see any writing in it at all."

"Let me see it, dear," her grandmother says idly taking it from Mary, but instantly cries out, "Oh, My! Where did you find it?"

"In the library. I pulled out a book to look at and this one must have been behind it because it came out at the same time. It almost fell on my foot." Mary's grandmother looked the book over for almost a full minute before replying.

"This was my book when I was a little girl about your age."

"But what good is it? There's nothing in it to read." Her grandmother just smiled for a few seconds and then leaned over to show Mary something in the book. "There's writing here all right, it's just very dim. It's simply fading away—as I am," she concluded, almost to herself.

"Let me see," Mary said. "Oh, I see now, but it's too faded. I can't make a thing out of it."

Mary's grandmother took the book back. "No, I suppose not. You would have to know the story."

"And you know the story?"

"Oh, yes. You might say I lived it."

"What do you mean?"

"Not now dear, I'm a little tired. One day I'll tell you all about it. Why don't you go down to the beach. It's turning out to be a fine day. Oh, and take the book with you. You might be able to read it better in the bright sun."

"All right, Gram," Mary said, looking out the window as she carefully put the book in the pocket of her light jacket "I'll just get my hat. I'll be back for lunch."

When Mary went through the house to get her hat she noticed something lying on the floor that looked like a crucifix attached to a fine gold chain. She picked it up and after a quick examination she dropped it into her pocket. It must have fallen out of the book. She'd ask her grandmother about it later and she headed for the beach.

Long ago before she was born a path had been cut into the rock face of the high cliff by her grandfather and Mary was able to climb down to a beach made mostly of pebbles, but she soon found a small patch of sand where she laid out her blanket. Curling up on it she began to study her curious library find. It promised to be a fine day and Mary relaxed to concentrate on her study when she was startled by a large shadow that swept over her and fearing that it might be a rain cloud to spoil her day she jumped to her feet dropping the book into her pocket, but it was too late. The shadow was not a cloud, but a gigantic wave that must have been ten feet high that was beginning to curl. With no time for Mary to move, it immediately crashed over her and, bouncing off the cliff, went back out to sea, dragging Mary with it. Under water Mary struggled tumbling over and over until she thought her lungs would burst before she finally broke the surface gasping for breath. It was several minutes before she realized she was still alive. Mary was a good swimmer and after wiggling her feet feeling for a bottom that wasn't there she realized that swimming was what she would have to do. She looked around searching for her beach, hoping that it wasn't far, but instead all she saw was fog surrounding her. This was bad news. Not knowing where the beach was she might swim in the wrong direction, swimming away from land instead of to it and that would not do. As she considered her situation, she noticed that the fog was clearing and for a moment she had renewed hope, but it didn't last long. When it had all cleared, she saw that there was no land at all in sight. The entire horizon was empty.

Mary began to panic. She knew that with a clear horizon she must be at least twelve miles from shore—or more—and that was a long way to swim. "Calm down," she told herself. "I seem to be floating pretty well and the water is warm—but that's not right. The water at this latitude is always cold, almost freezing. This is very strange indeed." As she mulled over these peculiar conditions she spotted not far away something floating in the water. At first it looked like a log and she started swimming toward it. Soon she realized it was a small boat floating low in the water and her spirits began to rise. It was not far away and she soon reached what looked like an old wooden life boat and she grabbed the gunnel and began to pull herself up. As soon as she could see over the side, she saw somebody huddled up in the bow. Unfortunately at the same moment that somebody saw her.

"Not so fast!" it cried, and Mary saw that it was a boy about her own age. Mary tried again to pull herself into the boat, but was greeted with a loud thwack next to her fingers as the boy struck at her with an oar.

"What are you doing?" Mary screamed. "I'm drowning. Let me into your boat!"

"Oh no you don't. You think I'm dumb? You're from the ship, come to get me."

"What are you talking about you little fool," Mary yelled back, "Let me into your boat this instant!"

"You think *I'm* a fool? You seem to be the silly one, splashing around out there, thinking I'm going to let one of you pirates into my boat."

Mary thought that maybe she should be a little more diplomatic. "O,K, maybe your not a fool," she conceded, "but then why are you floating around out here by yourself. Your boat's half full of water."

"If you're from the 'Black Bird," the boy said, "you know very well why I'm sitting here in a sinking boat."

"I'm not from any 'Black Bird!' you little—what ever you are," Mary yelled back at the boy.

"Well then, who are you and why are you swimming around out here a thousand miles from any land? Out for some exercise?"

Mary was getting too tired to fight. "If you help me into your boat, I'll tell you all about it. I'll even help you bail this tub out so that maybe we can stay afloat. Do I look as though I could do you any harm? You're a big strong boy and I'm just a feeble girl." *That ought to do it, she thought.*

He looked at her for a good long time and finally got up and helped her into the boat. "You stay in the stern then. I am strong and I'll throw you back overboard if you try anything," and he went back into the bow area.

Neither one said anything for several minutes and then Mary said after catching her breath, "So, what's your name?"

"You really don't know who I am?"

"No, I really don't." Mary said wearily.

"Well," he said, after some consideration. "You can call me Windom"

"How about Winnie?"

"Windom!" he said huffily.

"All right, Windom, that makes it easier."

"Easier for what?"

"Easier to talk, Windom. We need to talk."

"That's right. You were going to tell me some long story about why you're swimming around out here in the middle of nowhere."

"All right, it's a deal, if you then tell me why you're doing the same thing."

"I'm not swimming."

"No, but you soon will be. We're about to sink or hadn't you noticed? Have you anything to bail with?"

"There's this manual bilge pump, but it seems to be plugged up."

Mary got up and went over to where a bilge pump was bolted to a timber. "Did you try to clear it?"

"No. I don't normally have to do that kind of work—I don't know how."

"Good grief! Even though you are about to drown?"

"There's usually someone like you to do it for me."

Mary looked at him in disgust and put her head under water and started pulling stuff out of the intake side of the pump until it started working again. When they had the boat clear of water Mary told Windom her story.

When she was through, Windom scoffed. "You expect me to believe that story, Mary, if that's really your name?

You're out her in the middle of the ocean. You swam all that way? You must be part mermaid—Oh, Oh,—I'm dead and dreaming or maybe you really are some kind of sea creature. Have you come to harm me?"

"Stop being so silly, Windom. My story is true and I don't know why I'm here any more than you do. Tell me your story and we'll see if it makes any more sense than mine."

"You really don't know who I am?"

"No, Windom, I don't."

"Well, you do seem harmless enough. I am Windom Cesar—Prince Windom Cesar, the son of King Amon Cesar, ruler of the Kingdom of Zarz"

"Right. You win."

"What do you mean, I win."

"Your story is much better than mine."

"You don't believe me," Windom said.

"Don't feel bad, I think you are a grand story teller. I really do. That's a great beginning for a gothic tale."

By then the sun was just beginning to set and as they watched the sun going down they both jumped to their feet. Silhouetted against the setting sun, still far away, were three masts. "Quick," Mary cried, "have you anything to signal that ship with. It looks like it's coming this way." Windom seemed to hesitate far too long to answer her when there was help in sight.

"You don't want that help." he finally said. "We've got to get out of here," and he picked up an oar. "Do you know how to use one of these?"

"Of course, but what are you talking about? That can be help," Mary said pointing at an old full rigged sailing ship that seemed to be coming their way.

"No it's not. That's the "Black Bird". That's the ship I've just escaped from and they're coming back looking for me. Don't argue with me now, just grab this oar and pull for all your might. It's me they want, but you won't last a minute on that ship, they'll have you for breakfast! Trust me, I'll explain everything as we go. If we can avoid them until it gets dark, we might have a chance."

"All right, Windom, I'd better trust you, but you've got to tell me what this is all about. You promised."

"Right. Just pull will you? They're getting closer! Over to that fog. Maybe we can get lost in it."

Mary pulled on her oar as hard as she could toward what looked like the same kind of fog that she had just experienced an hour before and after a minute or two they couldn't see beyond the end of their boat.

"O.K., now we'll change course and head up in that direction for a little while as long as we can stay in this fog. Maybe they'll keep going straight and miss us." Mary was too tired to speak at that point and followed orders. In a few minutes Windom put his oar down. "We'd better stop, the fog's getting thin", he said. "We'll spend the night here and hope he's gone in the morning". Mary was exhausted and agreeing to that idea curled up on a coil of rope and went immediately to sleep.

2

It seemed as though Mary had been out only a few minutes, though probably much longer, when something woke her from a sound sleep. When her head cleared she seemed to hear something and she nudged Windom awake motioning to him to be quiet. Out of the fog they could hear distant voices saying things like—"He can't get away—We've got him now—A little further and we'll heave to and wait for morning". And then the voices drifted away as a little wave, probably from the bow of a ship, rocked the little boat.

"That was the Black Bird," Windom whispered, "and the sailors talking. Unless there's a miracle, they'll be waiting for us out there some place when the sun comes up. Pray this fog is still here."

But when it was light enough to see, the fog was gone and several miles away the pirate ship was getting busy. It seemed that it had seen them at the moment they had seen it and they were now slowly turning in their direction and hoisting sail.

"Well Mary, we're done for now. I'm really sorry. I thought we could get away". Mary didn't say anything, but stared at the ship that was heading in their direction. Then she turned and looked at Windom to see what he was doing and saw something in the distance over his shoulder.

"Wisdom," she said. "What's that in back of you?" Windom turned around and immediately cried out. "Oh, no! It's my father's ship! The Black Bird will destroy him."

"What do you mean?"

"My father's ship is not a war ship and the pirate's ship is a 40 gun ship of the line. He'll blow my father right out of the water".

"Well, then what's your father trying to do?"

"He thinks he can save me but it's hopeless", and Windom tried to warn his father away, waving his arms and franticly pointing at the pirate ship that was fast approaching. And then he stopped what he was doing. His father's ship was doing something and it looked as if it was running up a signal. "Oh, oh, he's going to try a flying lift. It'll never work," he seemed to say to himself and then Windom started running around the little boat gathering up rope.

"What are you doing."

"We might as well try it, we've nothing to lose do we?"

"What are you talking about?"

"Never mind. Just do what I tell you to do". Windom then grabbed Mary and quickly tied one end of the rope around her waist and the other around his own. By then the pirate ship was coming up fast and Mary saw a puff of smoke followed immediately by a great boom and a cannon ball bounced off the water just to starboard of their boat.

Windom glanced up and then said, "O,K, over you go", and pushed Mary over the side into the water. She came up sputtering in time to see Windom also jump over the side and start swimming away from their boat. They were now tied together with twenty feet of rope between them and then there were more even bigger booms and cannon balls were falling all around them, but fortunately hitting nothing.

Mary turned then just in time to see Windom's ship almost on top of them and Mary could see that the ship had run out a long beam from the foremast. What looked like a man was standing at its outboard end dangling a rope with something attached to it hanging just above the water. It was a grappling hook and at that moment it dropped into the water as the ship flew by and Mary was flying. The hook had caught in the center of the rope that connected Mary to Windom and they were both whisked out of the water and banged together as they were swung back over the ship's rail and dropped onto the deck.

Mary landed face down stunned by the fall and when she was again aware of what was going on she heard someone talking. "All right now me lassie, you're safe now. I'll just get this rope off of you and then we'll go see the captain." She could feel a pair of strong hands untying the knot around her waist and then she was helped to her feet. Mary turned expecting to see a gnarled seaman helping her and she almost fainted. A large muscular monkey at least five feet tall with twinkling eyes was looking down at her and talking while he gently lead her over to where Windom and some others were standing around the foremast. By now she was thoroughly confused, but didn't have time to think about it because the whole crew who were also monkeys were jumping around in the rigging and cheering as loud as they could. Mary was happy to see Windom being hugged by a normal man and woman and when they noticed Mary the man spoke up. "And what have we here? A bit of flotsam no doubt," he said as he looked her over from head to toe. Mary just stared at the man as a last cannon ball fell harmlessly astern.

"Don't worry about that," spoke up Windom who glanced over his shoulder at the splash. "They'll never catch us now."

"Well Windom," said the man. "I don't know what it is you've caught here, but you had better tell me whether you want it kept or have it thrown back.

"We'd better keep her for now, father. She actually helped me a little bit when I was trying to get away from the pirates." A *little bit*—thought Mary. *If it wasn't for me Windom would still be floating around out there in a sinking boat*, but she didn't say anything deciding to keep that to herself.

"Well then, what will we call it?" said Windom's father.

"Her name is Mary—or at least that's what she calls herself."

"Well, we'd better go below and get you both cleaned up, said Windom's father. Bring the deck mop with you Molly," referring, Mary deduced, to herself. Molly was obviously the man's wife.

They all retired to a large great cabin that took up all of the stern quarters with a large window that looked out at the swirling wake of the ship and a view of the pirates now just a speck on the horizon.

Molly turned out to be Windom's mother who told Mary her husband's name was Amon and that he truly was a king, but that it was a long story that she would be told later. She then took Mary into a small cubicle off by itself and soon had her cleaned up and dressed in some of Windom's dry clothes. Back in the main cabin a large table had been spread with food and hot tea which Windom was seriously attacking and Mary quickly followed suit. Amon let her have her fill and then spoke. "While you were getting cleaned up, Mary, Windom told me something about you— as much as he knows—and now maybe you can fill in the blanks. How exactly did you come to be splashing around beside his life boat. I understand he helped you in or you would have drowned".

Mary looked at Windom who was trying to communicate 'Please don't tell on me,' by shaking his head, no.

"Is that what he told you?" Mary said knowing that Windom had tried initially to drown her.

"Is it not true?" Amon said sternly. Mary looked again at Windom and decided to leave it alone. "Close enough," she said.

Amon looked sternly at Windom who appeared to be a picture of innocence and back to Mary. "Well, how did you end up there—beside the boat?"

"First of all," Mary replied getting tired of being treated like old seaweed, "I was not splashing around, I am an excellent swimmer, and was not in danger of drowning, but I'll let that one go. As for why I was there, I haven't the faintest idea. And for why I am here—I wish I wasn't, I want to go home," and she started to cry, but just a little.

"Now, now," Molly said quickly moving over to comfort her. "Amon sometimes acts like a fool, but he doesn't mean it. Now see what you've done?" she said, directed at Amon.

"What? What have I done?" Amon protested. "I'm just trying to find out what's going on. Good grief, women!"

When Mary had told her story again to Amon he looked at Molly and then they both looked at Mary. Windom looked at all of them. And then Amon spoke. "We are at least a thousand miles from any shore and even then the land would be nothing like what you describe." Mary said nothing.

"You say you were reading a book on this beach?"

"Wait just a minute," Molly said as she got up and went into the room where Mary had changed clothes and returned with Mary's book. "Is this the book you meant?" and handed it to Mary.

Mary immediately saw that it was. "Yes this is it!" she exclaimed. "Where did you find it?"

"It fell out of your coat when I hung it up and I just remembered."

"May I see it?" asked Amon, and as he reached over and took it the gold cross and chain fell out. "What's this?" Amon wanted to know.

"I'm not sure," Mary said. "My grandmother seems to know all about it, but hasn't told me yet. She was a little tired."

Amon turned the cross over and then back. It looked at first glance to be a crucifix of some sort. However it was a remarkable piece of jewelry. It was made of fine iridescent crystal and covered with intricate and strange carvings and it seemed to almost glow. "What are these holes in the arms for?" Amon asked Mary. There seemed to be three holes, one at each end of the cross bar and one at the end of the main bar.

"I don't know. I haven't looked at it closely."

"Mmm," Amon mused. And then he picked it up and blew into each hole in turn. "I guess it's not a whistle," he finally said.

"Try covering up one of the holes," Windom suggested.

"All right," Amon said and covered the main bar hole as he blew into the left cross bar hole creating a loud shrill whistle. "Wow!" Amon exclaimed. "That would do it!"

"Do what?" Mary wanted to know.

"It's a whistle for when you get lost. Blow this and it can be heard for miles".

"Try the other side," Windom said and Amon blew into the right side hole which produced no sound at all.

"Nothing," Amon said and tried again blowing harder and there was still nothing.

"Well, I guess that one sound is loud enough to do the job. Let me see the book."

"The Quest Of Mylja, it reads on the cover." Amon said. "Do you know what that means?"

"Nope," Mary replied.

"There's no writing inside."

"When I first looked at it there was some very faint writing. It probably got washed off."

Amon looked at Molly. "Did you see this?" he said, pointing to the cover of the book.

"Oh, yes," she said, knowingly, and then one of the monkey crew stuck his head in the door.

"You'ld better come topside, Amon, somethings wrong with Clearview," he said.

"By the way, Mary, this is Monkeyone," Amon said referring to the monkey that had just spoken. "He's the first mate of our crew of monkeys that I'm sure you've noticed. They're the best seaman in our area and we were lucky to acquire them."

Clearview, Mary found out, was an eagle hired by Amon to be his lookout and when Mary and the others got on deck they saw that he was extremely agitated, jumping up and down in the crows nest and jabbering to himself.

"What's his problem," Amon asked Monkeyone.

"I don't know. A minute or two ago he just leaped clear out of his nest and started screaming."

"What's your problem, Clearview?" Amon called up to the bird.

"If it was someone down there making that terrible sound, knock it off!" he screamed. "You just about blew out my eardrums."

Amon looked at the people around him. "Any of you make some terrible sound," he asked and it seemed no one had.

"Wait a minute," Windom piped up. "Mary, give me your whistle." Mary still had it in her hand and she gave it to Windom who promptly blew softly into the right side. Immediately Clearview flew into a rage. "All right! That's enough! One more of your little jokes and I'm off. I can find my own way home!" Clearview screamed down at them.

"No, no, Clearview, don't do that," Amon called back. "It's all my fault. It was an accident. It won't happen again."

Clearview then stopped jumping around and with a sideways stare settled back down in his nest.

They all knew then what the problem was. The sound emitted from blowing into the right side of the whistle was simply too high pitched to be heard by human ears, but was to other species an ear piercing sound. It was similar to a dog whistle.

"Well," Amon said, "I'm glad we got that straightened out. Could be of use I suppose."

3

Back in the cabin, Amon, deep in thought, suddenly spoke. "What's your grandmother's full name, Mary?"

"I told you, it's Mary Brent—well it's really Mary Lyttle Brent." Lyttle was her maiden name. My parents were killed in an automobile accident when I was very young and my grandmother raised me".

"What kind of an accident?"

"An automobile accident."

"What kind of an accident is that? Something on a farm?"

Mary looked around the room. "You know what an automobile is?"

"How do you spell it?"

Mary then realized that she was truly in another world, and time. "It's a kind of cabriolet."

"I see, horses went wild I suppose."

"Yes. Like that."

"And your grandmother has told you nothing of her life."

"I know quite a bit about her, but now that you mention it, she is a little mysterious."

"But you know nothing about her relationship with this book?"

"No, I just found it and she said she'd tell me later."

"Well," Amon mused, "if what I think is true, your grandmother is a famous person in our world."

"That was three hundred years ago," Molly said, "how can she be that person?"

"Most of our scientists think it possible," replied Amon, "that time between different worlds is not relevant to one another. A moment in one world could be a year in another.—but let's get back to the present, and you, Mary, seem to be caught up in it."

"I seem to be, all right, but if it's all the same to you I'd rather go home, my grandmother will worry."

"I'm afraid that's not up to me. It's possible that you have been sent here to help us with our problem now as your grandmother was many years ago, but I'm sure when we're finished here you will find your safe way home." But Mary wasn't at all sure of anything.

"What do you mean, I'm here to help you?" She wanted to know.

"I have no idea. Mary Lyttle, your grandmother, seems to have had some magic or other and was instrumental in solving our problem at that time but, in your case, we'll just have to wait and see. If you're really here to help, we'll find out soon enough."

"Is that ship, the one that was chasing us, part of the problem?"

"Only in a minor way. That's my brother. He wants my kingdom".

"Your brother!" exclaimed Mary, "He wants to kill you!"

"Molly, will you please explain the situation to Mary. I have to go topside and check our course," and Windom followed him up on deck. Amon didn't really have to go topside. He simply wanted Molly to do the explaining and so she was stuck with it.

"Well, now that the boys are gone (Molly called Amon and Windom, 'The Boys') we can talk. But first do you have any questions so far?"

Mary had plenty of questions, but one in particular. "Why is Amon's brother trying to kill him?"

"Amon's brother's name is Brem and he's not really trying to kill anyone. I've known my husband's family since I was a child, long before I married Amon and they're all good people, it's just that Brem got sidetracked."

"How?"

"Amon and Brem are twins, you see, with Amon being the older by fifteen minutes. Amon's father feeling that Amon would make a better king made Amon heir apparent. And as the two grew up it seemed to be the case. Amon was the good boy without imagination enough to be bad, and Brem turned out to be bad without enough imagination to be good. We each of us have some of these characteristics within ourselves, but in this case, according to the kings belief, these characteristics were separated and doled out to each individual."

"One person separated into two people," Mary mused.

"Something like that."

"Anyway, I don't believe Brem is really bad, he just got off on the wrong foot."

"How?"

"When our people made Amon King, Brem was furious because he wanted to be king and he's been working toward that end ever since."

"But Amon is king. How can Brem unseat him?"

"He can't. Our people know he's not suited to be king and would never allow it."

"Then what's the problem?"

"You've seen Amon. He's getting along in age and will have to give up the throne soon. Windom is next in line, but is still too young. Brem knows he can never be king himself, but thinks if he can somehow get hold of Windom and control him as a puppet king then Brem can be the real power behind him."

"That's why Brem had him captured and placed on his ship—until I found him?"

"That's correct."

"Well my other question is, why are you all floating around out her in the middle of the ocean?"

"That, I'll try to explain. Windom is an unusual boy, probably because he has inherited some of his ancestors qualities."

"What qualities?"

"Well for one, he seem's to receive strange messages, but that's another story. I believe what you're interested in now is why we are at sea, and it's primarily because Windom has, never been a strong child and Amon thought that he could accomplish two things at once. He would take Windom on a sea voyage hoping that the fresh air and ships discipline would better prepare him for his future duties as king while at the same time get him away from Brem's possible grasp."

"Is it working?"

"Unfortunately Brem spotted us sneaking out of the harbor and has been able to follow us, so that part of our plan hasn't, but as for the other, I think the sea air has done Windom some good."

At that moment Amon came back. "All is well top side. I've set her on a course North by West. That will do for now I guess. Now, how are we doing down here?"

"Mary's been pretty well filled in for now but she may have some questions."

"Yes I do" Mary said, "and for one, how did Windom end up in that sinking boat?"

"He was kidnapped by my brother when he got separated from a group sent for supplies on one of these islands. Isn't that true?" Amon said looking accusingly at Windom.

"That's what happened all right. They took me on board the Black Bird and had me caged in a box on the fore deck when a huge wave washed me away. Fortunately it broke one of the life boats free and I made use of it—now that I think of it, it was about the time you said you were washed away, Mary. It could have been the same wave because it was gigantic. Maybe, father, if your idea of there being more than one world is true the wave could have been caused by our two worlds bumping together".

"Possibly," Amon replied.

"But that was your uncle's ship," Mary exclaimed, "Why did you tell me they were 'pirates'."

"To me they're pirates," Windom said stubbornly.

"So now maybe you believe my story," Mary said.

"We believe you Mary," Amon spoke up, "because your story is too fantastic to have been made up."

"Where are you going now?"

"Right now we're heading into the great unknown because our charts are blank below the 40 degrees Parallel. We're trying to follow Windom's coordinates but I'm afraid it's hopeless. Unless Windom soon receives another one of his messages I think we'll be lost. So that's our problem. Maybe you're here to help."

"What messages?" Mary wanted to know.

"Those are the messages I was telling you about," Molly interjected. "The mysterious messages that Windom receives when he's asleep at night. We have no particular destination in mind, just to sail for two years, so we've agreed to follow Windom's directions."

"In this case they've been compass bearings pointing us to a mysterious island or land fall but we've recently run out of directions," and Amon looked accusingly at Windom.

"Don't blame me," said Windom. I don't know anything about it. I wake up in the morning and have these strange things going around in my head and I write them down. I just haven't had one recently. Only that one I told you about that said, 'beware the Misty Sea' where mysterious swirling mists drive sailors mad and trick unwary sailors into sailing forever in great circles."

"And your destination is supposed to be a thing of great value?" Mary asked.

"It's sometimes referred to as a great treasure. I don't think anyone here really believes me, but It's something important I know. I can feel it deep down inside!"

"We believe you, Windom," Molly said, and Mary did too.

It was getting late in the day by then and as the others retired Mary and Windom stayed on deck just a little longer to close the day and Mary wanted to know a little more about Windom's dreams.

"Tell me more about your dreams, Windom, they fascinate me."

"You really want to know?"

"Yes, I'm in kind of a dream myself."

"Well, that's grand. Nobody else even believes me. They think I'm making it all up. But I'm not. I've known from my childhood that there's something out there for me. Just waiting."

"What do you mean 'out there'."

"I don't know. Out there someplace," said Windom as he pointed his finger into the distance in a great arc. "It's like—well, I don't know. Have you ever looked, Mary, at a spectacular sunset and wanted to be in the middle of it? Wanted to pull it around you like a blanket? Now if I tell you a secret will you promise to keep it?"

"Of course. You can always trust me."

"You know, I believe you. I've felt it all along. We're kinsman, so to speak."

Mary wasn't sure about that, but they did seem to have things in common.

"So I'll tell you. My parents think this voyage is all their idea—to prepare me for kingship, but there's more to it than that. I believe it's my destiny playing out. Why am I directing the voyage with my mysterious directions? It's the way it's supposed to be. This whole adventure is for me to find my treasure—what ever it is."

This was quite a lot for Mary to absorb, but somehow, coming from Windom it made sense. "I may be going out of my mind, Windom, and that's for sure, but I believe you."

"You're a corker, you are! Your the best," and Windom gave Mary an embarrassed hug.

By then it was dark and the two of them with a new bond between them went below to retire.

4
....

The next day they were all topside getting a little sun when the lookout cried "land ho" and in a few more minutes those on deck could see a low island dead ahead. Monkeyone however was looking at something else and Amon asked him what he was seeing.

"There's a water spout just off the entrance to that small bay on the island and there seems to be more blocking our course."

"You're right," Amon said now that he too could see them. "What do you think?"

"I don't know. They look dangerous."

"All right, Monkeyone, does it look as though we can make it into the bay? If we can we'd better put in there until the spouts are gone."

"Yes, sir," replied Monkeyone and he piloted the ship into the harbor where they turned the ship around and tied up to a derelict dock that appeared to be hundreds of years old.

"What do you think, Monkeyone, do you think this thing will hold us?"

"I know it's it's in pretty bad shape, but I think it will do. We won't be here long." Amon hoped he was right.

The next day Amon decided to send a shore party onto the island to look for fresh fruits and vegetables.

"Can I go too?" Windom wanted to know.

Amon looked at Windom for a moment before answering. "I'm sure you can," he said. "The question is may you?"

"I know, that's what I meant."

"Well I guess it will be all right if you promise to stay with the group. No wandering away. And you, Mary, go along too to keep an eye on Windom."

"All right. I can do that," she said as Windom looked disgusted that Mary would have to look after him.

When ashore they found what they were looking for and spread out to gather it all up. Mary started to pick some fruit that look good and noticed that Windom was missing. Finally she spotted him on the edge of the wood looking into the distance. Windom!" she called. "What are you doing?"

"See that hill over there," he said, pointing to a slight rise in the landscape.

"Yes, so what?"

"Let's go climb it. From up there we can probably see the whole island."

"I don't believe that's a good idea, Windom. Your father said to stay with the group."

"It's o,k. It will only take a few minutes. We'll be back in time before the crew is finished," and he started off at a brisk pace. There was nothing to do but follow and Mary soon caught up with him.

They were already out of breath by the time she caught him and so didn't speak. What she was doing instead was watching little animals of all sorts watching them as they passed. She would like to have known more about them, but there wasn't time and she hurried on with Windom leading the way.

They finally reached a rise in the ground that meant they were beginning to climb the small hill. It soon got steeper and more difficult to walk on the slippery grass that seemed to cover the entire mound. Finally they reached the top and then Windom disappeared. Mary soon realized why. The other side of the hill was steep and covered with the same slippery grass that they had been climbing up and they both slid unceremoniously to the bottom.

"Now we've done it," Mary said getting up and brushing herself off. "I hope we can get back up."

"No problem," Windom said, "we'll just find a place that's not so steep."

This was not as easy to do as Windom had thought. It seemed the hill ran entirely across the island from sea to sea and appeared to be just as steep for its full length.

"This won't work," Mary said. "Let's go back to where we first fell down. Maybe it's not as bad as we thought," and they went back to their original slide.

No matter how they tried, on their knees, on their hands and knees, with shoes on or off, they couldn't climb back up the hill, and they finally sat down to think about it. After a few minutes Mary got the strange sensation that they were being watched and peered into some trees that were not far away.

"Oh, oh," she said to herself, but Windom heard her.

"What do you mean, Oh, oh," he asked her.

"Look there in the trees. Do you see what I see?"

"Oh, oh," He said. "You're right. I believe it's a bear. What do you think we should do?"

At that point the bear spoke up. "Well, you two are a sorry sight. What are you trying to do anyway?"

"We're trying to get back up this hill that we fell down,—Uh, are you a friendly bear?"

"Am I a friendly bear?" it said, amazed. "Of course I'm a friendly bear. What other kind is there?"

"Well, where I come from bears aren't always friendly."

"Is that so?" You must come from a strange place."

"I don't like to impose upon you, Mr. Bear, but we're in kind of a hurry and I wonder if you could help us get back up this bank?"

"How far do you have to go?"

"We have to get back to the bay. That's where our ship is."

"Well you can't make it now. Don't you see, the sun's setting"

Sure enough, it was setting. Mary and Windom had completely lost their sense of time.

"Oh, dear, we were supposed to be back before dark."

"Well, it will be all right. You can stay the night with me and we'll somehow get you back in the morning," and the bear ambled slowly over to where they were sitting.

"We'd better run, Mary! Here it comes." At this point Mary realized Windom hadn't understood a thing the bear had said.

"It's all right, Windom, The bear says we can stay the night with him."

"What are you talking about?" Windom squeaked out. "Can you talk bear? And what do you mean 'stay the night with him'? He probably wants us for his dinner."

"What's the matter with your friend?" the bear asked. "He seems upset."

"Yes, he is a little. He doesn't speak bear, you see, and he thinks your dangerous."

"The bear looked hard and long at Windom and then said, "Tell your friend that I am normally friendly, but if for some reason I get upset I can be very dangerous."

"Follow my led, Windom" Mary abbreviated. "We need to keep the bear in a good mood."

"Hear, hear to that," Windom agreed.

And so they followed Mr. Bear back to his cave where they were introduced to his wife and two cubs.

"I don't know if you two want something to eat before going to bed for the night, but we usually have a bite."

"That sounds good to me!" piped up Windom who had quickly lost his fear of the bears at the sound of food. "What have you available?"

"Oh, lots of good things. Fresh Roots of a Tobango tree, or leaves of a Bramle bush, and here are some other things over here. See anything you like?"

"Not yet," Windom said his hopes for a warm meal waning. And then he spied something in the corner. "What's this?" he asked?

"Those are Black berries. We have them for dessert."

"I think those will work."

"Well, dig in, there's plenty for all."

So Mary and Windom found something to eat after all

and although not entirely filling the berries tasted good, and after their long day they had no trouble falling asleep.

On waking up the next morning, Mr. Bear, Mary and Windom set off, with little breakfast, to Windom's disappointment, to find a way over the hill.

"It's not difficult," Mr. Bear explained. "Just extend your claws so that they will dig into the ground and you'll easily be able to climb up like this," and he clambered right up the incline.

"I say, did I miss something?" he said when he turned around and saw that they were not following.

"It might be that we don't have claws Mr. Bear," returned Mary.

At that Mr. Bear slid back down the hill to investigate. "Why indeed you're right. I hadn't noticed that affliction before. We'll have to think of something else."

"It's not an affliction," Windom said a little miffed at the Bear's lack of understanding. It's the way we're made."

"Oh, that's a shame, well let's try something else. I'll pull you both up. You boy cub hold on to my tail, and you girl cub hold on to the boys tail and we'll scoot right up. Are you ready?"

"Mr. Bear" spoke up Mary. "I hate to correct you again, but we have no tails"

"No tails?" the surprised bear replied. "That is unfortunate! You must be an early species. Anyway we'll make do. You, boy, can still hold on to my tail and you girl grab anything you can of the boy's—er— strange attire and we'll be off."

Mary had just enough time to grab Windom's belt when she found herself being dragged up the cliff.

At the top of the hill they all sat down on the grass and surveyed the country before them.

"I take it," Mr. Bear suggested, "that you have come from that bit of water over there?"

"Yes!" Mary said excitedly. "And their's our ship!"

"Well, then, You'ld better leave now. That's a long way." After hesitating for a moment he added, "I must tell you something. It might be important or not, I don't know but, I've seen something like your ship before—in that same place. I was a very small child, traveling with my father. There were creatures like you fathering it."

"So, people like we have been here before?" asked Mary.

"They were the only ones—and they never left"

"What happened to them?" Windom wanted to know.

"They all died right there where your ship lies. Oh, they tried to leave for years, but eventually they all died and the ship sank into the water."

"I wonder why they couldn't make it?" Mary mused.

"My father said it was the whirling water"

"It was there then?" exclaimed Windom.

"The whirling waters have always been there my father told me"

Mary and Windom didn't know what to make of this new news, but it was time to go and set off back the way they had come which now seamed ages ago.

Things went well until upon nearing the bay one of the Monkeyshine crew came out of the woods and grabbed Windom.

"So there you are!" he cried. "We've been looking all over for you. You've scared you father into a frenzy. Never mind, I'm sure your father will want to hear all about it," and Windom didn't like the idea of that.

By then the other parties of the search team had found them and they all marched back to the ship.

On board, Amon stood with his hands on his hips staring down at Windom. "So you decided to take a walk in the park?"

"Something like that I guess."

"You knew you were not to leave the group."

"I just wanted to know more about this Island."

"If it hadn't been for Mary, you would not be here now—or ever would be again."

"I guess she saved my life."

"This kind of willful disobedience calls for twenty five lashes you know," Amon said seriously. Windom didn't say anything. "As this is only your first—or maybe second offense, we'll overlook the lashing and instead give you three months probation. Monkeyone, get some of the crew and haul the ship away from this place and anchor off shore. I want no more Shenanigans, and then everyone, back to your stations. The rest, come below."

Back in the cabin Amon took over. "Now, everyone, we have a problem. If as you say the waterspouts don't move this is definitely some kind of enchanted island and we want no more of it. We've got to get out of this roadstead. Mary, tomorrow take the boat and some rowers and do a little reconnaissance. Go up to the point and see if there's anyway to get by those waterspouts. I can't believe that there's no way out of this place."

"I want to go too," Windom said sheepishly.

"A good idea. Mary, put him to work on an oar. He can use a little discipline."

Windom opened his mouth to say something and quickly shut it again when he saw Amon's expression. There wasn't much more to say and as it was getting late they all turned in for the night.

The next morning Mary was up bright and early anxious to get started. A little boat trip is what she needed to forget the previous days ordeal, and she put a crew together and they shoved off. She felt a little sorry for Windom as he pulled on one of the oars, but decided it would do him some good.

As they approached the point of land that terminated the island they could see that the whirlwind was far too close for the ship to get around it, and for a few minutes they rested their oars wondering what to do.

"What do you think, Wando?" Mary said speaking to the shore boat's captain.

"There's no chance getting around the point," he said, "we might as well go back. We're almost outside of the whirlwind so we'll go around it's outside making a loop." So that's what they did making a big loop so as not to get caught up in the whirlwind and headed back to the ship. Suddenly they were brought up short. At first they thought they had run aground, but looking over the side they could see deep water.

"Oh, oh," Mary said, looking behind her. "That coiled rope in the stern somehow got over board and has been dragging behind us". Almost all of it had gone over the side. It was a float able rope and they could see how it had dragged out behind them to circle around the whirl wind. It was so long that the bitter end, the unattached end, was lying in the water beside them. They had towed the rope in a great loop around the whirlwind and now the rope had brought them to a halt.

"Better cut it loose." said Waldo, but Windom spoke up. "Wait a minute. Fasten the loose end at the stern with the other end."

"That's not wise Windom," said Waldo, if it gets dragged into the whirlwind there's no telling where we'll end up."

"It's already in the whirlwind," Windom said, "Look." sure enough it was tight around the base of the whirlwind which looked like the trunk of a tree. "I've noticed that when we row it seems to drag the whirlwind along with us. What do you think?"

"Well," said Waldo, "Let's row a little and see what happens," and sure enough they seemed to be dragging the whirlwind along with them as they rowed. The stalk of the whirlwind seemed to be so solid the rope didn't pull through it but instead pulled it along.

"Well now that we've got it, what shall we do with it?" said Waldo.

After a minute or two Windom spoke up. "The only place it will be out of the way is at the back of the bay."

"You're right Windom. O,k, boys, to the back of the bay it is, pull with a will!" and they started slowly to move.

It was slow going however with sweat running down their faces as they pulled at their oars. An occasional moan or grunt helped them in their slow progress as they made a wide detour around their ship to avoid any contact.

"Now what will we do?" said Waldo as they approached the back bay's tall cliffs.

"We've got to let it go sometime," said Mary, "It might as well be now. Cut both ends loose and pull for the ship as though your life depended on it—and it probably does." And so they quickly cut the rope in two and took off as quickly as they could. As they franticly rowed, Mary looked back. "Look, Look," she exclaimed and they all turned around to see what she wanted. "Look what's happening to the whirlwind." The whirlwind as it brushed up against the cliffs began to slow down. The cliffs were causing friction that slowed the spinning of the wind slightly and it was spreading out. The larger wind was also heading slowly in their direction which was also directly at the ship and no one had to tell them to get back to the oars. They pulled so hard that a small rooster tail was spinning off the stern of their boat.

As they neared the ship everyone on board was hanging over the rail watching them. "Quick, haul us up and cut the anchor rope. You'll soon have more wind than you need." The monkeyshines already had a rope ladder over the side and Mary and the boat's crew scrambled up it. The Ships crew was franticly hoisting all the sail they had before they realized what the little whirlwind had become. Brushing along the cliffs that circled the bay it had spread out to encompass the entire bay and it was quickly approaching.

"Quickly," Monkeyone cried. "Down with everything but the jib. "She's come a gail."

And when she hit she was. The ship was knocked clear down to her rail and stayed there shuddering until they all thought they were heading for Davie Jones Locker. When it appeared that the ship was never going to recover, it slowly started to right itself and began to move. There were three men on the helm and as the ship righted itself it immediately began to sail All the canvas that had been left up was one jib and the spanker and they were sailing at hull speed as they rounded the point. The whirlwind which was now a full gail rounded the point behind them, and as if in anger, sent a huge wave that overtook them almost capsizing the ship a second time before they were completely in the clear and sailing normally.

It didn't take long for every one to be cheering and doing somersaults in the rigging as monkeys are wont to do, and as soon as he could be heard Amon shouted, "Well done, Well done! I knew you could do it, Mary."

It was only when things had calmed down that Mary spoke.

"It wasn't my doing. If it weren't for Windom, we might still be out there." After she had explained how it was Windom's idea to tow the wind, Amon looked proudly at his son. "Well Windom, you've redeemed yourself! I was getting ready to throw you to the fishes. You're off probation.

5

Sailing south again with the wind at their backs the swells that were following them were building up. On the second day orders were given to the helmsman not to look to the rear because the waves were so big they might influence his steering. As it was it took two helmsmen to hold the wheel as a swell came up and rolled under the ship. That night in bed Mary, who had become used to the ship's gyrations and actually was enjoying it, suddenly woke from a sound sleep when a particularly huge wave lifted the ship so high it seemed as if it were going to take off and fly, and then dropped the ship with a crash so precipitously that Mary flew up out of her bunk striking her head on the deck above her before falling back. After being dazed for a few seconds she noticed that all was calm. Calmer than it had been for days. In fact there was almost no movement at all. She got up to see what was happening and when she got on deck there was a full moon lighting the night sky almost as bright as day. "What happened?" Mary said to Amon and the others who were all standing about quietly observing the situation.

"That last wave" Amon answered, "picked us up so high as to carry us over that reef over there and deposited us in this lagoon," Sure enough, they were in a lagoon where the water was smooth as glass with only a tiny ripple now and then. The crew had immediately anchored the ship so as to better assess their next move and were now looking at an island that the lagoon surrounded. It was a tropical night with the moon reflecting its light off of palm trees and casting their shadows onto a white sand beach.

"Could be worse," Amon said with a smile and they all laughed because on the surface it seemed a paradise. "This will be a perfect place to get the ship back in shape and to revictualize her. We must have cleared the reef completely when that wave lifted us over. I see very little damage. We should be on our way in a few days."

"Assuming we can find a passage back through the reef," added Monkeyone.

"Your right, I hadn't thought of that," mused Amon. "Well, we'll not worry about that now. As it's several hours before dawn, maybe we can get a little sleep before breakfast," and they all turned in to get some rest leaving two monkyshines to keep watch.

After breakfast They were all on deck not knowing what to expect. There seemed to be no life on the island. No natives, and no fire breathing monsters as Mary was beginning expect. 'Isn't this what was supposed to happen in such a fantasy?' she wondered.

"Pretty quiet, Monkeyone. What do you think?"

"It's a small island, probably deserted. I think we can go ahead and work on the ship. We can have her ready to sail in two days".

"Sounds good to me. Carry on, then."

It was around noon when they all heard a distant boom and looked up from their work. Outside the reef which was about a mile away sat the Black Bird with a puff of smoke rising from a gun port. It's cannon ball had fallen short of their ship and they hadn't noticed it.

"Oh dread!" was the first thing Amon said. "We're in trouble now. He's found us in a vulnerable spot. There's no where to run."

That certainly was the case, Mary thought. Now what were they going to do?

As they watched, the Black Bird swung her yards around and began, what they thought would be, to sail away, but soon realized that was not the case. She was only going to circle the island probably looking for a pass through the reef. If the Black Bird found its way into the lagoon there would be no escape for their own ship.

"Not much we can do," Amon said. "They out gun us ten to one. To fight in here would be suicide." So they all half heartedly continued what they were doing and waited to see where the Black Bird would show up.

In about two hours the Black Bird reappeared but, still outside the reef. She soon had her signal flags out and Amon reported to the others what he read.

"It seems there is no pass in the reef. My brother seems to be happy about that because, although there is no way for him to get to us, we also cannot escape our imprisonment. Let's see, he say's, "With no way for you to escape you'll be there forever, Ha, Ha'." reading on Amon continued, "But, he says, to show his good will, if we join his ship he will see that we all get home alive."

"He just wants me." Windom said resignedly.

"That's true," Amon agreed. If we all agree to Arturo's wishes we'll have to turn Windom over to him. That's what he's wanted all along."

"It seems we don't have much choice," Windom said with a groan. "I'm willing to go back to that slave ship if it's the only way of saving our lives."

Amon knew what Windom was willing to do and spoke for the whole ship when he said, "Not on your life, Windom, and it may come to that but, we'll find a way. I would rather rot on this island than turn our lives over to Arturo."

Everyone cheered because they were all thinking the same thing.

"Quick," cried Amon, "warp us in to the shore as close as you can. See if we can get out of the Black Bird's range," and as the crew feverishly towed the ship in to where she was almost resting on the sand Amon ran up her own flag which said, 'Phtewey', or something similar.

Immediately the Black Bird raised her own signal. "Have fun on your island."

It took a few minutes for the Black Bird to get her guns to bear, but, then she began to fire. The first ball fell short and the next one just cleared the stern by about a foot so there was no hope left, the Black Bird was fully capable of sinking their ship. Finally, after one bounce, a ball hit their ship amidship at the water line tearing a three foot hole in the planks. The crew had an old sail ready for just such an event and rushed to the side of the ship to cover any damage but it was too late, they were already sinking.

And then the gunfire from the Black Bird stopped. They knew that their target had been hit and was doomed and sinking and Arturo sent up another signal. "Sorry about your ship, Ha, Ha. She was a good one. Farewell, brother, may we never meet again!" And Arturo and his ship sailed away.

Amon didn't have time to mourn their situation and rushed over to the rail of the ship and looked over the side. "Monkeyone, come here," he called, and Monkeyone joined Amon at the rail. Just then the ship shuddered a little bit and began to heel over. "Look at this," Amon said. "We're on the bottom." Sure enough they were sitting on the bottom of the lagoon. When they had moved the ship in shore they hadn't noticed how shallow the water had gotten and now they could see that it was only about eight feet deep. The ship drew about eight feet of water and so they were now sitting on the bottom with most of the ship still high and dry.

"Could be worse, eh, Monkeyone?"

"You're right Amon. I think she'll sit here where she is. I don't think she'll heel over any more." The ship was sitting on her bottom leaning over only slightly and seemed to be pretty stable.

Just then they heard what sounded like a loud bird chirping and Monkeyone rushed over to the opposite rail. When the others joined him they found him in some kind of strange talk with a dolphin. Several minutes went by and then the dolphin swam off.

"What was that all about?" asked Amon.

"That was Dolly Phin, an old friend from my fishing days," said Monkeyone. "She saw the whole "dastardly episode"—her words—and is ever so sorry. She also has some news that might be of help. She's very familiar with the sea down here and she says that in about two days there will be an exceptionally low tide right here and wondered if that would help us any."

"Let's take a look at that hole," said Amon, and they all peered over to look at the hole in the hull that the cannon ball had made. "I think that's repairable, what do you think, Monkeyone."

"I agree," said Monkeyone. "If Dolly is right, and the water recedes enough, we might be able to reach the hole, but we'd better hurry if we're to get the materials together."

So all that day and the next they gathered together what they thought they might need for the repair job and when they had gathered together all the supplies they could they sat back to see what the tide would do.

It wasn't until the third day that the tide began to go out. It started slowly and Mary and the others began to be discouraged but, it kept going and sure enough soon the hole in the hull was fully out of water. They quickly folded an old sail over the hole, nailed boards over that the best they could and started to pump what water was left in the ship over the side. As they pumped the tide began to come back in. It came all the way back in covering the patched up hole and with a little shake the ship was again afloat.

"How's she holding?" Amon called down into the hold. "Pretty well so far," called back Monkeyone. "A little bit of pumping I think will be all she needs."

When Monkeyone was again topside they discussed what to do next. The temporary patch would not hold for long.

"We have to get the ship up on the beach as far as we can so that we can heel her over 'til the hole is out of the water and then we can do a real repair. What do you think?"

"That's right," said Monkeyone. "We'll run some winches ashore to a couple of trees, and haul her up as far as we can and then heel her over. I think we can do it."

For two days they rigged up the winches and slowly hauled the ship up to the beach until she wouldn't go any further and then healed her over on her side.

"Well done! Monkeyone," Amon cried when it was all done "the damage is free and clear. Now let's get to work."

From shore they cut two trees with trunks that had just the right shape to make new ribs to replace those that were crushed and from their own stores they found the necessary lumber to use for planks. Within a week they had the hole repaired as good as new.

In the meantime Dolly Phin was a so called sidewalk superintendent watching the proceedings from the bay. She also informed them that another high tide was due in another month. This was good news because while working on the hole the ship had become high and dry.

Now that the ship was ready to go all they had to do was revictualise her which they did with breadfruit, coconuts, bananas, water and what ever else they thought was edible, then sat back to see if their ship would ever be afloat again.

With nothing much to do as they waited, Mary rested in her cabin and picking up her book she casually leafed through its pages. A little surprised she found at the back several pages that had been blank know had strange markings on them. She had never seen them before and wondered from where they had come. Maybe they had been stuck together and were now separated she thought. As she was pondering this mystery Amon came into the cabin.

"What are you so absorbed in Mary?" he asked.

"It's peculiar but, I just noticed these pages I hadn't seen before."

"Oh? let me see," and Amon peered down at what Mary was studying. "What is all this?"

"I haven't any idea," Mary said. "I've never seen it before."

"I think I'd better have Frendo look at it."

"Who's Frendo?" asked Mary.

"Frendo is our historian. You haven't seen him because he's very old and keeps to his cabin."

Amon left and soon came back with a withered old man. "This is Frendo Mary and—"

"I know who Mary is" Frendo said interrupting. "You have something interesting Mary?"

Mary showed Frendo the book.

"This is interesting," Frendo said as he poured over the jottings on the page while Amon and Mary waited. "This is a chart, these figures are compass headings written in an ancient language that must be a thousand years old. I'm just able to make it out. What's even more strange is the course it indicates looks like an extension of the one we are trying to follow. The last message received by Windom"

"You can read the compass headings?" asked Amon.

"Yes I can said Frendo. This is a nautical chart with directional headings that are read from the stars. I can recall from my school days—a year or two ago—at which they all laughed, how to transpose them into compass headings."

"Does it make sense to you?" Amon asked.

"If this notation here?" said Frendo pointing to a strange mark on the map is the island we just escaped from, which is only a possibility, then these could be compass headings. If so they correspond to an easterly path. What is our course now?"

"We're on an east by two degrees north," said Amon.

"That follows all right. But to be more exact I would bring her around to a direct east course. Assuming that smudge is our island."

"Well," Amon said, "it's the only reference we have so we'll just have to believe it. This whole map is a mystery. For instance, what are these occasional smudged along the route?"

"I'm not sure about those. Could be something important though. Possibly something to be aware of, maybe danger."

"Well it's all a mystery to me."

"I've found," said Frendo "there are many mysteries in this life of ours."

Mary was lost. She had no idea of what was happening and was ready to go home if she could only find out how.

"Here's your book back," Frendo said after thoroughly examining the writings. I've made a copy of the chart. If we ever get back to sea we can use it. Can't be worse than what we've been doing". Frendo then went back to his cabin where he spent most of his time and the rest of them went back on deck.

While they waited to re float the ship Mary and Windom swam in the clear green water of the lagoon and collected sea shells and explored the island. It seemed to be deserted, or rather, never to have been inhabited and having found nothing to get excited about they sat down under a palm tree to rest and cool off. They dozed and when they woke up it was getting late and they went back to the ship.

Finally it was time for the high tide that Dolly Phin had told them about to come in and they prepared the best they could to be ready. They cleared away as much sand as they could from the ship and then watched the water creep toward them. Slowly it came up the beach, but it seemed to be moving awfully slow, but that's the way something does when you watch it too closely 'a watched pot never boils' and they all peered over the side of the ship as patiently as they could.

Occasionally a little ripple would seem to push the water along but, it was slow going. Finally the water had surrounded the ship and started to crawl up the side of the hull. Higher and higher it crawled and the ship began to roll on the sand as the monkeyshines pulled on the winches that were now attached to anchors offshore. The ship was almost afloat when it stopped. The water didn't rise any more but, just sat there.

"Is that it, you think?" said Amon. "Have we lost it?"

"I don't know," said Monkeyone dejectedly.

And then a small wave washed up and the ship began to move. Slowly at first the ship bumped a few times on the sand and then it slipped and was free of the bottom and was floating.

"Hooray!" went up a cry and everyone was dancing and cheering.

"Well we did!" Amon said. "It was that last push that did it."

"You mean that little wave," Windom said.

"Yes that was it," Amon said, and the crew began to secure the ship.

Mary and the others helped out where they could until they realized Monkeyone was talking to someone and they peered over the side just in time to see Dolly Phin swimming away. She had just informed Monkeyone that in searching the reef she and her friends had found a possible way the ship could get through to the open sea. It would be difficult but, it was a possibility with the help from her cousin Porpoise Gigantis. He was one of the oversize porpoises, a very rare species that grow to be thirty feet long. In fact it was he that caused the wave that broke them free from the beach. When he saw there plight he did a flip causing the wave that floated them when he fell back into the water. Dolly had now gone to find him as he was supposed to be still in the area.

"I hope she's right," said Amon.

"Well," said Monkeyone, "I do too. After all our work we don't want to tear the bottom out of the ship on coral heads."

The crew went about preparing the ship for casting off and in about an hour Dolly returned leading the largest Porpoise any of them had ever seen and Dolly explained to Monkeyone what was to be done. They were to prepare a rope with a large loop in the end about three feet in diameter and throw it over the bow. Gigantis would slip it over his nose and tow the ship through the maze of canals that would get them out to the open sea.

"Is she sure there is enough clearance for the draft of our ship?" asked Amon.

The answer came back in the affirmative. Dolly had swum under the ship and through the entire canal system and assured them that there was just enough depth as long as they didn't stray out of the canal. That's why they needed Gigantis to tow them through with a short rope.

And so it was agreed. The rope was prepared with a loop tossed over the bow and then secured to the capstan of the ship with the other end. Gigantis slipped his nose quickly through the loop and began to pull and nothing happened as the line became taught.

"This isn't going to work," said Monkeyone. I knew that porpoise wasn't going to be able to pull this ship," and for a minute it did look hopeless. And then there seemed to be some movement. Dolly and some of her friends had put their noses to the stern of the ship and it was just enough to get the ship moving.

"Well, you could have fooled me," said Monkeyone, and they began to pick up speed until Gigantis was able to handle it alone. They had gone about a half a mile down the lagoon when Gigantis made an abrupt left turn toward the reef.

"Oh, oh," said Amon, "here we go." They were headed straight for some waves breaking on the reef and Monkeyone yelled over the bow, "Hey, where are you going," and he reached for the ax to cut the rope when Dolly squealed up at him and he stopped with the ax in mid air. They were entering the reef now and Gigantis made another abrupt turn to the right and the waves broke behind them. Nobody on board said anything because they couldn't get their breath. They'd been holding them since the first turn. A few more turns and Gigantis came to a halt. Then he turned and came back alongside the ship which slowly turned the ship completely around. According to Dolly who was swimming alongside supervising, Gigantis had missed the last turn, but everything was all right, he would go back and find it. And he did making another left turn.

And then suddenly where the coral had been under the ship there was only deep blue water and the ship knew it was in the open ocean.

"Hooray!" cried everyone. People were crying, "It's a miracle!" "We made it! "Never thought we'd make it!" and then they pulled up the rope that Gigantis had quickly slipped off his nose as he began swimming away.

Amon asked Dolly, through Monkeyone, where he was going. It seemed he was a little shy and had more important things to do.

"Is there any way we can repay you all for saving us," Amon wanted to know.

"Just throw us a fish now and again when you run across us," she said and they all swam away doing somersaults and back flips until they were out of sight.

"Well, well," said Amon, "We've been given second lives. We had better make the best of them. The last heading given to us by Windom is east by two degrees north which is somewhat confirmed by the headings in your book, Mary, so Monkeyone we'll leave her there for now."

"Ay, Ay, Sir," said Monkeyone and took over the wheel.

"All right now," said Amon, "let's the four of us go to my cabin and talk over this new map of Mary's," and Amon, Molly, Windom and Mary went below. While looking the book over Amon decided Frendo should join them and notified one of the crew to request his presence who soon arrived.

Frendo had made an enlarged copy of Mary's map and it was spread on the table where they could all see it. "As you said, Frendo, This map of Mary's looks almost like an extension of the last map we received from Windom. You can read the compass points?"

"Yes. I'ld say continue on our present course."

The upshot of the matter was that they turned the ship due east and settled in for a long cruise.

6

....

For two weeks it was smooth sailing. The color of the sea was a brilliant azure blue indicating deep ocean water speckled with tiny whitecaps blown by a whole sail breeze that scooted their ship along at hull speed. Mary, now able to handle the ship's rigging almost as well as the monkeyshines themselves, joined Windom in climbing the ratlines, the cross pieces between the shrouds, up to the small crows nest where they looked for whales or watched dolphins frolic in the bow wave.

One day while at the stern watching a school of flying fish play Mary began to watch the ship's wake trail out behind her further and further until it finally disappeared over the horizon. But it didn't stop there. She saw it as a timeless ribbon stretching out behind her going on forever and when she turned around looking to where the ship was going she imagined that she saw the same ribbon now going forward also forever. It was as if she were standing on the moon looking down and seeing herself as an infinitesimal speck somewhere on this vast ribbon of time.

Suddenly she was brought back to earth with Windom's, "Hey, Mary, wake up!"

"What—" Mary said, a little startled.

"Well, you're alive. You've been standing here for five minutes not moving."

"Not true," Mary replied. "In five minutes I've moved an eternity," thinking how far she would have traveled in five minutes on her ribbon.

"What are you talking about," Windom retorted impatiently.

"Nothing, Windom," Mary said wistfully, and Windom turned around to watch a whale spout, putting his attention to better use.

The next morning sitting with her back against the bulwarks of the rail Mary looked at the map in her book wondering what those mysterious squiggles meant. It was difficult to tell how soon they would encounter one. While musing over the map, although mostly out of the wind, the pages of her book began to flutter until she had to put it away. When she stood up the wind almost knocked her down. The ship was beginning to heel over dramatically until the opposite rail began to dip into the water.

"Better get below, Mary" called Monkeyone who was directing the crew to reduce sail. "It seems we're in for a blow".

And a 'blow' it was. For awhile they were able to struggle along on course, but finally gave it up and and had to run with the wind under bare poles. All the bunks on the wind'rd side of the ship were useless because everyone just rolled out on to the floor and Mary, just as every one else had to do, hung on for dear life as the ship pitched and rolled her way into unknown seas.

When things finally calmed down and Mary and the others could again go on deck Amon and Monkeyone took readings of the stars and concluded that they had indeed been blown far to the south of their true course.

"Well, what do you think, Monkeyone? We're so far down south we don't even have charts of this part of the world."

"That's true, Amon, and it's not a good place to be."

"What do you mean."

"The old tales told by our people hint at great evil this far south."

"Anything specific?"

"Just that it's evil. Something about an island that spews fire creating demons".

"Ah, said Amon, "we have similar stories—in fact one that tells of a mysterious girl from another world that was instrumental in saving us from destruction. It's possible that our own Mary is somehow connected to that ancient person—" at that moment Monkeyone interrupted Amon.

"Right now," he said, "we had better think of other things, Amon. Take a look." and Monkey one handed him the glass that he'd been searching the horizon with.

"Well, well," said Amon. "A ship. Friend or foe, do you think?"

"There are no friends at this latitude, Amon. We had better get up sail," and he immediately ordered the crew to get everything up that the ship could handle.

When the ship was well underway Mary and the others took turns looking through the glass to watch the progress of the other ship.

"We don't seem to be losing her," Amon finally said.

"No, for a big ship she's moving fast." That night when they all turned in except for the eagle lookout the mystery ship remained the same distance behind as when they first saw her.

At dawn the next morning Mary and the others were up with the sun anxious to see how things lay and were a little shocked to be able to see the other ship without the glass. It had actually gained way on them so as to be seen with the naked eye.

"She's a fast ship," Monkeyone said, "there's no doubt about it. A large square rigger at that. I've never seen a ship that size that could overtake this ship. At this rate she should be in cannon range by sometime tomorrow." With trepidation they observed the large ship through the day reduce the distance between it and them and went to bed fearful of what they would find in the morning.

At first light they were all on deck and it was worse than they had expected. The ship that now loomed huge with towering masts had cannons that already were in range to reach their stern was only waiting for first light to fire the first round which it soon did. The ball not only reached them but sailed entirely over the ship landing a few yards off their bow.

"They're playing with us," Amon moaned. "That was just a warning shot."

"We'll never be able to out run her. We're going to have to stand and fight," Monkeyone said resignedly.

"We haven't a chance," Amon replied, "She's a first rater. She must have thirty two guns."

"Well, we have no choice, but I know a few tricks. If we can hold her off until we get into that fog bank we might have a chance." While they had been worrying about the other ship they hadn't noticed a fog that had been rolling in just off their bow.

The other ship was now getting serious sending a ball that bounced off the water missing their stern by only a few feet just as they penetrated the fog bank. They were now momentarily hidden in the fog and the next ball missed them by several hundred yards.

"Now boys," cried monkey one, "drop the foresail and come around 'til we're to starboard of that bounders course. In the fog she won't know where we are and then boys jibe to port which should send us cross her bow. Then we'll give her everything we've got!" The crew had run out the guns while they were being chased and they were now ready to fire. Just then the pirate ship suddenly loomed out of the fog. When it saw them to starboard it corrected its course to starboard and at that moment Monkeyone cried out, "Jibe ho" and they jibed to port. Mary and the others watched breathlessly as they bore down on the fast approaching pirate ship. It was coming up fast and for a minute it looked as though they may have miscalculated their speed and would be run down by the other ship but at the last moment they cleared its bow by only a few feet while at the same time firing all their guns as they came in range. They had only five guns, but they did a good job taking down the pirates foremast. Unfortunately the pirate ship quick-wittedly kept bearing to starboard until all her port guns were in range of Amon's ship as it passed by, letting fly with a broadside of twelve guns. Fortunately the pirate ship hadn't expected the turn and their guns were not well aimed or Amon's ship would have been blown clear out of the water. But, as it was the pirate ship did its job by taking down Amons mainmast causing the ship to come to a halt and to essentially put her out of commission. The pirate ship still able to sail jibed around and began to bear down on them, and Mary could see them readying grappling hooks in preparation for boarding.

Three hundred pirates with their cutlasses raised were in their own ships rigging prepared to board Amons ship, as Monkeyone cried, "Here they come boys give'em what they deserve!" And the monkeyshines, all thirty of them were ready to defend their ship to the death with what small arms they had.

Just before the two ships came together there was a tremendous roar sounding as though the whole sky had exploded and immediately the pirate ship blew up throwing men and guns and pieces of ship high in the air.

When the smoke and debris cleared enough to see again, the pirate ship had completely sunk and Mary noted that all it's crew left alive had fallen into the water and had turned into sea snakes scurrying away to the south. And floating across from their own ship was the Black Bird with Amon's brother Arturo standing by the rail with his hands on his hip's with a big smile on his face.

"Greetings brother! Are you glad to see me?"

Surprised speechless for a moment, Amon finally was able to respond. "Well, Brother, in this case I have to admit I am. You must have been hiding in the fog all this time watching us getting massacred. You are up to your old tricks I see, letting someone else do your dirty work for you."

"Brother!" Arturo cried, "you do me no justice!. I am mortified! I come to your defense, saving you from sure and painful death and you find fault with me. You should be ashamed of yourself."

"You're right of course, Arturo," Amon said sheepishly. "I apologize. I've been under a bit of a strain and I lost my head."

"Of, Course. I accept you're apology. Now will you come aboard and join me in a glass of fine wine that I've been saving for just such an occasion?"

Suspecting possible treachery Amon refused by returning the offer. "I have no fine wine but if you would join me on my ship I offer you plumb pudding."

"Ah, you devil you. You still don't trust your old loving brother do you? I'll tell you what I'll do. Send me over a line and I'll send you back by way of it a small cask of my offer and we will drink to each other across this great divide."

And so that was what they did. And as Arturo said it was fine wine and there was enough for Amon and Monkeyone while Mary Windom and Molly had tea.

"And now, Arturo," Amon said, when they were all finished with the pleasantries, "We are I'm afraid at your mercy. What do you intend to do with us?"

"With you?" I don't intend to anything with you. Do you think I would take advantage of an adversary when he's down? You insult me Amon. No, your time will come, but not now. You must regain your strength to be worthy of my attention. By the way, if your ship can still navigate a course north by east, in two days—or rather four days due to the shape you're in—you will find what I believe to be a deserted island capable of supplying you with the necessary trees to refit your ship. Do hurry. I look forward to our next visit. Toodeloo."

As Arturo's ship was simply hove to with the mainmast backed so as to hold her position it was easy for them to get under way and they were soon hull down on the horizon.

"What do you think of that, Amon?" said Monkeyone.

"Well, it was a bit of a surprise but, when I think about it I realize he couldn't have done anything else. He may be a renegade but he's an honorable renegade and it would have been against his nature to do anything else."

"Is this the end of it then?" asked Mary.

"Oh, by no means. The next chance he gets he'll be at me again."

"It seems such a waste."

"It's just the way it is, Mary," Amon said and then he turned to Monkeyone. "I believe Arturo means well Monkey, what do you think."

"He could have just destroyed us right here so there would be no point in more trickery. We might as well believe him and see if we can find this island of his."

Amon agreed and so they cleaned up their ship as best they could, and with the mainmast gone set a jury rigged sail on the existing foremast, and headed north by east to see what they could find.

For the next three days it stormed with lightning and thunder and a fierce wind that kept blowing them off course, The jury rigged ship was not easy to control and they soon had no idea where they were. And then the sky cleared, the sun broke through scudding clouds and except for what looked like a fog bank to the east it turned into a beautiful day. With their chores done, Mary and Windom were able to climb to the masthead where they sat dozing in the crows nest. They were suddenly brought to attention by the screech, "Land ho." and they both sat up excitedly.

"What do you see, Windom?" Mary said, "Can you see anything?"

"Over there, on the port bow," Windom said, pointing.

"You certainly have good eyes," Mary said, "all I can see is a smudge on the horizon."

"Well," Windom admitted, "that's all I can see, but the lookout has eagle eyes and I take his word for it." In fact the lookout was an eagle hired on for just that work and that was why when it cried out, "Land ho," it was more a screech than anything else.

7

It was late in the day when they saw land and it wasn't until the next morning when Mary came on deck that the crew was just dropping anchor in a quiet lagoon off shore from what looked like a fair sized island.

"Well we've found an island although there is no telling whether it's Arturo's or not. We've been so thrown off course that we might be anywhere."

Monkeyone who was searching the shore with a glass thought the island might do in any event. "I see no signs of life anywhere and there's some fine trees we can use for timber so we might as well get to work."

It took all day just to get the ship ready before they were ready and what with locating all the tools they would need and rigging tackle booms and cradles to get the timbers aboard it was decided to wait until morning to go ashore and all night a lookout kept watch on the island looking for any sign of life. By morning all seemed clear and with two of the ships boats along with the crew who were to fell trees, Mary Windom and Amon, set off.

Ashore they began to select the trees that they could use. Mary looked around for Windom and saw that he had climbed up a low hill where there was a small clearing and was standing in the middle of the open area looking off to the south. Mary climbed up to see what he was up to. "What are you doing?" she said, "we should be down below cutting trees".

"I know, I just thought I'd see what I could see from up here."

"Well you can't see very far, with this fog." And Mary was right because there was a thick haze covering the entire area.

Just then a giant bird of some kind swooped down out of the overhanging cloud and flew over them and began a slow turn as it began to circle.

"Windom, let's go!" Mary screamed as the great bird began to dive. They began to run for the cover of the trees but not in time. The bird was huge with a wing span of twenty feet and with one grab had both Mary and Windom in each of it's claws and was flying off to the south. Every time it flapped it's wings it's legs banged the two children against each other until Mary was able to grab Windom's shirt and hold them together for a minute.

"Quick, Windom, slip your belt through mine so we don't bang around!" Just then they flew apart again but, with a few more tries they got themselves secured.

"You've done it again, Windom, what is it with you, now look what you've done."

"Oh shut up Mary! It wasn't my fault. How did I know this buzzard had it's eye on me? I'd rather we try to find our way out of this mess than quibble."

"Right." Mary agreed, "Sorry about that. What do you think."

"Well, I suppose this thing has to land sometime," Windom speculated.

Mary thought about that for a minute. "To feed it's babies."

By now the fog had lifted and they saw that they were being flown south over a river that they seemed to be following. Windom had left all his tree cutting equipment in the clearing but, Mary was still clutching her knife in one hand and she started swinging it at the underside of the big bird.

"What are you doing!" cried Windom, "you're going to get us killed."

"We're going to die anyway when we get back to her nest. I'd rather drown," and she kept swinging her knife at the bird. Finally one of her swings was successful and she cut halfway through one of the birds legs. The bird screamed and the leg released it's grip on Mary. Of course Mary was still attached to Windom but, hanging from only one leg they were being swung about violently. The bird was screaming in pain and anger and finally unable to hang on to them any more let go. By now the bird had shot up into the sky and was several hundred feet above the river and as Mary realized all was lost she turned to Windom who was still attached to her and cried above the roaring wind noise, "Good by Windom, I'm so sorry." Windom was so terrified that he couldn't say anything as they seemed to be falling to their deaths.

But the great bird would not give up it's treasure so easily and just before Mary and Windom hit the water it swooped down once more as birds do when they've dropped something and grabbed them again with it's one good claw and was able to hang on only for a few seconds before it dropped them again. Which was fortunate because they were now only a few feet above the water. They both hit the water at the same time and water skied across it for fifty feet before sinking.

Mary dropped her knife and started scrambling for the surface as Windom was already doing. They were not far from the shore and began to swim toward it when they saw the great bird making a large circle above them.

"Hurry!" Mary cried. "The bird— we've got to get to the trees!" They swam so fast they almost made a rooster trail as racing boats do. They scrambled up the shore just as the bird made it's dive and threw themselves into the trees as the bird just missed them. They lay in the trees recovering as the bird made two unsuccessful passes before it flew away screaming at it's loss.

"You can unhook us now" Mary said when she got her breath back because they were of course still tied together.

Windom quietly undid them and then turned and slowly looked at Mary. "You are something else, you know that?"

"I know," Mary said demurely.

"You almost got us killed."

"Ah, but I didn't did I."

Windom just shook his head in disbelief.

As they were picking themselves up off the ground Mary said hushedly, "look," and Windom looked to where Mary was pointing. What had just come out from behind a tree was a small animal possibly a mole and it was looking at them.

"Well hello little fellow," Mary said, more in jest than anything else because she certainly didn't expect a reply. "What are you doing here?"

"I'm traveling much as you are I dare say" It spoke back. Well, that was such a shock for Mary that she sat back down and leaned against a tree.

"This is too much," she said almost to herself but, I guess the mole heard her.

"I say, are you all right?" the mole said sympathetically stepping forward.

"I don't know anymore but I guess so. It's just that moles don't talk where I come from."

"How peculiar," the Mole mused. "How do they communicate I wonder? Anyway about you. That was a spectacular dive. I've never seen anything like it. Do you do it often?"

"Not often thank goodness. While we're getting personal, who are you?"

"I am the Mole, Mortimer, Mort for short and I am traveling North. Will we be traveling companions. I should like that."

"Well we'll have to find our bearings first but, in fact we may be."

"Well if you've lost your bearings I should like to help you find them what ever they might be—-Oh, Oh—" Mortimer or rather Mort stopped his sentence in mid stride and slipped behind a tree as three small men strode up. They couldn't have been over two feet tall.

"Welcome, indeed! Yes, yes, welcome indeed! You are most welcome, tall people," the spokesman said. "My name is Ring rhymes with King, easy to remember you see. And what might I call you."

"My name is Mary, it doesn't rhyme with much of anything and my friend is Windom.

"Mary and Windom, rhymes with contrary and kingdom—almost. Anyway I am here to invite you to my humble home for a repast, better known as dinner, or food if you like. Just follow me and we'll be there in a Jiffy, and he began to march off.

Mary looked at Windom and vice versa and there being free food available they decided to go along. As they looked back at where they had been they saw Mort standing behind a tree violently shaking his head. It seemed he wasn't in favor of their decision but being hungry they followed Ring and his companions out of the forest and across what eventually became a desert. It took longer than a Jiffy to get to Rings little village, more like an hour, but eventually they arrived at a cluster of modest sandstone brick houses. Here, Ring and his companions furtively conferred among themselves looking back occasionally at Mary and Windom before Ring's friends left to go to their own homes.

"I wonder what that was all about," Mary whispered to Windom, but Windom just shrugged his shoulders as Ring returned to address them.

"And here we are my friends," Ring said, as they walked up to a tiny house far too small for Mary and Windom to even get through the door. "Well, this won't do at all will it?" Ring said as he looked the children up and down. "I'm afraid you're just too large for my little house. How about a picnic? It's a lovely warm night so I'll just have my wife whip something up that we can all have out here under the stars. It will only take a minute. I'll bring a rug out that we can sit on and it will be fun."

It only took Ring a few minutes to have them all sitting around a large pot of stew of some kind ringed with various fruits and nuts. Mary cautiously tried the stew that turned out to be delicious which she hungrily devoured. After a desert of fruit she leaned back against the wall of the little house and watched Windom clean up what was left.

"I must congratulate you Mr. Ring," Mary said. "You've made us very happy with what you've done. Thank you."

Ring looked at his wife with what Mary thought was a strange smile and thanked her for her part. "And now," he said "a little night cap to celebrate the end of a perfect day and he opened with a flourish an ornate bottle filled with a wine red liquid. "For this special occasion I will share with you a very rare tee that I've been savings for a time such as this," and he filled four glasses with it and passed them around.

Mary automatically sniffed it first which she always did with strange food. It had a strange pungent aroma but not at all bad and so she took a sip. As she sipped it it tasted better and better and she soon had her glass empty. Windom she noticed had finished his and his head was on his chest. Mary looked over at Ring and his wife and noticed that they still had all or most of they're drink still in their hands. The last that she remembered was them looking at each other with that same queer smile until she woke up the following morning.

When Mary woke up it was because someone or something was pushing her. It was light and the day was warming up when she opened her eye's and with a terrible headache she looked around and saw Ring and his three companions standing over her. She started to get up but, couldn't quite do it. Something was wrong. She soon found out however what the trouble was. She was bound hand and foot with some kind of heavy rope. She quickly banged Windom who was lying beside her with her elbow. "Windom!" she cried out. "Wake up!" Windom woke up with a start and looked around. "We've got guests Windom," Mary said. When Windom had completely realized what the situation was he erupted. "What is this!" he cried. "What's going on! Untie me this instant! Do you know who I am? You are in big trouble now. If you don't untie me immediately my father will have your head!"

All through this tirade the four little people who had been so nice to them the day before were now looking down at them with a sneer. "Quiet! overly large person!" Ring shouted. "If you wish to live another day you had better listen to me."

Windom was just about to begin all over again when Mary nudged him. "We'd better hear what he has to say before we destroy him," she said sarcastically.

"At least one of you has some sense," Ring said. Now listen carefully, it could mean your life. You've been brought here specifically for only one purpose—to help us with a little problem we have. It's not difficult and when you're finished you may go home. We are without water because our well has caved in and we are in great need of it being repaired. You can see that we are of normal size and that it's beyond our ability to do the repair but, as you are for reasons unknown, abnormally large we believe you can do us a great service as we have done for you in saving you from probable disaster. In any event you have no choice in the matter and you are about to begin day one. Untie their hands Grisle," Ring ordered one of his companions.

Mary looked at Windom with a look that meant do what they say for now we'll figure something out later and they were both lifted to their feet. Grisle walked around behind each one took a key out of his pocket and unlocked a lock that was attached to their binding. Mary had to give Windom a severe look to convince him not to get violent just now because it would only cause more trouble.

Their hands were now free and they were both given a large shovel. Far too big for the little people's use the shovels must have been fashioned from their dining room tables just for Mary and Windom. With their feet still bound together with just enough slack to hobble along they approached the work site with mincing steps As they looked down at what they were supposed to dig out they realized that they wouldn't be able to do it in their entire lifetime. For now they slid down the side of the cave in and began to dig. At the top of the well Grisle stood and watched them. These little people were armed with bows and arrows that were probably poisoned, and slings in which they hurled stones, and every time Mary or Windom slowed up Grisle would send a rock down to remind them to get back to work.

They worked all day in the hot sun with only a cup of water each and planned an escape. Unfortunately they couldn't come up with anything reasonable and decided to bide their time. Something might come up. On their trip back to the village they passed the back yard of one of the houses and saw a group of the residents laughing and playing some sort of game while drinking large glasses of water. So much for their water emergency. That night they were given no more drugs but were re locked to a stanchion in the house wall and exhausted they fell asleep. Mary who was a light sleeper awoke in the middle of the night to the sound of someone talking. Whoever it was must have been standing right over her probably making sure she was asleep.

"They were a little slow today," the voice was saying, "probably the effects of the drug, but they'll have no excuse tomorrow. We'll work em to death."

"Don't kill 'em before they get the job done." the other said, "You're too eager to taste their bones," and they both laughed and walked away. Mary had suspected all along that the little people weren't going to let them go and so this news didn't surprise her. She thought of waking Windom and telling him what she had just heard but she knew there was nothing they could do just then anyway and decided to wait and tell him in the morning and she went back to sleep.

Almost immediately Mary woke up to something bumping her feet and she tried to brush it away and then to her surprise saw that it was Mort knawing at her binding. "Shh," he whispered. "I'll have you freed in a flash." It wasn't a flash, but in a few minutes he had her feet free and in a few more he had her untied from the wall. Mary woke Windom who had been sleeping soundly and after a scare when he almost gave them away with a loud grunt he was also quickly freed. Mort motioned to them to follow him and they quietly slipped away after grabbing one of the bottles of water left over from the last nights party.

When they were well away from the village Mort stopped them. "It's all right, we can talk now."

And Mary exclaimed, "Mort, how did you find us! You've saved our lives. They were going to kill us."

"What makes you think that, Mary," Windom spoke up.

"I heard them talking last night," Mary told him.

"They would have too," Mort said. "I know them. But, there's no time to waste here. We've got to keep moving."

"But, how did you find us?" Mary repeated, as they started off again at a good clip.

"Oh, I followed you. I know these people and I knew you were in trouble. I tried to warn you back in the trees but I guess you didn't notice." Mary didn't say anything and they kept moving for awhile before Mort stopped them. They were headed for the river but, now Mort had other plans. "This is as far as we should go in this direction. It was only to misdirect any followers. Now you two head back toward the desert and I'll follow and cover your tracks."

"What are you talking about, Mort," Windom complained. "It's only a mile or two to the river. Let's keep going," and he started to keep going.

"Stop there!" Mary said. "Let's hear what Mort has to say."

"Listen to me folks! If you ever want to see your friends again. You'll never make it to the river before light and by then the little people will be hot on your trail and believe me they would have caught you by noon. What we must do is throw them off our track. I know this country and to put it simply, I can save you."

"All right," Mary said, "I'm with you, where do we go?"

It was a clear moonlit night and Mort pointed to a large sand dune that looked to be about a mile away. "See that dune where it comes to a peak? Well, head for that. We must get to it and over it before the sun comes up. That's when the little people will be looking for us and hopefully they will follow our original tracks toward the river."

"O, K," Mary said, and started off. "Come on Windom." Windom was still standing where he was and finally grudgingly followed while Mort brushed out their new tracks with his tail.

The dune was farther than it looked and they didn't reach it until the sun was almost up as they dove over the crest. Out of breath they lay back against the dune and rested.

"It's fortunate that they partied last night." Mort said. "Otherwise they would have been up by now and maybe have seen us go over the dune. You stay put and I'll pop my head over the top of the dune and see if I see any activity."

After a minute or two Mort slid back down the dune. "They're up all right, running around in circles and seemed to have taken off in the direction of the river. So far our trick has worked. We'd better move out. We need to cover some ground. Now if we continue in this direction there's supposed to be an oasis somewhere over there," and he pointed off in a general direction. "We'll need to resupply our water. We have a long journey ahead of us."

"What do you mean there's 'supposed' to be an oasis? I thought you knew this area," Windom demanded.

"Well, I might have exaggerated a little. I've never actually been anywhere near here. I'm on my first adventure. However I did a lot of research before I left home and studied a lot of maps of this area and feel confident that I can remember most of them."

Mary didn't say anything and Windom looked at Mort in disbelief. "You mean to tell me that you've dragged us out here into the middle of the desert and and now tell us that you 'may' be able to save us when we could have been back at the river by now?"

"Yes, you could have been back at the river, and been recaptured or dead by now," said Mort calmly.

"Stop the bickering," Mary spoke up. "We're here now and had better do something about it. Lead the way Mort. Let's see if we can find this oasis of yours," and they started off in the direction that Mort had indicated.

A little after midday Mort pointed to something in the distance. "There, that looks like it. The oasis. See, over there." They all peered in the direction that he pointed and there seemed to be something there. By night fall they had reached it.

"So this is your oasis," Windom said.

"I guess my map was a little outdated," Mort replied chagrinned. What they had found at one time had been a productive oasis with a well and date palms surrounding it, but now the well was full of sand the date palms were dead and fallen down and what had once nourished weary and thirsty travelers had now mostly returned to desert. Being exhausted they decided to spend the night there and to keep out of the wind they collapsed behind one of the large fallen date palms.

8

In the morning as the sun was coming up Mary awoke to the sound of voices. She raised herself up just high enough to look over the trunk of the palm and saw two bedouins scrounging the old well. They seemed to be content that there was nothing there that they could use and left walking back across the sand. She woke the others and they watched the bedouins return to a long camel caravan going north about a half a mile away.

"It's a good thing we picked this spot behind the tree trunk to spend the night or they would have seen us for sure," Mort offered.

"If we had gone back to the river we wouldn't have had this problem in the first place," Windom said.

"Will you stop it, Windom, Mort's trying to help us."

"It's all right Mary, just ignore him," Mort said, and before Windom could respond which he was ready to do, Mort continued. "In a way it's a good thing that that caravan came by when it did. It's bound to be heading for another oasis that's replaced this one and we'll just follow along, out of sight of course," and that's what they did moving along behind the dunes peeking over the top occasionally to see that the caravan was still in sight.

It wasn't long until, sure enough, they came to a large oasis where the caravan settled in as if they were going to stay for awhile.

"What are we going to do now?" Mary asked. "They could be here for days and we need water now."

"We had better wait through tomorrow. I'd be surprised if they stay too long. These caravans are usually on a schedule."

"Maybe we could just walk in on them. They might not bother us at all," Windom said.

"See the black hoods they wear?" said Mort. "That means they're the Wantons. They are a murderous clan feared by even other clans. You wouldn't live to see another sunrise."

"Is this also one of the details marked on your maps," Windom said sarcastically.

"This is one detail you can prove for yourself if you wish, be my guest," and Mort waved toward the Bedouins encampment. Windom didn't take him up on his suggestion and they spent the night knowing they couldn't hold out without water much longer.

In the morning Windom and Mary woke up to peer over the dune and suddenly realized that Mort was no where to be seen. What they saw in the camp below were Bedouins throwing a bag of something back and forth and laughing in glee. Every time it flew through the air a screeching sound came out of the bag and Mary and Windom realized at the same time with horror that inside the bag was Mort.

"That's Mort they're throwing around," whispered Mary in dismay.

"I know," Windom said. "I wonder how they got him."

"I know how," Mary retorted. "He was tired of you criticizing him and went down there to prove something to you."

"Well, he didn't need to do that, I was only joking."

"It's done now" Mary replied, "and we have to get him back."

"Are you crazy?" Windom retorted. "They'd have us for their dinner. The main course!"

"Well, you can at least keep an eye on him with me. See if you can see what they do with him." And so they watched the Bedouins all day who finally tired of the game and then surprising Windom and Mary they began to feed Mort through a small hole in the bag scraps from their own meal which they were eating off a blanket placed on the sand.

"I believe they plan to keep him as a pet," Mary said.

"Well thank goodness for that," Windom said in relief, "Now we don't have to worry about him."

"What are you talking about?" cried Mary. "It doesn't change a thing. It just means we may have more time to save him."

"That's crazy, Mary. We haven't a chance to save him."

"You'd just leave him?" Mary cried in disbelief.

"Well, how are you going to save him, tell me that."

"I don't know yet but, I'm sure going to try."

They were still watching the bag when the sun went down and by the light of their fire they watched the Bedouins one by one retire. The bag was tied to the back of one of them as he stretched out by the fire and went to sleep. Windom decided that that was all they could do for now and went to sleep. Mary on the other hand didn't take her eyes off of the bag until the fire had died down to the point where Mary couldn't see anything in the camp anymore and then she began to slip down the dune. She stopped at the edge of the camp and watched and listened until she was sure it was safe and then crawled toward the sleeping Bedouin who had the bag. Slowly she crept inch by inch until she was next to the bag. The Bedouin was snoring loudly and smelled of alcohol and Mary realized he was probably drunk. She reached over and began to drag the bag toward her, but it was tied fast to the bedouin. She tried to untie it but it was hopeless. The Bedouin had a curved dagger in a sheath and Mary eyed that. What were the chances that she could relieve him of that without waking him? A long shot but, what could she do. She reached over and grasped the knife and then waited. Nothing. She began to draw it out and it slipped out of its sheath like butter, probably made to do that. The Bedouin slept on unaware of Mary. Mary quietly sawed at the rope holding the bag to the Bedouin and finally cut it in two. She started to move away when she saw a large water bag beside the sleeper that seemed almost full and she reached over and grasped that too. Suddenly the Bedouin rolled over and opened his eyes. Mary didn't move and the Bedouin spoke something that Mary didn't understand, rolled his eyes and went back to sleep. Mary realized he must have passed out again from drink and waited until he was snoring and then began to slip away. She crawled back up the dune and over the top sliding down the back side accidentally bumping into Windom who woke up with a start.

"Hey what's happening! What's going on?" he said half asleep.

"Here," Mary said tossing the stolen water bag to him, "but, only drink a little, it's all I could get."

Windom took a drink and asked, "Where did you get this? Oh, you have one too," pointing to the other bag that Mary was holding.

"This isn't water," Mary said, working at the binding that held it closed.

"Well, what is it then?"

"This is Mort," she replied still working at the string just as Mort rolled out onto the sand.

"What are you talking about. What have you been doing?"

Mary picked Mort up who seemed to be dazed. "Are you all right, Mort?" Mary asked.

"I'm all right. It was so stuffy in there," he said, "that I guess I sort of passed out. And how in the world did you do it? How did y out get me out of there. I thought I was done for. You saved my life! Thank you, Mary, Thank you, thank you!"

"That's what I would like to know, Mary. What have you been up to?" asked Windom.

"I just sneaked down the hill to see what I could do and found the Bedouins all drunk and asleep so I snatched Mort."

"I'm sure it wasn't quite that easy," Mort said, skeptically.

"I bet it wasn't either," retorted Windom. You are out of your mind. I've known it all along. You are intent on getting us all killed.

"What were you going to do?" Mary replied patiently.

"Well, not something dumb like that."

"So, you probably would have left him there."

"Well—I don't know—but, don't get me wrong, Mort, I'm sure glad Mary got you back—I just don't know."

Through all this Mort was sitting in the sand watching Windom with a slightly sardonic smile on his face when he spoke up. "You are both very entertaining, but may I make a suggestion?" Both Mary and Windom turned and looked at Mort questioningly. "In about two hours the sun is coming up and the Bedouins too. And when they do they will be all over these dunes like hungry rats looking for me and my suggestion is that we make haste getting our little bottoms out of here," and he got to his feet and started to do just what he suggested.

Windom grabbed the water bag and followed Mary as they headed out across the dunes.

"We have been paralleling the trade route of the Bedouins," Mort spoke up, "but we better separate ourselves from it. At least a half a mile. The Bedouins will probably look for us for awhile but, probably not for long. I don't think I was that important to them. You didn't bring away anything of real value to them, did you Mary?"

"There was a deadly stiletto that I used to cut you free with but, I thought the same as you. They might miss that more than they would you so I left it there,"

"Wise girl," said Mort.

"Brilliant," was Windom's only sardonic comment.

The sun did come up just as Mort had predicted and they had made good progress away from the Bedouins rout when Mort climbed up a tall dune to peak over the top. "Just as I thought. They seem to have stopped looking for me, they're all back in line on the trail. They've also just made the turn where the trail splits and have gone west. That, if I remember correctly from my maps, will take them to Borumbo a major trading center. The right turn goes east and that is the one we want that will get you to the sea and your ship.

"We're lost for sure," said Windom shaking his head.

"Maybe you'd rather follow the Bedouins," Mary said sarcastically.

"Oh, no. In for a penny, in for a pound."

Of course Mort was correct and after another two hours of plodding through deep sand they came over a ridge and there was the sea.

"Oh, thank goodness!" Mary said excitedly. "Nothing has ever looked so good to me!"

"So it does to me," said Mort — "even though it means my adventure is coming to an end."

"Your adventure?" said Windom skeptically.

"This has been quite an adventure has'n't it." Mort went on. "Anyway for me it has probably been the adventure of my life. But, of course, you don't understand. You see my parents are the reason I'm here. They sent me away from home telling me that I needed an adventure. That it would be worthwhile and maybe of value later in life. And here I am having my adventure. If nothing else, when I'm married and my children ask me what life is all about I can tell them of my great adventure."

All this time Windom was rolling his eyes and shaking

his head occasionally. Mary was listening intently to Mort and scowling at Windom.

"So where is the ship?" asked Windom.

"We are a good two miles from the river," said Mort, "and you said you were tied up at it's mouth as I recall so we probably can't see the ship because of the way the coast curves right here. We should see it soon."

In about an hour Mary called out, "Look, there it is," and it was, just off the beach at the edge of the trees that lined the river.

"And they have the new mainmast stepped," Windom observed. "They've been working hard, we'd better hurry."

"That is a magnificent ship," said Mort admiringly," as they set off toward the ship.

The sun was just beginning to go down as the little group started running along the beach. Wanting to reach the ship before dark they made good time on the hard sand.

As they approached the ship they cried out, 'Hello! Ahoy ship, Hello! waving their arms until they finally saw someone waving back and soon a boat put out from the ship and they were all back on board including Mort.

As they climbed on board Amon, Molly, and Monkeyone were waiting for them at the rail and helped pull them on board.

"Thank the good Lord you're all right," Amon exclaimed. We were so worried the way you were snatched away by that giant bird. We immediately sent a search party out to look for you—in fact that reminds me—Monkeyone, have a green flare sent up so that the search party can return to the ship and—well what is this?" Amon had just noticed

Mort for the first time. "So you've found a new friend, Mary, there must be a story here."

"Mort, this is Windom's mother and father, Amon and Molly. And this is Mortimer called Mort by his friends. And he's not just a friend, he's our savior. He saved our lives."

"Well, well, we thank you very much for that, Mort, if I may call you that."

"I would be honored, sir," Mort said with a slight bow.

"You said you liked ships, Mort?" Windom interjected.

"Oh, yes very much so though I've never seen one this big."

"Come along then and I'll show you around," Windom said and as he led Mort away Mary heard Windom explaining to Mort how all his silly criticism of him was all in fun and that he meant nothing of it, and Mort said that was all right he hadn't taken Windom seriously anyway and they headed for the bow as new found friends.

"Well, Mary," Amon said, "you're going to have to tell me all about your adventure."

"I will do that, in the morning. It's a long tale. You'll be amazed. But right now I'd just like to rest, I'm pretty tired." It had gotten dark by then and Mary was looking forward to curling up in her bunk and having a long snooze.

"Of course," Amon said. "Your cabin is as you left it so be my guest."

"One thing Amon before you go. I see that you've already got the new mast stepped and it looks like you're just about ready to pull up anchor."

"That's right, we've been working pretty hard. Are you anxious to get away?"

"Yes, pretty much."

"We'll be ready in the morning. Your search party should have returned by noon and as soon as they're back we'll up anchor." Mary then retired to her cabin and collapsed.

9

The next morning Mary told everyone the story of her and Windom's adventure with Mort, which was a great success. Mort had spent the night on board curling up in a coil of rope in the bow but was now ready to embark on the rest of his adventure.

"You wouldn't like to come along with us, would you?" Windom asked.

"It sounds like a great adventure all right, but I've had mine, and it was a good one wasn't it? No, I have to return home now and settle down. Maybe I'll have another one day but this one will carry me for quite a long time."

The search crew had just returned and as Mort was lowered into one of their boats to be taken ashore, Mary called down to him, "Stay clear of the little people, Mort."

"Oh, they won't bother me. My people have had a long history with them, not always pleasant, but never dangerous. I'll be all right. Good by, good people. Bon Voyage." and the last they saw of Mort was him waving back at the ship as he disappeared into the forest that ran along the river.

The ship soon had all it's sails up and with a strong whole sail breeze they headed out to sea. Amon and Monkeyone were at the helm going over charts and Mary walked up. "Where are we headed now," she asked.

"Well, Mary, Monkeyone and I have concluded that we must have been blown south about two hundred miles. We've just taken sightings of the sun and believe that by taking a course North by East we should reach the point where we were blown off course in about two and a half days and then we'll see what to do then."

"You may need my book again I guess."

"We may want to look at that again".

Mary turned in early that evening still a little worn out from her adventure but, was up early the the next morning. She could tell it was going to be a beautiful day warm and clear with strong steady wind blowing them along at hull speed and she sat down on the deck where she could lean against the mast and soak in the sun. Finally feeling more adventurous than that she went forward to stand in the bow and look over the rail where dolphins were at play in the bow wave. A long swell had begun to roll under the ship and as it did the bow rose up and up and the sea fell away until the ship crested the swell and began to drop into the trough. When that happened the sea rushed back up until it looked like it was going to roar clear over the bow and sweep Mary away, but it always stopped just in time only reaching the bottom of the bowsprit and then the sea would fall away to repeat it all over again. Mary watched mesmerized by the scene until getting a little wheezy she decided she'd find something else to do.

Windom had during all these days, time to teach Mary many things about life at sea and one of them was how to climb the rigging and now she climbed the ratlines to the peak of the main mast to a small platform where she could stand and observe far below her on the deck the crew going about their business. The platform wasn't as large as a true crow's nest on a full rigged ship but served the purpose. Just under her feet the gaff, that long boom that supported the sail's peak on a gaff rigged ship, was secured to the mast and it now moaned and groaned as it shifted back and fourth. Being a Brigantine rigged ship it carried a main sail on the main mast and a square sail on the foremast and now that huge main sail was spread out below her trimmed in tight as they sailed along close hauled and making knots. From here she watched the two streams of foam that rushed along the port and starboard rails leave the stern to recombine in a long straight ribbon of white as its wake receded in a deep azure blue sea. As the wind picked up the ship healed over even more occasionally rolling her lee rail under and when it did Mary found herself looking down at the boiling sea instead of the deck of the ship and visualized herself taking a high dive into the sea and decided it was time to go back down. It would be better than diving onto the deck but, still not fun.

On the morning of the third day Mary was standing at the stern rail watching the ship's wake when she felt the ship turning. She turned around to see Amon heaving on the wheel to bring the ship onto a new course as Monkeyone cried out to his crew, "Let her run a bit and then trim her up. That's good."

"What's up?" Mary said.

"We've reached our old course," Amon said, "and we've decided to look for that original island my brother talked about. We've got plenty of stores except for fruit. There wasn't much that we could find at our last landing and without some fruit scurvy is possible. What we had last night was all that was left."

"Think you can find it?"

"I think so, it should be around here some place."

It took two days to find the island, time in which Mary spent on deck relaxing in the warm sun. In the late afternoon of the second day the lookout cried out, "Land ho! Four points off the the starboard bow," but it wasn't until the next morning that the others could get a good view of the island. Mary and Windom were at the rail when Mary asked "Look promising?"

"I think so. See those leafier trees? Looks like some kind of fruit tree to me."

"I see what you mean," Mary said. "You think the island is uninhabited?"

"I guess we'll soon find out".

By then the ship was entering a lagoon though a small opening in the reef that surrounded the island. It was a high island probably volcanic in origin and covered with forest unlike the low flat islands that were more common in that region and so looked more promising for what they needed. They dropped all the sails except the flying jib to give them steerage and coasted toward the beach until they were in three fathoms of water when Monkeyone called out, "Drop anchor!" and down went thirty feet of chain, at the same moment dropping the jib. With the bow anchor secured they paid out the anchor line as the ship drifted backwards about three hundred feet and dropped the stern anchor. They then paid out the stern line taking in the bow line about one hundred feet until they were anchored bow and stern when Amon called out, "Secure! That will hold her for now I think as long as we don't get a serious blow." He then walked forward to the bow and leaned on the rail studying the island. "See any signs of life?" he asked the group that lined the rail. After a minute or two Windom said he didn't see anyone and then the others agreed.

"All right," Amon said, "it's getting late so we'll wait 'till morning to go ashore. In the meantime Monkeyone, post a look out for the night." They all watched the shore for signs of habitation until it got too dark to see and then turned in.

As there had been no problems during the night, they sent a reconnaissance party ashore early the next morning to make sure all was safe. When the ship received their signal that it was all clear a boat went ashore carrying several monkeyshines, Amon, Mary and Windom. Windom had promised to stay with the group and not wander off to get in trouble again.

"Look at this," Windom said, "A kind of orange wouldn't you say," as he plucked one off a small low tree.

"If you say so," Mary replied, "but, not like any that I'm familiar with."

"Maybe not, but, close enough I think. Anyway the crew seems to think they're all right. They're filling the barrels with them." That they were and Mary and Windom joined in. When the barrels were almost full a voice boomed out of the forest making everyone jump to attention. It hadn't really boomed as it wasn't particularly loud but it had a presence that no one missed.

"Good day, gentlemen and lady, do you like my fruit?" the voice came from a tall figure that seemed to have stepped out from behind a tree.

Dumbstruck at this apparition everyone was for a moment speechless until Amon stepped forward. "Sir, I must apologize for being so rude as to invade your domain without first introducing ourselves but we were convinced this island was deserted. May I now do the honors. I am Amon Arturas, the Captain of our group and this is my son Windom and his friend Mary."

"I am honored to meet you all," the visitor said, "and it's quite all right for you to pick my fruit. That's what it's here for."

Amon hesitated for a moment and Windom blurted out, "It is?"

"Why, yes," the visitor explained. "It is for the benefit of sailors in need that have found themselves in these waters."

"Are you responsible for this orchard such as it is. It seems a little out of place this far south."

"Not exactly responsible. I am simply this islands caretaker."

"Are there others?"

"No. I am the only one."

Mary and the others began to look this stranger over more closely. He was tall, just a little taller than Amon, well built standing straight with a look of confident assurety and dressed in a single robe that reached to his feet. It was difficult to tell how old he was because his hair was snow white and yet he was unwrinkled and he looked at you with penetratingly clear eyes. He seemed to be totally at peace with these strangers who could possibly do him harm.

"But, I see that you are almost finished with your work and I wish not to hold you up. Will you be returning to your home or are you adventuring?"

"No, we are not ready to return home yet," Amon replied as the monkeyshines continued stuffing their barrels. "We have to attend to some important business. In fact maybe you can help us with a little information. What lies east of here?"

"East? Nothing lies east of here that would interest you."

"Oh, but it would. You see, I have important directions that point me in that specific direction."

"I am sure you have been misdirected" the man said with authority.

"I think not. Our communicate is backed up by two sources and they have always been accurate," which was not always true but why go into detail.

"I am only advising you, firmly, not to go any further east in your travels. It is not safe."

"Pray tell me then why it's not safe." Amon was beginning to question this man's sincerity or even sanity.

"I don't know with certainty what lies there as I have not yet been there but, I can tell you what I do know. Many ships have come this way and some have continued on in that direction and never returned—except one. That one was a black ship, a pirate ship, an evil ship with an evil captain crewed with murderous villains. I warned the captain as I must to be aware of what I said, but he just laughed and told

me how he and his crew had never been defeated in all their
bloody affairs and was certainly not afraid of the unknown,
and then sailed away east. It was less than three weeks when
he returned. I didn't recognize it at first as the pirate ship,
or as I should say what was left of it. It was barely afloat
stripped to the waterline of all its rigging, masts on deck rails
torn away and a captain gone completely mad. Standing at
the helm, he spun a useless wheel that no longer steered his
ship, but by then was sailing itself south, singing at the top
of his voice a tune that sounded something like this:

> 'Fly for your lives, boys,
> Fly for your lives,
> Drop all your pistols,
> Drop all your knives
> Look to the wind, boys.
> Trim all the sail,
> Beelzebub lurks
> Over that rail
> Pump with a will, boys,
> Pump when you're told,
> Water's a'risen
> Deep in the hold,
> Pray for your mothers,
> Pray for your wives,
> Pray for your ship now
> Pray she survives
> For see how she creeks
> rattles and moans
> Beelzebub waits

to gnaw her bones
Hear how her timbers
shudder and shake
You'ld better pray for
Your black souls sake.

That was what he was singing to his fearless crew who were then cowering in the scuppers."

"That's quite a tale, sir," Amon said. "You've almost convinced me, but I'm committed."

The stranger didn't say anything for a moment studying Mary who had walked up to stand next to Amon. It was as if he had first noticed her.

"You have not been with your friends long I believe," he said addressing Mary directly. Mary didn't know what to say to that and anyway it wasn't necessary, it being a statement, and the man continued, turning back to Amon. "There may be more to your group than I know so I'll not keep you any longer. I'll just point out one thing. Do you see far to the east what looks like a fog bank?" and he pointed to what Amon and the others hadn't noticed, but now observed as a low cloud or fog as the man had suggested. "That is where the trouble seems to begin. If you change your mind, turn back before you enter that unknown."

"Well, for all it's worth, I do thank you for the provisions. They will save us from a host of problems. And though I may appear skeptical I believe you're sincere and I take everything that you've said seriously. It's time to be off now so thank you again for everything. Good bye," Amon said, shaking the man's hand who took Amons hand with a strong firm grip. The man said nothing more but, waved to them as they returned to the ship.

When the new stores were stowed away securely they set sail again on their original course that did indeed seem to be taking them toward what appeared to be a low lying fog bank. All day they sailed but it didn't seem to be getting any closer. Amon finally spoke to Mary who was standing next to him. "That bank must be further away than it looked".

"It looks that way," Mary replied. "What did you think of that man's story, back on the island?"

"I think he believed what he said," Amon said thoughtfully. "It was a pretty detailed story. But I wonder what was his state of mind. Isolated out here for no telling how long in the hot sun can can get a person's mind confused. That might be the case. Anyway that's what I believe. That's what I have to believe." That's what Mary preferred to think too and yet she wasn't sure.

It was two more days before they reached what had looked like a fog bank but now appeared quite different. It smelled different with a suggestion of decaying seaweed and was not cool as you would think but was damp and warm, almost hot.

"A bit uncomfortable is it?" Amon said as they entered the fog and Mary began removing her sweater.

"A little bit," she said. "Is this normal?"

"A little unusual I'd say," Amon replied, trying to peer into the gloom that then surrounded the ship from bow to stern.

Several hours went by before the fog began to thin and then as quickly as they had entered it they were out into a clear day. The sky was blue, the sea was blue, and they seemed to be able to see forever.

"Well, this is more like it," Amon said. "What do you think, Mary?"

"I think it's a lot better. What was that thing we just went through?"

"I don't know, Mary. Some kind of unusual atmospheric condition I presume. I've never run into such a thing before."

10

The next morning as it was getting light every one was on deck when it began to get dark again. Looking to the sky they saw a dark cloud that was almost black obscuring the new sun so sinister looking that they couldn't take their eyes off it. And then it began to thin like an early morning fog becoming transparent enough for those on deck searching the sky to see that something was going on over their heads. At first it was difficult to make out just what was happening, but it soon became apparent that the shapes dancing overhead in the cloud were alive. There seemed to be two groups facing each other. One group was made up of animals foaming at the mouth that looked like a mixture of mad dog and crocodile with green hair that seemed to be missing in large areas and claws the size of an arctic bear. With blood red eyes they watched their opponents while they dashed back and forth trying to gain an advantage. Opposite them were dragon like creatures with long necks supporting large pointed heads and beaks that were breathing fire and strong tails that kept swinging back and forth. The two groups seemed to be eying each other in preparation for attack when they received some kind of signal. The cloud soon dispersed, which seemed to have been the signal and as those on deck watched, the two groups begin the war. Their dancing was a war dance and they first began throwing balls of fire at each other that seemed to come from their claws. That was a warm up. Then they rushed at each other being careful to strike their opponent in exactly the right spot. If they were successful it would blow their rival in to tiny pieces. If it wasn't a direct hit in which their opponent was destroyed their foe was simply divided into two pieces which then continued fighting.

It was a ferocious battle and as they watched, the animals on both side were being destroyed and multiplied at about the same rate, so the war went on with neither having an advantage, their numbers staying about the same. Those on board ship watched this battle going on over their heads for about an hour as the thousands of pieces from the destroyed animals drifted like snow flakes down to fall into the sea around the ship.

Although fascinating it was a violent and gruesome affair, but then it got worse. One of the animals looked down and spotted the ship. This caused the others to do the same and soon their war came to a standstill with them all looking down on the ship. Seemingly more interested in the ship than their own grudges they began to direct their fire at the ship. The fireballs were about one foot in diameter of pure fire and at first were falling harmlessly into the water where they shot geysers of foam and steam into the air, but soon began to come closer to the ship. With a good breeze the ship was sailing well when a fireball went through the center of the mainsail. The sail stayed intact but now had a four foot hole in it. There were now so many fireballs going into the sea that the air was getting hot and the water was literally beginning to boil.

Through all this Amon was doing his best to keep the ship on course while everyone was dousing each other with water trying to keep cool. And then with a great rocking of the ship a sea serpent flew up to the surface of the water causing a small tidal wave. They soon realized that it wasn't a sea serpent at all but a Poseidon like being who was waving a long spear at the heavens. It seemed as though the water was getting too hot for this creature and he was vehemently complaining to the warriors to knock it off which they promptly did, Poseidon seemingly having the last word.

"Well, that was good timing," Amon said. 'Poseidon,' as Amon called him, "must be our savior," and he walked over to the rail and called out, "Thank you, whoever you are, we are indebted to you," and waited for a reply knowing that he probably wouldn't get one. Instead Poseidon looked at the ship for the first time and roared. It was difficult to tell what mood he was in but the ship soon found out. Not far away another Poseidon had emerged from the sea. This one came half out of the water and seeing what seemed to be his friend came over to the ship to look it over.

"Oh, oh," Amon said, "I guess I should have kept my mouth shut".

The giant Poseidon leaned down to peak at these strange tiny people on this toy ship and then broke out laughing and put his hand on the stern of the ship and gave it a great shove that sent it scooting across the water. Amon and the others were taken by surprise and were thrown to the deck.

"Hang on, everyone! Hang on," Amon cried, and they did just that for their dear lives.

The Poseidon's had devised a game in which they began scooting the ship back and forth between them and each time the little ship shot forth on another trip they would both break out in ear shattering laughter. This was great fun for the Poseidons, but would soon tear the little ship apart as the strain on the sails were already just about to pull the masts out of their steps.

"Get the sails down! Quick," Amon yelled to Monkeyone between pushes and monkey one with his crew had them quickly down. It turned out to be a better move than anticipated because the sails had acted as a wind break slowing the progress of the ship down when shoved by the giants. Now with the sails down the ship shot across the water flying by the receiving giant who was not ready for it. One of the many cloud banks in the area was near by and Amon, quickly steered the ship into it.

"Throw that life preserver over board!" cried Amon. "and some of that lumber on deck that was left over from our refitting". Amon then spun the wheel and sent the ship off on a tangent course. "Quiet now everyone, not a sound," whispered Amon. "Maybe they'll see the debris we've just thrown overboard and think we've been sunk."

Everyone on board was quiet as a mouse as the crew quietly re hoisted the sails. There was a nice breeze and as they sailed away undercover of the fog they could hear at first the giants angrily yelling at each other and then less so, their voices fading into the distance as they seemingly fell for the ships ruse. Amon then reset the ship to its original course. They were still sailing blind in the vast fog bank and it was several hours before they broke out of the fog. During that time no one had said anything. They were wondering what was to come next.

And then they suddenly came out into a clear blue day. There was nothing in sight but a vast horizon and a speck in the distance.

"Well, thank goodness for a little peace!" Amon said. "It looks like good sailing for awhile."

"What's that over there?" Windom said, pointing at the little speck.

"I don't know," said Amon, "but it's pretty much on our course so we'll go over and have a look."

It took all that day and night before they found themselves in the morning about a mile offshore from a forested island.

"This looks interesting to me," Amon said, "I think we'd better go ashore."

They were on starboard tack and soon realized they would never reach the island on that course and came about. They soon realized that they would never reach it on that tack either. All that day they stood off and on trying to get to the island.

"There's something peculiar about this island," Amon finally said. Both the current and the wind were against them and it appeared that the ship would never be able to land, but Amon didn't immediately turn away he just, kept staring at the Island. Mary noticed this. "What is it?" she asked, looking to where Amon was staring.

"I can't get over the feeling, Mary, that I've seen this island before."

"Where could that have been, father," Windom said, "you've never been here before".

"No, not here. I've seen this island in our history books. This is the island where I was born, as it was then."

"Too much sun, dad," Windom said, looking at his father sideways.

"I know it's not possible, Windom. And yet—well, you never can be sure, can you?". They finally had to give up trying to reach it and resumed course leaving the mystery island behind.

For several days they sailed in fine weather through a seemingly endless sea with just enough swell to gently rock the ship allowing Mary and Windom to scamper up and down the rigging which by now they did with ease. When they tired of that they would watch dolphins reveling in the ships bow wave and one day were startled to hear the lookout high in the rigging call out, "Land ho, dead ahead." Though Mary couldn't see anything just then the next day she was on deck early and there in the distance was a low lying island that the ship reached just before sundown. There was no immediate sign of good anchorage and so the ship stood offshore until morning when they would have more time to look for a landing sight.

At sunup the ship began to slowly sail up and down the coast that was forested right down to the sea. There was no beach or harbor of any kind but, soon the lookout pointed out a small river that entered the island between tall trees that might possibly be navigable. The ship slowly approached its mouth sounding the bottom for depth and finding it just deep enough with room for some minor maneuvering, and followed it as it led them into the island. For the last couple of days the wind had been following them and it now pushed them down a beautiful river just fast enough to give the ship steerage. After about a mile Amon who was conning the ship told the crew to drop anchor.

"What a delightful spot to spend a day or two," Amon said. "We can rest a bit, refit and restore before we plan our next move. What do you all think?" Everyone thought that was a dandy idea and after all the sails were down and furled and a lookout was posted to keep an eye out for unwanted intruders Amon went below to update his log and Mary and Windom stayed on deck at the rail examining their new home. The river had come straight in from the sea and seemed to continue straight on as far as they could see and was lined on each bank with an almost impenetrable forest that came right to the rivers edge.

"This is a beautiful place," Mary finally said to Windom, after visually searching the trees, "but do you think it's safe. What about hostile natives?"

"Oh, they'll wait till dark to slaughter us. They always do. They'll sneak on board, probably sometime late tonight when we're all asleep and chop off our heads."

Mary turned and looked at Windom losing patience. "Windom," she said, "you are really too much. I'm serious. Do you really think there might be a danger. We have a lookout you know."

"A poison arrow will take care of him. Never know what hit him."

"I give up," Mary said half to herself.

"No, no," Windom replied, "Don't give up. You're the only one I can count on."

"Count on?"

"Yes. You're so unreal, with you I can be comfortable." Mary didn't tell Windom, but she did give up.

After a brief search along the shoreline by two scouts it was deemed safe to leave the ship and the crew of monkeyshines were given permission to go ashore for the rest of the day. Amon, Molly, Windom, and Mary stayed on board to attend to their chores. Frendo also stayed on board in his cabin where he spent most of his time.

Just as the sun was going down at the end of the day Monkeyone and the other monkeyshines came back on board. At first Mary thought that they had been disappointed with their trip ashore because they seemed subdued. But then she realized they were just being thoughtful and thinking something over among themselves. There was no normal monkey play or jubilation. They simply went forward to the bow area where they settled down and began talking quietly to each other. Monkeyone sat with them which was not normal as he usually kept separate from the crew. Amon also sensing that something was amiss approached them and speaking to Monkeyone asked him if there was anything wrong.

"No, Nothing wrong—exactly, he said hesitantly. The crew is just going over what they've just seen ashore—nothing important really—it's just that they've not been home for a long time—and well—I guess maybe they're homesick."

"I see," Amon said, not convinced that there was no more to it than homesickness. "Well, let me know if there is anything I can do. We should plan to get away by noon tomorrow I think.

"All right," Monkeyone replied but before Amon had taken more than two steps away Monkeyone suddenly added "Wait a moment. I think maybe we had better have a talk Will you be available in about an hour?"

"Sure, I'll be in my cabin," Amon replied walking away.

"What was that all about?" Mary asked as Amon walked by stopping a minute to look back at the monkeyshines who now seemed to be more agitated as Monkeyone sat in their middle seriously talking about something that seemed important to them.

"I don't know exactly," Amon answered, "but something seems to be up. I guess we'll know more in about an hour. I'll be in my cabin if you need me."

Mary watched him go and then turned to Windom who had been standing beside her. "What do you think of that? she asked him.

"I don't know, but something is definitely going on. I've never seen the crew so serious."

It was a warm night and Windom and Mary were standing at the stern rail when Monkeyone knocked on Amon's door and went in. Being as warm as it was the large aft cabin window of Amon's was kept open and it just happened that Mary and Windom could easily hear what was being said below.

"All right, Monkeyone, what have you come to talk about." Amon was saying.

"Sir," Monkeyone began, "I want to talk to you about the crew."

"I thought you might," Amon replied.

"Well, I guess you know this is an unusual place, this island, and—well— this is going to be difficult," he finally stammered.

"I can see that and I understand," Amon replied, "but feel free to say whatever you like. We go back a long way. Nothing can affect that."

"That's just the problem," Monkeyone said. "We go back a long way. We've had some good times and bad, haven't we?"

"We sure have so fear not. Tell me what's on your mind."

"Well, I'll just have to be out with it. The crew has fallen in love with this island. That's it I guess. As you well know they've all been with you from the start and love you as they do their own kind but they're getting old. In fact I think you've noticed a few slipped hand holds and such that could be dangerous, have you not?"

"You're right, Monkeyone. You're very observant."

"It's my job, anyway they're old and getting tired and this island is unusually well suited to be their home. It's so much like where they came from. Do you understand what I'm saying?"

"It's clear as a summer day, old friend. The crew want's to jump ship."

"Well, I wouldn't put it quite like that, sir. In fact they have all, to a monkey, said that if you seriously need them they are willing to stay on, but I know them and they are worn out. It would be their dream come true to be able to spend the rest of their lives on this island.

"I know. I well understand. I was just joking with the 'jump ship' remark. I believe, as you say, to a monkey they would stay aboard if they thought I needed them. And now the big question"—and when Amon didn't continue Monkeyone spoke up.

"And what's that, sir".

"I think you know but, I'll tell you. How do you feel, I mean about yourself."

"I was afraid of that—well, you know I'll stay on board as long as you need me. You know that. About the island—I love it too as well as the crew. It looks to be a place where I could spend the rest of my life in great comfort and peace. However, as I said, we go back a long way. This is a good ship and you're as good a captain as anyone would want so if you wish, I'll be happy to stay. I wouldn't even consider leaving if I didn't know that you can sail this ship as well as I can."

The two on deck could hear Amon get to his feet and walk across the room. Finally Amon spoke up. "As for the crew they deserve a rest. Tell them that they are free to 'jump ship'— just joking. As for you—I'd miss you as a fine seaman and a good friend but you must find your own way and if this place suits you—well, I'll wish you all the happiness that you can stand and send you on your way."

"Thank you, sir, with all my heart. I'll inform the crew now. As you can imagine they will want to know as soon as possible. As for me—I will sleep on my decision and let you know in the morning."

"That's fair enough, and be assured that whatever you decide will make me happy."

Windom and Mary looked at each other as Monkeyone came out of Amons cabin going forward to inform the crew what had been decided. "Well, this is a fine kettle of fish," Windom finally said. Who'd have expected this?"

"Nobody I guess," Mary said, wondering what was going to happen next. "What about the ship? Who's going to sail the ship. Monkeyone say's Amon can sail it as well as the monkeyshines, but how can that be?"

"Well," Windom began hesitantly, "we all—even you I believe— know the ropes and we can probably get by by ourselves in a pinch. We could probably sail this ship in peaceful weather."

"What about bad weather?"

"Then we'd be in trouble."

It was by then time to turn in and Mary went to bed wondering what new adventure was about to take place.

11

M orning found Mary and Windom again at the aft rail watching the sunrise when Monkeyone returned to Amon's cabin. As before they could clearly hear the conversation below them.

"Well, friend, good morning to you. I see it's another fine morning. You have something to tell me I presume?"

"Yes I do," replied Monkeyone. "I've decided to stay with the ship"

This decision was not unexpected. Monkeyone, was as dedicated a person as Amon knew and would probably feel an overwhelming loyalty to the ship. Amon didn't say anything for a moment as he strode across the room. "Monkeyone? tell me one thing—and be as honest with me as you've ever been—would you really prefer to be on my ship than to be on this island with your friends?"

"Well—" Monkeyone hesitated, I would love to stay here with my friends of course but, I just wouldn't feel right. I belong here."

"I believe you've answered my question, even if you didn't know it. As of this minute you are relieved of duty. You are no longer my first mate but will forever be a good friend—"

"Wait! What are you saying?" Monkeyone interrupted.

"You know what I'm saying," Amon replied. "You are relieved of duty. You are now retired with my good wishes. You may join your friends and spend the rest of your life in leisure."

"But, I said I would stay with you—on this ship."

"I know what you said, friend, but, I know that in your heart you long to stay here in your paradise. And you must know that I could never live with myself if I were to keep you on board just to help me out. Time is running out. There is no telling what this ship is now going to encounter and it may not be to you and your crew's benefit. No, it's time you found your peace and it seems to be here—now don't argue with me."

Monkeyone was going to insist on staying but realized that Amon was right, he really did want to retire and was simply being loyal to his old friend. "Thank you, Amon," he finally could say his, emotions almost overtaking him. I guess it really is time, but it's hard after all these years."

"Yes it is, but it's not goodbye. The next time I come through here we will meet again and then if you wish you may again sign on with me." They both smiled at that because it was obvious that Amon was not ever going to be near this spot again.

Windom and Mary hearing all this said nothing but, watched the sun continue it's ascent knowing that things would be different now.

The official dismissing of the crew occurred at noon when they were all lined up at the rail. Presenting each with a single part of the ships engraved dining service, a spoon here and a knife there. As there would be little use for money where they were going to be Amon thought it would be more appropriate to leave them with something in which they could remember their voyages. When he reached Monkeyone he presented him with one of the ship's bells that was engraved with the ships name and home port. For the time it took to complete the ceremony no one spoke and for a few moments there was absolute silence. Then a cheer went up from the crew as they one by one scampered up the mainmast to where they could leap onto the branches of the overhanging trees and race into the forest. Monkeyone was the last to take his departure and just before he leaped into the trees he looked down and saluted the ship.

Amon wished to be away by noon and they all set about getting the ship ready. One of the crew had earlier by going to the top of one of the tall trees observed that the river seemed to transverse the entire island and that Amon could probably sail straight on through the island to its opposite coast. This was fortunate because the river was too narrow in which to turn the ship around and go back out the way they had come. With help from the large windless Windom and Mary were able to get the outer jib up and sail slowly up to the anchor and winch in its rope and chain. When the anchor was up and down, meaning off the bottom, they secured it and hoisted the mainsail, and were soon making good time down the river.

Sure enough and luckily for them they were able to sail entirely through the island and out the other entrance.

After a day or two of experimentation Windom and Mary realized that for the good of the ship they had better handle a minimum amount of sail. The large square foresail was too difficult for just the two of them to manage and so with great effort it was brought down along with the sky sail which was not necessary, and keeping up only the large for and aft mainsail, the small working jib and the larger flying jib. This was the most efficient system that the two of them could work and even then only in reasonably fair weather. If the weather really closed in they were in trouble anyway. For three days they sailed comfortably under this shortened sail plan, under a warm sun, through a blue-black sea with only a slight swell to rock them to sleep.

On the fourth day the wind picked up and Windom and Mary began to pay more attention to the sails. A following swell was growing that lifted the stern slightly letting it down again as it passed under the ship. The wind kept growing stronger and the swell as it barreled into the stern began to effect the course of the ship.

"Windom!" Amon yelled trying to be heard over the wind that was now howling "Better get the main down, Windom! It's only going to get worse." Windom and Mary who were thinking the same thing jumped to the task. With the wind as strong as it was and being short handed they did what they could running down wind. First they winched the main boom in to a mid ship position so as not to cause an accidental Jibe and then with just a slight flutter they got the mainsail down and booted. The flying Jib had already been blown away which was good because the working jib was probably already too much for the ship to carry but they left it up to help with steering.

The seas now were getting huge and frightening to see as they continually rolled in under the stern lifting it and pushing it one way or another. Mary who loved the sea and had read many seafaring books remembered how she had read that in the old days of sail in her own world sailors when rounding the horn in a gale were ordered never to look back at the waves because a fifty foot wave would be two terrifying and now Mary believed it. From where she was huddled in the waist of the ship the huge waves seemed taller than the masts.

"Mary! Windom! Get up here!" Amon was screaming to be heard, and they both scrambled up to where Amon was fighting the wheel. "Take over here for a minute. Try to keep her from broaching. I've got to rig a sea anchor," and he went below quickly returning with an old torn sail. In a few minutes he had it made into what he wanted attaching one side of it to a long piece of line. He then tied the other end of the line securely onto a large davit at the stern of the ship and slowly paid the anchor out until it was a few hundred yards astern. Then he came back to the wheel where Windom and Mary were. The minute the sea anchor had gone over the stern the ship had settled down and was now sailing a much calmer course.

"There's nothing more we can do here!" Amon yelled to them over the screaming wind. "She's under the control of the elements. Wherever the good Lord takes her now! We'd best go below and hang on!" So after lashing the wheel to its course they all went below.

And hang on they did tying themselves into their bunks to keep from being flung out as the ship rolled rail to rail in the raging the sea.

Trying to make head or tails out of what was happening Mary realized that on each wave the ship was rising higher and higher before cresting and falling into its trough. Up and Up the ship would rise and then reaching the wave's crest it would drop and Mary noticed that the interval was getting shorter between each wave and that they the waves were getting steeper and that the ship was now overtaking each wave. The ship would rise on the back of the wave as it overtook it and then surf precipitously down the front taking her breath away. And then the ship started up another wave and just kept going Up, Up, Up it went and then slowed and stopped for just a moment before it took off and seemed to be flying. There was no crashing about in the waves then, just a howling wind breaking the silence as the ship dropped off the top of the wave as the wave broke. "This is it," Mary thought just as there was an earth shattering crash and then blackness.

The next thing that Mary was aware of was soft warm sand. She seemed to be lying in it on her side and she carefully opened one eye. And then she opened the other. And then she began to check herself out, first an arm and then a leg and when they seemed to work she rolled over onto her back and sat up and looked around. Not far away Windom was stirring and there was Amon and Molly walking her way with Frendo beside them striding along like a young man.

"Are you all right, Mary?" Amon called.

"I seem to be fine, how about you?" Mary replied looking herself over.

"Oh, we're fine." Amon answered. "And look at Frendo, here," and Frendo did a little dance. Just then Mary saw another figure striding up the beach."

"Who's that?" Mary said pointing at the figure. The others turned just as the new arrival walked up.

"Hello, brother," it said with a big smile.

"Arturo," Amon said in amazement, "What in the world are you doing here. Where is your ship."

"There with yours, my good friend," he said pointing to a pile of lumber and tangled ropes that used to be their respective ships being destroyed in the surf.

"Well, it looks like we've both been sunk," Amon said watching the debris disappear in the waves. "Now what do we do, brother?"

"Why, love each other, brother, as we should have been doing all along. I seem to have followed you all over this strange world for some reason but I've forgotten why."

"Just as well, Arturo, I've forgotten too."

Windom then did a somersault and ran down the beach and back. "Say," he said joyously, "I've never wanted to do that. I wonder what's come over me."

"I don't know what's happening, but we all seem to be feeling pretty good."

"So, what do we do now?" Mary asked.

"Good point, Mary," Amon replied as he began to look around. They were standing on a narrow spit of sand with the ocean waves breaking on one shore and a calm stretch of water lapping the opposite beach. Across this quiet water was land that seemed to stretch for ever in both directions but was far to distant for them to reach without a boat. As they watched that far shore something seemed to move and it appeared to be a tiny person waving.

"Look there," Arturo said. "It looks like there's man pushing off in a boat."

"Just one man?" asked Arturo.

"Seems to be." Arturo answered.

"Must be friendly, then," Amon said as they waited the stranger's arrival.

"Soon a tall man standing in the middle of a small rowing boat ran it gently up onto the sand and jumped out to stride up the beach to them.

"Welcome! all of you. So you finally made it. I was beginning to worry."

"Father!" Amon exclaimed, for this was Amon's father who had been lost at sea some years before. "So this is where you've been?"

"This is the place, and now we're all here, you, Amon, Molly, Windom and Arturo. And who is this?" he said turning to Mary.

"Father, I want you to meet Mary Lytle."

"Mary Lytle?" he said surprised.

"Well, her full name is Mary Lytle Curtis but, we just call her Mary. Her grandmother's name is Mary Lytle," Amon said pointedly.

"Well, well," Amon's father said, "the world repeats itself. Welcome, Mary, I trust you've had an interesting voyage."

"That's putting it mildly," Mary said, at which Amon's father laughed.

"Mary was paramount in looking after Windom," Amon added. "You know how he gets in trouble."

"Oh, that I do," Amon's father said. I assumed Mary was along for some reason, but now it's time to go. If you'll just get in my boat, I'll soon have you ashore."

As each one boarded the little boat, that had originally been only large enough for Windom, it grew large enough for the next one and then the next one and so on until they were all in, but Mary. When Mary began to board, Amon's father stopped her. "Not just now, Mary. Make yourself comfortable here on the beach and your time will come."

As the little boat pushed off Mary watched it move away. She felt no fear or anxiety as you might think being left all lone on a strange shore but she was surprised to realize she was completely at peace, as though this was how it should be.

When the boat reached the far shore its occupants all got out and stretched their legs.

"This is a remarkable place," Amon said. It feels familiar but, how is that possible? have I been here before? Everything seems so new."

Amon's father looked everyone over for a moment. "You have not suspected where you are? No I suppose not. You will however. Soon. It seems to be new to you because it is new, and also old. Old as all time. Windom, you will never be ill again. The rest of you will never grow old here—but come along, you must come and meet the others—and there are so many."

Mary watched her old friends moving into the interior of the land that was disappearing into what appeared to be a fog, but it wasn't a fog. The view was simply losing it's concreteness. It was dissipating like a cloud as it melts away and then it was gone. Where once there was land and people there now was nothing. Not even the sea. Suddenly a huge wave swept over and around Mary and though they were no longer visible to Mary, her friends turning around for one last look were able to see, for just a moment, Mary disappear as the sea broke over her. They all cheered seemingly to know that that was how it should be and then they turned and entered their new world.

A large wave just then fell gently on the rocky beach splashing Mary Curtis where she was seated with her eyes closed. Startled, she looked up and around and brushed herself off. She was still holding the little book that she had brought down to the beach to read and it was perfectly dry. It must have been protected from the flying salt water she thought and then she began to remember something about ships and adventure. And it all came back to her. 'It had to be a dream,' she thought while gathering her things together and dropped the book that fell open on the sand. She picked it up and noticed that it had fallen open to the last few pages and where there had been only one empty page there were now several pages filled with charts outlining ships courses. Mary knew that those pages had not been there when she had first sat down. She decided she had better talk to her grandmother about the book and quickly climbed up the cliff back to the house.

As Mary rushed up to the front door of her house she saw Martha the housekeeper who came on Mondays standing in the doorway.

"Oh, hello, Martha," Mary said, "I had forgotten it was Monday, isn't it a beautiful day?" and as she started through the door Martha gently stopped her.

"Mary, will you please come with me for a moment. I have something to tell you."

"I will in a minute, Martha. I have to see gram first."

"That can wait, Mary. This won't take long," Martha said, and there was something in her voice that made Mary wonder what all this was going to be about. It wasn't like Martha to take this kind of control. "Why don't you just sit here with me, Mary," she said and patted a spot on the couch where Mary sat down waiting expectantly to hear what was so important. After some hesitation Martha spoke to her.

"Mary, I'm terribly sorry to have to be the one to tell you this, but your grandmother has passed away. When I entered her room to tidy it up I saw that she had gone back to bed—to take a nap I thought—but it wasn't a nap, she had passed." Mary, for a moment didn't comprehend what Martha had said. "What do you mean, 'passed away'." Mary said. She well understood what 'passed away' meant but, couldn't accept it at that moment.

"Your grandmother has gone to heaven, Mary. I'm sorry but, she's no longer with us, do you understand?"

It then sank in and Mary realized that her grandmother had died but couldn't quite believe it. "But I had something to tell her—" Mary said and then knew she wasn't making sense of it. "May I see her?"

"I should think that would be all right. Maybe you'd like to say good by."

They went into the bedroom which at that moment looked normal to Mary. Her grandmother was in bed as Mary had so often seen her except that now a sheet was covering her face. Mary walked up to the head of the bed and reached out for the sheet looking first at Martha who nodded her head. Mary lowered the sheet just enough to see her grandmothers closed eyes and then drew back.

"She looks so peaceful, don't you think," Martha said, "I know she's now in heaven."

She did look peaceful to Mary, almost happy. "Bye, bye, gram," Mary said in not much more than a whisper. She knew now that her grandmother had moved on in her adventures and that it wasn't necessary to tell her of her own. She knew all about it. Mary was sure of that, still she would have loved to discuss it with her. Maybe someday. There were no tears that day. Only later when her loss had sunk in did they flow.

Mary went to live with her aunt and uncle who gave her a good education, took her traveling with them all over the world, and she went on to live a long and good life.

She never told anyone about her big adventure. She would have liked to tell her grandmother. Maybe someday.

MYSTERIES OF
MACO MARU

1

"All right then, we agree? said Mr. Dolot.

"Yessss!" was the enthusiastic answer from twelve year old Mollie Dolot and her mother. And why not a unanimous yes? They were all going to Hawaii for a three weeks vacation! That would be their home base from which they would search out the south sea island called Mako Maru. It was supposed to be located somewhere east of, Tahiti. Mollie's father had inherited some property on this island from his brother who had mysteriously died recently and they were going to look for it. It was thought to be an uninhabited island and probably the property was worthless, to be disposed of, but the Dolot family being an inquisitive group decided to make it an adventure and search it out and in three days the three of them were settled into a comfortable room in Hilo on the big island of Hawaii.

Before leaving for Tahiti and the first leg of their adventure Mr. Dolot took the family to the the Hawaiian Museum. "Do you now what this is?" Mr. Dolot asked Mollie showing her a framed paper hanging on the wall.

"Not exactly," Mollie said, examining it closely. "Something to do with the ship—.

"Exactly. It's the ships manifest."

"What's a manifest?"

"It's a record of the ship's cargo, including the passengers. Now look here," and Mr. Dolot ran his finger down the page until he reached some names. "Do you know who these people are?"

"Those people there?" Mollie asked peering at the paper and then answered her own question. "It says Ted and Sara Wolmsley."

"Do you know who they were?" Mr. Dolot asked.

Mollie thought about it for a minute. "Don't we have ancestors named Wolmsley?"

"That's right. These people right here are they. Your ancestors were with the first load of missionaries to visit Hawaii in 1820."

"These very people? I didn't know that. They were missionaries? Do you know anything about them?"

"Yes I still have some old letters from them. When we get back home I'll show them to you," Mollie was curious about her ancestors, but it seemed she would have to wait until they got back home to learn any more.

From Hawaii they took a plane to Tahiti and then, because no one locally had ever heard of Maco Maru, they hired an old broken down inter island freighter to search for it and eventually found what they were looking for. Only it was not a desert island at all. Although very small it had trees and fruit, animals and birds, and more importantly it was inhabited with a small population of Polynesian islanders. They were friendly and greeted Mollie and her parents as long lost relatives. Mr. Dolot's property was located atop a small mountain in the interior of the island with a commanding view of the blue south pacific ocean. It even had a small cabin that could be fixed up. Just fit for three Mollie decided having fallen in love with the place. Mr. Dolot wrote articles for various magazines and was able to easily communicate electronically with his publishers and thought as Mollie did and so here were the Dolots two years later.

Manawella was thirteen years old, one year older than Mollie who was now twelve, and in the two years that Mollie had been on Maco Maru he and Mollie had become good friends. Today Mana, as he was called by the locals, along with his two ten year old twin sisters and Mollie were headed for the small cove that provided the only beach on the island. They had been given permission to spend the night there on their pandanus mats while Mana explained the stars to Mollie as they were different than the ones with which she was familiar. But as often happens their interest soon turned to ghost stories. Mana had just told one that had them all shivering in the warm tropical night.

"That was a good story, Mana. Where did you hear that?" asked Mollie impressed.

"My Uncle is the official story teller of our people and has many more like that. They're all supposed to teach us something."

"Ah, they carry messages. Do you believe in miracles?"

"No."

"Why not"

"Because they're not real."

"Was that story you just told real?"

"My uncle thinks so."

"Well, here's a story I heard myself. It's supposed to be true. But a kind of miracle too. Do you want to her it?"

"Sure. If it's a god story."

"I think it is. And it's about your island, too."

"My island? What do you know about my island?"

"Listen, Mano, do want to hear my story or not?"

"Yes I do. Mano want to hear story."

"Now stop that. I've already apologized. I didn't know you knew the kings english. This was a reference to an early mistake she had made when tying to communicate.

"O.K. carry on old girl."

Mary gave him the bent eye and then continued. "I don't know if you know it, but you're island is a little difficult to find—

"That's the way we like it."

—and we finally had to secure an old tramp steamer to find you. It seems an old, really old, native knew where you are and told this story.

"Will you get on with it?"

"I might," Mollie said exasperated, if you will just shut up. You want to hear this story or not?"

"Yes I do, I really do. I'll keep quiet. Please carry on."

"This old native, Polynesian, was at the time very young acting as a cabin boy for the current captains father who told him this story that must have happened over a hundred years ago. The original owner of this ship was once sailing uncharted waters when he discovered this island and with three of his crew went ashore to investigate. A little later the first mate who had been left in charge of the boat saw the captain running for his life calling to the mate to get under way immediately as he himself swam to the ship crawling aboard in a panic. The other three of his crew were never heard from again and the captain who had been ashore went completely mad. At his inquest conducted because of the loss of his crew he maintained that they were devoured by giant snakes with human heads. No one could ever exactly identify the island and so nothing was proved and the captain was released. But to the day he died he swore it was all true.

"Where's the miracle?"

"I'm coming to that. For the rest of his life he walked the beaches talking to himself and telling anyone he met his story. And then one day a large bird wandered over to where he was sitting on a rock and he told the bird his story. It was a huge bird probably a —- and as he told his story the bird seemed to pick up its ears and pay attention. When he was through it flew away. The next day at about the same time the same bird flew overhead and then another and soon the sky was full of birds. It took ten minutes for them to all pass by. He didn't think much of it until several days later a visiting ship captain related a strange tale about hundreds of bids flying over his ship that seemed to be carrying snakes in their beaks. From then on the old man was more at ease and never told his story again unless someone asked for it. Instead he quoted poetry mainly this one:

> I spoke to a bird today
> Oh, yes I spoke to a bird
> It may seem strange and a little absurd
> A little deranged to speak to a bird
> But we had so much to say

"That could have happened before your people settled here. You said you've only inhabited this island for about two hundred years?"

"That's right. And we certainly have no snakes. That's some story I have to admit. By the way, I've been meaning to ask you about that thing around your neck. What is it?"

"Oh, this? It's a whistle. I know it looks like a cross, but it's a whistle. Actually I think it's a key too. It's even a little bent where someone must have forced a door lock or something. My father inherited it from a great aunt and he gave it to me. I kind of like it."

"Well it looks unique. I was just curious."

By then they were all pretty tired and turned in for the night.

MOLLIE'S MIRACLES

While Mollie, Arny and the twins slept, secure on their mats, five miles away deep beneath the surface of the southern ocean a sea mount not yet an island began to rumble and shake and a few boulders slid down its steep slopes. And then a much larger temblor occurred causing a huge portion of the mount to collapse and fall several thousand feet to the ocean floor drawing a large part of the ocean down with it. When the sea came back up it formed a swell a foot above the surface. A foot may not seem like much, but is more than you think when it covers a mile of ocean. As though you had dropped a pebble into the sea at that place a ripple was formed that spread out in all directions racing across the sea at five hundred miles an hour. When this one foot ripple began to reach shallower water it began to grow as a wave grows on reaching a sandy beach and soon it towered twenty feet high before it no longer cold support itself cresting over in a cascade of white foam. In this case right into the cove where the children were sleeping.

Arny and the twins were swept up the hill that formed the back of the cove into a grove of trees where they held on for dear life until the water had receded and were relatively unhurt. Mollie however found nothing to hang on to and was swept far out to sea.

Mollie was a good swimmer and finally she could stop fighting the turbulent ocean and look around to see where she was. The dawn was just arriving and she found herself alone with no land in sight. Only the broken hull of a small outrigger canoe was between her and the bottom of the ocean and she swam over to hit and clambered aboard. There wasn't much left of the canoe, just enough to float her and keep her out of the water.

It was several hours before she realized she wasn't alone. First she saw a fin slowly cruise by and then quickly reverse course coming back to look her over. And then there were more fins circling her. Mollie watched them as they circled eying her and it seemed to her that they were smiling and not in a friendly way. More like a satisfied momentary observation just before one eats a delicious looking lunch.

What a way to die, Mollie thought. She knew it would hurt, but for how long she wondered. Suddenly a huge pair of jaws opened next to her and snapped down on the canoe just missing her foot. That shocked her out of her lethargy and she grabbed her whistle and blew as hard as she could. She was more angry than afraid and had to do something even though it had little effect. There were no more attacks for several minutes the bite of wood apparently not being satisfactory.

And then there were more fins. There seemed to be thousands of them. But these Mollie realized were not shark fins, but dolphins, and they were leaping out of the water and landing on the sharks backs. They were huge and much faster that the sharks and within several minutes of ferocious fighting the sharks had been beaten off. It seems that blowing on her whistle to frighten the sharks away had instead alerted dolphins that were in the area.

The dolphins were leaping into the air, doing flips and Mollie was sure they were laughing. They seemed to have thoroughly enjoyed their little rumble. One came close by and seemed to be saying something to her and then with another three it sped away while the others kept circling and playing as if they were keeping her company. Maybe protecting her.

Exhausted, Mollie had dosed off for what she thought was no more than a few minutes, but was actually several hours, and when she awoke a hand was reaching down to grab her as a huge outrigger canoe sailed by. As she was hoisted over the side she saw all the dolphins swimming away frolicking as if greatly relieved to see Mollie on board the boat. Mollie thought later that the dolphins had somehow found the boat and brought it over to save her. She had read about.

"Thank you! Thank you so much! You've saved my life," Mollie stammered when she was finally able to speak. My names Mollie, who are you?"

This was the biggest canoe she had ever seen in person although she had seen their pictures in magazines. She recognized it as a discovery canoe canoe sent with whole families to search out new homes on distant island. But what was this one doing out here in this day and age. Maybe a celebration.

There was a boy about her own age sitting across from her and he answered, "What do you mean saved you?"

"You saved my life—and what in the world are all you people doing out here? Are you celebrating ancient voyages? This has to be some kind of miracle—that you were out here when I needed you".

"We are on a voyage. A long voyage. With you we have finally found all of you. And now we will soon be home."

"You mean you're lost?"

"No, not exactly, we just haven't found our final home yet. And you shouldn't use that term any more."

"What term?"

"Saved your life."

"But you did."

The boy looked at Mollie for a few moments before speaking. "I'm sorry," he finally said, I didn't realize you don't yet know."

"Know what? you're not making sense."

"That you're dead, of course."

"Are you crazy? I'm not dead," Mollie blurted out, and then realized maybe she shouldn't have used those words. Maybe he was a little bit touched in the head.

"You were dead when we picked you up." the boy insisted.

"Oh, ha ha," Mollie laughed, "no I was just sleeping." The boy leaned over and took her hand and then jumped back.

"You really are alive!" and then he called out the man steering the boat who seemed to be the captain. "Father, I think we made a mistake!"

"Yes, we've made a few, what is it now?" the man called back.

"This girl is alive. Really alive," said the boy.

The man who was apparently the boys father after a few moments silence called back. "Bring her here," and Mollie was directed up to where the man was sitting with one hand resting on the big steering oar. "What's your name?" he said, looking her over carefully.

"Mollie."

"Well Mollie, my name is Lana Mar. Or just Lana. This is my son Marana and if he says you're alive you must be. He's never wrong—or maybe this once—because he thought you were dead when we retrieved you. How did you get out here in the middle of the ocean all by yourself?—never mind, we have more serious things to think about now that we know that you are not really dead."

"Of course I'm not dead," Mollie said in exasperation." What game were these crazy people playing. "I'm as alive as you are."

"More, I'm afraid," the man said.

"What do you mean more?"

"Well, you see we on this boat, all of us, are only souls. The souls of people like you. People who were alive and active, but are now only bones lying on the bottom of the sea."

"I don't understand you. Are you teasing me because I'm a little girl and won't know any better?"

"Mollie," Marana spoke up. "My father may not have explained it clearly. We—all of us in this boat—are not of your world. We are no longer living beings. We are only souls of the dead. Here, take my hand," and he held out his hand to Mollie. Mollie took Marana's hand and immediately drew back. Marana's hand was ice cold and without substance. It was as if she had grasped a half deflated balloon. "You see?" Marana said. "You might think us unreal, but we are as real as you are. Only we've moved on." Mollie looked around the boat and noticed that all the passengers seamed to be sleeping. "And that brings up a problem."

"It seems to be a problem for me, all right. What in the world am I doing here".

"Yes, that's the question. Only it's a problem for us too."

"How so?"

"I'll try to explain. Our mission, my fathers and mine, has been to rescue the souls of certain worthy people and deliver them to what will be their final destination. We have seventy seats in this boat and we must fill them all before the final voyage. We must deliver seventy souls no more or less. And you, who are still alive, are occupying the seat reserved for the seventieth soul. You see the quandary?"

"I am an interloper."

"We, my father and I, have so far been directed to retrieve only those souls worthy of delivery, which poses the question, why did we pick you up?"

"You made a mistake?"

"That's what I thought at first, but now I'm not sure. You may be here for a special purpose."

"But you can't make your delivery. Maybe you should throw me back," Mollie said but her joke fell flat.

"That would solve the problem," Lana said changing course slightly with the steering oar, "but we are not allowed to do that. You see we have been sent to save souls, not to create them. But we will never find our last island this way," Lana mused.

"What last island?"

"The island where we will spend eternity."

These people had to have been out in the sun far too long, Mollie thought.

"Mollie thought over her situation again and had to admit they were right. She definitely did not belong on that boat and the quicker they solved their problem the sooner she could return to some sanity and decided to help if she could.

"Maybe I could give you my soul," Mollie said without thinking.

"Can't be done." Lana said as a matter of fact. "The souls we need are the ones that have left the body. Mmm," he thought. "Take the oar, Marana,' he said to his son, I'm going to have a talk with our wise man," and he began working his way to the bow.

"What wise man?" Mollie wanted to know.

"We people always travel with a wise man. Someone who has access to more knowledge than the common man."

About an hour later Lana returned and again took the oar. "I have talked it over with our wise man," he said, "and you were closer to the truth than we thought. He informs me that according to an old legend there is a possibility if you are in agreement. It requires for you to give an oath that it is your wish to offer your soul temporarily to us for the purpose proposed. What do you think?"

"Tell me your proposal and I'll consider it."

"Wise answer. It amounts to this. You offer your soul to us for the sole—pardon the pun—purpose of finishing our work, not to exceed thirty days, and in return we offer you another life because there must be an equal gift to you."

"What kind of life?"

"Oh, a birds life, or an animals, although there are no animals here at see. Maybe a fishes life."

Mollie thought it might be fun to experience another life and thought about it. "The dolphins were good to me. Maybe a dolphin."

"Is that your choice, then?"

"Yes, a dolphin."

"All right then. Ruen—That's the name of our wise man—will prepare the magic that you must consume and then we'll see if it works."

"See if it works? What is this concoction anyway?"

"Oh, just a few herbs and such as he might find in his medicine chest. He carries a complete chest."

Mollie was beginning to think she had made a mistake in her agreement. What was this drink going to be made of, mice and snails and puppy dogs tails.

A comfortable mat was prepared for her to lie down on and when the drink arrived Mollie with only a furtive glance at the brew drank it down and prepared to die. After a moment of panic she realized the drink had not tasted bad at all, but quite good, fruity and semi sweet with a touch of cumin and, resigned to her fate, Mollie, making herself as comfortable as possible, dosed off.

It was a slow process, waking up from her sleep, but finally with a start she opened her eyes to a soft green light and found herself swimming with a pod of dolphins. They were leaping and spinning and circling around her like they were celebrating the return of a long lost relative. And she found herself doing the same as if she had been cavorting like this her whole life.

The pod was following a large outrigger canoe that Mollie somehow recognized as if in a dream and as she leaped out of the water in one of her soaring dives she saw a boy at the bow of the canoe waving at each dolphin as it flew by. Day after day the canoe sailed on with its marine escort playing in the boat's wake, diving and spinning as only dolphins can and then just as Mollie the dolphin had decided she would like to do that for the rest of her life she woke up.

"Well, well, back with the living—or rather dead. How was your other life?" Lana was saying as he looked down at her.

"Delightful. Can I go back?"

"I'm afraid not. Your time is up."

Mollie's human memory was slowly coming back and she remembered why she had been flying with the fishes. "Did it work for you?"

"Oh yes! Come let me help you up. What do you see?"

The canoe was sailing, making good time, through a thick fog, but dead ahead the sky was glowing with light as though it were reflecting in a night's sky off the lights of a well lit city.

"We are here! We have arrived at out destination," Lana cheered, and beneath the light Mollie could now see an island. Not just any island, but the most beautiful island Mollie had ever seen. Surrounding the island was a lagoon of crystal clear water tinted green that washed a white sand beach whiter than snow and trees so green they looked painted.

"This is our island?" Mollie asked in awe.

"Not your island. Not yet anyway. But it is my island, my fathers island, and the home island of all these good souls," and Marana swept his hand across the contents of his boat.

"It's beautiful. Can I stay here for awhile anyway?"

"No. We'll be crossing the reef in a minute or two and you won't be able to follow us. Not just yet anyway. Your time will come I'm sure, but not now. We've outfitted the small boat for you and it's time that you be off. Here, let me help you down," and Lana and Moana lifted Mollie over the rail of the large canoe into the small outrigger that they had been towing behind them. "Thank you for your help. If it hadn't been for you we'd still be searching for our island."

"Are you sure I haven't been a hindrance?" Mollie wanted to know.

"Oh no. Not at all. It turned out a little different than we thought it would, but I'm sure it was in the original plan. It always is. Keep the sun as it travels east to west two points off your starboard bow and you should reach a small island in two or three days. It's there that you will continue your journey. We have finally finished ours. Good luck and Bon Voyage!"

The last thing that Bonnie saw as she turned to watch the large canoe negotiate the pass in the reef were many people standing on the shore waving and cheering as Mollie's ship of friends slipped up on the white sand beach. As she watched the fog closed in to obscure the scene and when again the fog cleared there was only empty sea where the island had been but a moment before.

Mollie's small canoe she found had been well stocked with food and water and so keeping the sun a little to the right of the canoe's bow as instructed she sailed westward. The weather was fine and under a blue sky with only a few white puffer belly white clouds they made good time the small canoe being very fast in a brisk breeze now and then lifting the amma out of the water and Mollie had to keep her mind well on her business.

On the third morning under a distant gray cloud she could discern a small island. It was off to her right meaning that Mollie's navigation was off slightly as she sailed, but only a little bit. By noon she was heading for a small beach when she spotted what turned out to be an elderly man relaxed in his canoe fishing and she changed course to intercept him so as to gain what information she could about his island. When she bumped his canoe the man who had been asleep woke up with a start.

"Hey, watch where your going—" the man blurted out before ha had observed the situation—"Oh pardon me. I was just resting a moment. Who are you?" he said looking her over carefully. "You are not one of us." Though by now Mollie was well tanned from the tropical sun she was definitely not a native.

"No I'm not," Mollie answered, and not wanting to get into a long explanation she simply said, "I'm just a lonely seafarer hoping to find a place to rest. Will your island welcome me?"

"Well, the man said looking at the shore. "I see I've drifted a bit while resting. We are where we do not want to be. Come along and follow me," and the man began to lead Mollie away from the beach she had first been heading for until hey were on the other side of the island. Here they pulled their canoes up onto another beach. "Come along now. We must see Ponto to find out what to do with you."

"Who's Ponto?"

"He's our chief. He'll know what to do. My name is Luana, by the way," and he looked questioningly at Mollie.

"Oh, I'm Mollie," she answered.

"Well, Mollie, how in the world did—oh, never mind, here's Ponto now, you explain it all to him."

"Well, Luana, what have you fished up there?" Ponto said as he walked up. "I saw you coming in with something strange aboard your boat and I had to see what it was."

"I'm not that strange," Mollie replied offended.

"Luana, she talks," Ponto said looking at Luanda.

"Yes she does and her name is Mollie. She wonders if we might welcome her to our island."

"Oh. Then she hasn't come from the other side?"

"No, she calls herself a seafarer."

"Oh, then I'm very sorry, Mollie for being so rude. I was under the impression that you were from the other side.

You are definitely welcome to our humble home, such as it is," and Ponto made a grand bow. "But where do you really come from? You are not one of us?"

Mollie quickly decided to eliminate the immediate past from her bibliography for time's sake and because it wouldn't be believed any way. "I was washed off the island where I was living and out to sea by a large wave and ended up here," she abbreviated.

"Yes that does happen, but you've come a long way. It must have been some wave," Ponto said skeptically.

"You don't know the half of it," Mollie said with emphasis.

"Well you are welcome to stay as long as you want, that is if you decide to."

"Why do you think I wouldn't? It looks like a beautiful island."

"A crab looks cute until one touches it's claw."

"And what do you mean 'The other side'?"

"That is why you may not want to stay. I'll try to explain. We, that is we people who live on this side of the island, were on an expedition to find a new land in which to settle when we came across this island. We've been here almost four years now. Unfortunately another clan lives on the opposite shore who have lived here a long time and consider us foreigners and originally wanted us gone."

"And you want to stay."

"No, no longer. We want to leave."

"Why don't you?"

"They are an evil and violent bunch and having superior numbers they've been able to force us to be little more than slaves giving them half our fish catch and working their vegetable gardens. And so of course now they wish to keep us here."

"I see you still have your large exploration canoe. Couldn't you slip away at night?"

"Not a chance. They watch us day and night and have five war canoes much faster than our canoe. You'll soon meet their leader. I'm sure they've seen your arrival and are as curious about you as we were. In fact I wonder how you'll be greeted. I don't think they'll harm you. They're a superstitious lot and will be wary of someone as different from us as you are."

As Ponto had suspected the next day Mollie did meet the leader of the other clan. He and a group of his armed warriors approached Ponto's camp and demanded to see the new arrival. They were of a definitely different race entirely. Not Polynesian at all, and their leader was more recognizable to Mollie than he would have been to the south sea islanders. He was tall and obviously european.

"Well, well, little girl, what are you doing way out here?" he said as soon as he spotted Mollie. You are not one of these snails," he snorted pointing to Mollie's new friends.

"I could ask the same of you," Mollie replied not at all impressed by this oaf.

"Oh, ho!" he laughed. "A little alley cat for sure! I'll send for you at sundown. Don't be late," and he and his bodyguards stalked off.

"What does he mean, he'll 'send for me'?" Mollie asked Ponto.

"He want's to meet and talk with you at his camp. He'll send someone to take you there. You'll be fine I'm sure.

There would be no reason to harm you. I'll send one of my men with you for moral support."

Just as the sun was setting Mollie's escort showed up and he, Mollie and her own guard set off for the strange man's camp. There Mollie's guards were left outside to guard an entrance to living quarters cut out of a limestone cliff. This apparently was the home of the man who now cordially invited her to sit down. At first she thought that only the two of them were present but then noticed a boy about her own age sitting in a corner of the room.

"Well, well, and right on time. Let me formally introduce myself. I am Enock Grandville, the chief of this island and this is my son Tory," and he motioned to the boy in the corner. "And who might you be?"

"I am Mollie Malone and my friends call me Mollie."

"Well Mollie Malone, why are you on my island. And more importantly how did you get here. You are alone I presume?"

"Yes I am, very much so," and she meant it.

"You are not a native of this area? I mean of these southern seas?" Enock asked as he looked her over.

"No, I was visiting an island south of here when I was washed away and now find myself here."

"How convenient," Enock mused. "You look more like you are from my land than from anywhere around here."

"You look european. How did you get here?" Mollie asked Enock.

"I washed up on this beach as you did. Twenty seven years ago and am now I'm king. How would you like to be queen?"

"Me, queen? You mean your queen?"

"No, no, not my queen. Your are far to young for that. But in time possibly my son's queen—when he takes over."

Mollie didn't say anything for a few moments. She was wondering if there might be an opening here in which she could help her friends. Finally she asked, "What did you have in mind?"

"I have been observing my people and they seem to be in awe of you as they were of me when I arrived. I looked so different from them that they thought I might be one of their ancient gods returning and I was quick to take advantage of it. And here I am their god. My son is in line to be their future king, but if you—a queen in her own right— were in the future be his wife it would better secure our position, if you understand me?"

"You want me to be a god so as to better strengthen your power over them?"

"Don't forget you would also be queen. Queen of this island. You will have everything. The fact that we look so different from them helps. And I have a few tricks.

"Sounds good to me," Mollie said. Her mind was whirling as to how she could use this opportunity to help her true friends and decided it would do well for her to appear amenable to this hair brained scheme. She glanced over into the corner where Tony, the king's son was sitting, and detected distaste in his moody expression. Taking it personally she thought she didn't appeal to him.

"Well, I think we understand each other. Drop by mid morning tomorrow and we'll begin your indoctrination. My son will walk you to the door. What good fortune has visited me," Enock said to himself, as he walked away, but was overheard by Mollie.

"What?" she said turning around. "Oh, I just was thinking what good fortune has come my way—but of course yours too," and he walked off smiling to himself.

"So you're going to be king some day," Mollie said just to make conversation as she and Tony walked to the front door.

"Not on your life. That's Enock's dream, not mine. Mine is to get away from this island as fast as I can. Are you really going to go along with Enock's idea. If so, take care, he is a dangerous person."

"Really," Mollie said surprised at Tony's tone of voice, and she turned around to face him. "You really don't want to be a king?"

"Of course not. And Enock is not my real father," Tony whispered. "He adopted me when my parents died in a fishing accident. He just wanted me to do his dirty work for him. He's quite mad. Don't trust him. He will use you and then throw you away like a dead fish."

They were at the front door and as Mollie sized Tony up she decided to take a chance and trust him. "I only said I would cooperate so as to gain his trust. I don't want to be Queen. I want to help those good people on the other side of this island to escape. Say—if you can help me I'll see that you can come along too, that is if you're really serious about getting away."

"I sure do. This is an evil island, the way it is now, and I can help. I'll be your spy inside. I'll find out his plan and let you know what it is. What a dream! To get away from this infernal island. I'll see what I can find out tonight. Enock has no idea that I want to get away and trusts me explicitly. Don't tell anyone or I'm dead meat" he said as he opened the front door for her.

The following day, as told, Mollie showed up at Enock's house. "Ah, good, right on time. I have some work to do so Tony will show you around. He's a good boy and will tell you our plan." He then left them and Tony gave Mollie a small tour of their encampment introducing her to the important people she should get to know.

"They're mostly good people really, but have been turned against your people by Enock. A way of gaining power. Divide and conquer."

"You sound educated. What are you doing out here?"

"My parents and I were going to sail around the world, but this was as far as we got."

"How long ago was that?"

"About three years. We washed up here after a storm smashed our boat. Shortly after that a shark killed my parents and this monster took control of me. What a miracle it is that you made it here too. Maybe there's hope after all. But let me tell you what Enock has planned. We have to come up with some magic to prove to the natives that you have great power. That way when Enock destroys you he will have strengthened his hold over these people even more. Do you have any magic up your sleeve?"

"What do you mean destroy me? Do you mean that after I do my magic he intends to kill me?"

"That's his plan. We have even a better one."

"We do?"

"You don't die, but come back to life. In that way you prove to be even stronger than he. I think then my people will listen to you and let you and your people go—and me too of course. You promised."

"Of course and I keep my promises. Have you a plan? It sounds as though this whole farce might be dangerous."

"My plan is to try and figure out a plan. Any ideas?"

I'm losing faith in your plan. I thought you might be further along."

"Well, let's take it step by step. First there has to be your miracle. Can you fly? Can you turn yourself into a bug?"

"Are you serious? Do you really think I have magic?"

"I don't know. You sure showed up here mysteriously."

"That's a long story, but not now. I'm just as simple as you are," then wondered how he would take that after it was said." He just gave her the bent eye as if to say 'be careful'.

The rest of the day was spent going over possibilities for their ruse which were all to far fetched or impractical and Mollie went back to her people with her head spinning and by the next morning she had an idea.

"I've an idea," Mollie said to Tony when they met the next day. "Listen to this. Are your people familiar with the 'red tide'?"

"I don't know, let's go ask Enock. He should be aware of this part of the plan and might be able to help."

"The red tide," Enock mused when they asked him about it. I haven't heard that term since I left southern Cal. many years ago. These people may know of the pheromone, but it's a rare occurrence and you might be able to use it. What did you have in mind?"

"I saw this red tide not far off your coast as I approached your island and I remember that it seemed to be drifting in this direction. As this tide makes the water look red I thought I might be able to predict it's arrival. I'll call it the blood of your peoples ancestors that I have brought to their shores because of their evil ways. As you know it's simply plankton colored red by omega that poisons their shellfish so that they it can't be eaten and I'll tell them that I will keep it here until the people change their ways. Eventually it will go away and I'll take credit for it leaving."

"Sounds good if it works. Carry on," Enock said and went back to his work.

"Enock's going to leave it up to you," Tony said to Mollie, "so let's go and drop some hints with the natives. This they did by warning them about their evil ways and that if they didn't straighten up the blood of their ancestors would visit them.

It worked almost too well because the next day the red tide arrived. Enock, Tony and Mollie then held a meeting with the native leaders, Enock pointing out Mollie's terrible power. Then Mollie took the stage telling the people that if all went well in a day or two she would send the poisoned tide away and they could again eat their favorite shell fish.

Sure enough on the next day the tide shifted and the red water began to drift out to sea. To celebrate the village had a luau. When the sun was down and the bonfire large Enock appeared. "You see how powerful our new god is," he proclaimed. Are there any gods more powerful?"

"No!" roared the crowd. "Then let's celebrate our good fortune. Come and drink with me."

"Oh, oh," Tony said. "Enock has brought out his favorite concoction."

"What's that?" Mollie asked.

"It's a psychedelic drink he makes out of fermented coconut milk and juice from a certain shell fish that's normally poison to eat. It's one way he has of influencing the natives."

"They won't get out of control?"

"Oh, no, it's a mild sedative when taken casually."

"Then there's no problem?"

"In our case there's a big problem. Tonight he plans to kill you, here in front of the natives."

"Tonight?" Mollie said.

"Now I know what he meant last night when he said today would be the great awakening. He means to kill you and take credit for being even more powerful than you. And I saw him making his drink. The powerful one.

"What will we do?"

"He means to kill you with the drink. Made more powerful it' poisonous. He's killed his enemies with it on occasion. But I have an antidote—well, not a real antidote—but I can outwit him. When I didn't want to participate in his parties I found that if if I mixed his drink with sea water it would make me sick and that I would vomit up the drink. When he gives you your lethal dose tonight I'll slip you the sea water, then we'll dodge behind a tree, throw up and I think you I be o,k.

"You think?"

"O,k, I'm sure. But one more thing. Can you swim?"

"Yes, pretty well."

"Good. As soon as you vomit it the drink out of your system throw up your arms and start screaming and race for the beach. I'll run with you. When you hit the water swim as far as you can until you can't be seen by the village and then go back to your people. I'll visit you there tomorrow and tell you the rest of the plan—Oh, oh, here he comes—don't worry I have the sea water right here," and he motioned to a bush at his feet.

"Ah, there you are, Mollie. What a night, eh! Oh, say, have a drop of this and you'll feel like a million," and Enock held out the poisoned drink which Mollie took holding it in her hand for a moment. Instantly Tony stepped between Mollie and Enock so as to conceal his movements and poured a cup of sea water into the fowl mixture before stepping back. Smiling he nodded his head as Mollie throwing caution to the wind drank some of the liquid. Immediately she threw up her arms and turned away from Enock. She was partly following Tony's instructions and partly because she was instantly sick throwing up the drink.

"Oh, oh,!" Tony yelled, "Somethings wrong!" and he nudged Mollie to start running which she did with gusto and the two of them raced to the beach. The natives were so startled they didn't follow and Mollie set off with a strong stroke for her people. Tony saw that she was well on her way before heading back to the party.

"What was that all about?" Enock asked Tony when he returned.

"It worked all right," Tony said with a smile. "That must have been some dose you gave her. She barely made it to the water. I watched her trying to swim until she had a convulsion and rolled over. The current caught her and I saw her body float away."

"You're sure?"

"Oh, yes, no doubt."

"Good, will you tell the natives just what happened?"

Tony gathered all the natives around him and told them what had happened. "People. What you have just witnessed was the death of a god. I followed her to the beach where I saw her die. You can be sure she's dead. Your god, Enock found her to be too powerful and not trustworthy and, so he being more powerful than she, he killed her. Now you know how powerful Enock is. Hooray for Enock!"

"Hooray!" the people echoed. Enock having drunk a little too much of his own brew went to bed early and Tony turned in with a smile on his face working on the rest of his plan.

The next day early Tony found Mollie already up walking the beach.

"You can't do this," Tony explained. "You have to get back into the trees. You mustn't be seen by my people or it will ruin my whole plan."

"What's your plan this time?" Mollie replied a little sceptically.

"Come on back to your people and I'll tell you on the way." And as they walked Tony told her his plan. "We have to discredit Enock's power. Your escape yesterday was just the first part of the whole idea. What we have to do now is establish your own superior power. Under cover of night, tonight, have your people provision your canoe for a long journey. Then tomorrow prepare a huge luou, big enough for the whole island and invite my people. Tell them it is to be a big surprise. Now comes your part. Keep out of sight all day. They must think you are truly dead for this to work. Now here is the spot where we build a big fire." They were then standing in front of a huge cliff of solid rock. We need flames seven or eight feet tall that will reflect your silhouette on that cliff. It's solid rock and will work fine for our display."

"What display?" Mollie was beginning to worry.

"Here's what we'll do. When the fire is at its highest you place yourself where you can't be seen between the fire and the rock. Maybe back ten feet. When you get the signal you raise your arms and all that my people will be able to see is your reflection in the rock. It will be huge. You then will loudly read what I've written here," and he handed her a piece of paper with a note on it. Read it into this Conch shell. You will sound like a god and your silhouette will appear unreal dancing on the rock. The result will be sensational!"

"Sensational," Mollie mused.

"Oh yes, my people will think that your spirit has risen from the dead and your word will be all powerful. More so than Enock's"

"It seemed like a hair brained idea to Mollie, but she agreed to Tony's plan and explained it all to her people.

That night they worked till dawn loading their huge discovery canoe with all they could carry and blessed it for a safe journey, assuming they could really get away. Then all day they prepared the luau. As the sun set that night they lit the fire and by dark it was blazing as Tony had directed and Mollie crouched in the bushes waiting for her signal.

As Enock's people arrived the Luau got underway and soon they were all well into the roast pig and fermented coconut juice when a blast from a conch shell horn split the air and everyone jumped up to see a vision broadcast onto the white stone cliff. The reflection of Mollie with her arms held high was spectacular and more than one mouth dropped open wasting good pig.

"Now, do you know who I am? Of course you do. I am the god you attempted to kill. That was a childish and foolish thing to do. As you can see you can't kill me. I am a god, a true god, not like that imposter Enock. He is nothing and will soon pay for his silliness." Mollie was dancing a slow island dance as she talked and it caused her reflection to rise and fall on the rock face holding the people in awe. "My purpose here tonight," she continued, "is to impress upon you the seriousness of your position. My people intend to leave your island first thing in the morning. You are not to harass, hinder or disrupt their departure in any way. You have only seen a touch of my power. If any thing as I have just described occurs I will descend upon you like a hurricane. Now enjoy your luau and have a nice time." Then Millie slowly walked toward the flames which gave the impression that her reflection slowly melted into the rock.

"That was sensational!" Tony whispered as Mollie slipped into the underbrush to join him. "It's too bad you couldn't have seen yourself."

"I felt like a fool," Mollie said as they slipped away from the party.

"You should have seen how my people reacted. The were completely convinced. You know that I've burned my bridges," he continued. "Enock is now aware that I've betrayed him. If I were to return he'd have my head on one of his pike staffs. So I'm off with you, right?"

"Of course. We wouldn't send you back after what you've done for us."

The party by then was drawing down for Mollie's people and most of them, along with Mollie and Tony, left the luau to prepare for their approaching journey.

As soon as it was light enough for them to see what they were doing they climbed aboard the large catamaran that was then anchored in the lagoon, and hoisted the one huge sail. Soon they were at hull speed crossing through the pass when they saw two of Enocks fast war canoes launched each with twenty five warriors.

"It looks as though Enock still has some followers," Tony said. "Let's hope the other three canoes are still in the shed." No more followed, but fifty well armed warriers could easily spoil their morning. Their catamaran was no match for the fast war canoes that were quickly approaching when several fins attached to porpoises flew by the catamaran heading for the canoes, closely following was a pod of killer whales, and as they approached the canoes they all shot to the surface causing a huge wave. Mollie had seen the same type of whale on T.V. using this tactic to slide seals off of Ice flows in alaska and it sure worked here because each canoe's bow as it encountered the wave was thrown straight up into the air and when it crashedhed back down the canoe was brought to a halt.

"If last night's exhibit didn't convince them to leave us alone I guess this magic did, they're turning around." Tony said as they watched the canoes heading back to the island. "I'm beginning to think maybe you really are something special."

"I had nothing to with this, but it does seem as though we just witnessed a miracle," Mollie replied a little awed herself at what had just happened. "I think the dolphins were some old friends, but the whales were new." Free at last they watched their recent home recede into the distance.

For three days the little group of adventurers sailed what appeared day after day to be an endless expanse of quiet ocean blue as a marble with occasional white capped ripples breaking the surface until swells began to form that grew into waves that began to splash over the side of their canoe and then a full blown storm fell on them.

"Quick! Down with the sail! Morano ordered and had a sea anchor strung out to keep the two bows of the catamaran facing into the gail. For several hours the rain came down in torrents keeping the people busy bailing the best they could barely keeping up with the water as it poured in to the two hulls. All night and half the next day they fought the water until the storm finally passed.

Morano had been using an ancient chart of sorts made from twigs of various diameter and length tied together. The large straight branches represented courses pointing to islands made by tiny shells while smaller twigs represented wave direction, bird migration routs, wind direction and other elements needed for navigation in those days.

"Well, that little episode set us back about fifty miles," he said looking at his chart," but I think we will still make landfall in about three days."

"You can tell all that with that bundle of sticks?" Mollie wanted to know.

"Not exactly, but it helps. My people have been sailing these waters for a thousand years and know where many of these islands are and have made these charts to indicate distance and direction to many of them. According to this chart there should be a moderate sized island here," and Morano pointed to a tiny shell half way up one of the sticks.

"That is fascinating," Mollie said amazed at the intricate string work.

"It was simply a matter of necessity. Many of these islands are small only able to accommodate a limited number of people. When the population grew new lands had to be found," Morano said thinking Mollie was referring to the vast distances these people must have traveled with only these sticks to guide them.

Morano was amazingly correct in his calculations because three and a half days later there was a clowd on the horizon. Soon under the clowd there appeared an island and after waiting for morning they dropped sail and coasted into a small lagoon.

"Oh, Oh," Morano said as natives began to line the shore in a threatening manner waving spears and bows and arrows. "We'd better anchor out a bit and I'll go ashore and find out if we're welcome. You two can come also if you like," Morano said to Mollie and Tony. Only minutes after Morano began talking to the chief the whole mood of the natives changed and they began cheering and waving for the rest of the adventurers to come ashore.

It was just a small lagoon and were told it was the only landing spot on the island. The islanders were just finishing the process of building a stone wall made from choral all along the beach.

"Why the wall?" Morano asked the obvious chief of the islanders.

"We are preparing for war. That's why we greeted you the way we did until we found that you are one of our kind. We thought you were the enemy. And so you see, maybe you should be on your way before they arrive. But if you'd like to stay you are certainly welcome. We need all the help we can get."

"What's your population here?" Morano asked the chief looking around at those building the wall.

"We've only been here a few years. We are about two hundred and fifty strong."

"How about the enemy?"

"We expect about five hundred."

"That's a little one sided. What is the trouble?"

"There's no real trouble. They just want our island. We have pearl shell and they don't."

"Well, as you an see we are about two hundred strong and so we could even out your battle."

"I noticed that. And so you'll stay?"

"Yes. I'm sure we'll all agree to that. Let's get to work.

Morano, Tony and the others jumped right in to help build up the wall while Mollie went over to help the women prepare food for the workers all the time thinking about the coming battle. The women had rigged a tall bamboo tree to help them lift a large pot of stew from where it was cooking over to where they could portion it out. It was far to heavy to handle otherwise and Mollie watched this with interest. Somehow it reminded her of ancient romans with their catapult. Suddenly she realised that this principal could be used in their own warfare and walked down to where the men were working. Lining the embankment behind the wall they were building was a forest of giant bamboo and Mollie within several minutes had an idea.

"Morano," Mollie called over to him.

Morano stopped for a moment looking over to her. "Can it wait? I'm pretty busy."

"This is important," Mollie called back. "It will only take a minute."

With a sigh Morano came over to join Mollie. "All right, what's so important?"

"Come with me just for a minute. I want you to see something," and she took Morano over to where the women were working. "See the device they're using to lift the pot?"

"Yes, how clever," Moran replied with little interest. "Now I have to get back to work."

As they again entered the bamboo forest Mollie stopped Morano. "Now look at this. I have an Idea. "Watch," she said as she pulled down a small bamboo and tied her handkerchief to it with a three foot piece of string. Then she pulled it down a little further put a small rock in the handkerchief and let it fly. It was like the way she catapulted a water balloon when she was a child, but this time it was a rock and it flew far out onto the beach.

"That's a cute idea," Morano said," but our arrows are more effective that that. I really have to get back to work," and he began to move away.

"No, wait," Mollie called after him. "That's not what I mean. We use a huge tree and a fifty pound rock. We can bombard the lagoon with them."

"Where did you get that idea?' Morano said slowly walking back looking up at the large bamboo and obviously thinking about Mollie's suggestion.

"It's not my idea. It was done two thousand years ago. By people called Romans. They built complicated catapults more sophisticated than this that they hurtled one hundred pound rocks to smash down castles."

What's a castle?"

"It's like this wall only huge. That kings lived in. Made out of stone."

"How were these weapons made?"

"We can't make ours like theirs because we don't have the material that they had, but we have something they didn't have—this bamboo—It's flexible and will work like a big spring when we let it go using the same principal as the Romans did to make their catapults."

"How will we do that?"

"Well, we'll have to work on that. Get a couple of men to help us and we'll see what we can come up with."

"I guess the wall can spare a few men," he said and soon Mollie and Morano, Tony and two warriors were at work. As close to the beach as they could get they selected a huge bamboo eight inches in diameter and twenty feet tall to work with. By weaving lengths of bamboo fibre together they made a twenty foot length of rope which they attached to the top of the tree. Then they made a pandanus mat in which to place the stone and tied that to the rope. Then realising that they need another piece of rope to pull the top of the tree down with, they made one and attached it also to the top of the tree. Now they had one rope to pull the tree down with and another to hurl the stone. The five of them pulled down the bamboo until the top of it was near the ground, put a fifty pound rock in the mat, and let it fly.

It was a total failure. First the stone kept hitting the trunk of the bamboo and then it either went straight up or straight down.

"This will never work," Morano said. There is no way of controlling it."

After more experimentation Tony came up with the idea of using two trees bound together at the top. In this way the rock would travel between the trees. Then by placing several different spots to secure the rope anchors they were able to vary the direction of the stone by several feet right or left.

"All right now," Morano said when they had it all ready and pulled down, "Let's see what we've got," and they let it fly.

"Hooray!" Morano cheered as the fifty pound stone flew over the beach and landed twenty feet offshore in the lagoon. It would have smashed anything or anyone coming in.

The enemy was expected any day and the islanders worked feverously to erect as many of these secrete weapons as they could in the meantime.

Soon the enemy were spotted. Four fast war canoos were heading there way with about one hundred warriors in each one.

The islanders were ready. In the two days that they had been working on the catapults they were able to construct only three of them, but they were dependable accurate and armored with plenty of fifty pound rocks from the river and now with three hundred and fifty able warriers to defend their homeland they stood prepared.

It seemed like hours that they watched the canoes approach under full sail with banners flying and rowers rowing, but was probably only minutes. Soon they were entering the lagoon. They dropped sail and the rowing stopped as they slowly coasted in toward the beach surveying the defenses.

One thing that the islanders had done was string a rope between two rocks in he middle of the channed where the canoes would obviously enter. It was hefty enough to stop slow moving boats and the catapults had been aimed so that their rocks would land right at that spot and the islanders waited expectantly and from them a war cry went up as soon as the first boat hit the rope and was stopped in its tracks.

"Fire!" the islander's chief cried and three large boulders sailed through the air towards the boats. The first rock to reach them fell just to the right of the first boat directly on top of several warriers who had just jumped out to come ashore. Those warriers would never see another beach as the water turned red. The second rock missed entirely, but the third rock made a direct it on the bow of the second boat damaging it severely.

By now the enemy was swarming up the beach in a suicide charge because the islanders behind their fortification were knocking them down right and left with spears and arrows before they even got to the wall. Three of the enemy did get over though killing one islander and wounding another.

It took two hours of hard fighting for the enemy to decide it was a lost cause. Those that could made it back to the two undamaged canoes waiting outside the fire line. The last the islanders saw of them was that they were heading home. As for the two enemy boats left in the lagoon the first one had been destroyed and the second unseaworthy with its bow torn off.

The beach however was another matter. There were twenty dead and fourteen wounded. The dead were carefully buried and the islanders then cared for the wounded. One of the wounded died over night and so the remaining thirteen were placed in the second canoe that had been repaired well enough to get them home and were given a message to take home with them. It was to be understood that no retaliation would be taken upon them as the islanders did not war. But as they could see (the enemy) the islanders were able to defend themselves and would tolerate no more skirmishes.

The next few days were spent cleaning up and repairing their wall. The catapults were left operable in case the enemy returned, but one day a lone canoe was seen approaching containing four wariers rowing and one warrior standing in the bow. Mollie and the others watched it enter their lagoon and run up onto the sand. The man in the bow was holding a spear point down and slightly to the rear which signaled peace and that he wanted to talk. The islander's chief signaled back that he could approach and they walked off into the bush where they talked for about an hour when the warrier returned to his canoe taking it back out of the harbor.

"What was that about?" Marano asked.

"They no longer want war. They have copra and we have pearl shell and they want to trade and have piece."

"Hooray," cheered the islanders near enough to here the conversation and soon everyone was informed.

"Stop work everyone!" cried the chief. "Instead get to work on a party. The biggest luau we've ever had. Now go," and they all rushed to get a feast together. This had been wonderful news.

The celebration lasted all night and much of the next day. Mollie and Tony of course joined in and had a wonderful time.

Several days later the island had been cleaned up and back to normal and Mollie and Tony were feeling adventurous and informed the chief that they were going to hike over to the other side of the island.

"Stay along the shore and don't travel too far. And for no reason ascend the central mountain. There's a mad hermit who lives there who is quite out of his mind and who occasionally takes a shot at anyone that he feels is invading his island."

'So this trip is going to be more adventurous than originally planned' Mollie thought, but being restless from so much recent activity they set off.

As instructed they kept to the beach when it was possible and only went inland when necessary. Around noon after climbing some vertical cliffs they returned to the beach where they fond what looked like some old rusted fittings rom a ship wreck. While they were examining the artifacts

Mollie said casually, "How serious do think that hermit might be?"

"I wouldn't worry about him, we'll be heading back in a minute anyway. Let's cut across this ridge, It'll save a lot of time over the way we just came." That seemed logical to Mollie who was getting a little tired. The worst part of it was the heavy brush they had to maneuver and suddenly Tony, who was leading, tripped over something.

"Ow!" he cried out as he fell.

"Tony, what happened?"

"I tripped over a rock. Boy that hurt!"

"I don't see any rock," Mollie said searching the underbrush, and then she exclaimed "Tony, look at this! This is what you tripped over," and Tony came over to see what it was.

"Well, I'll be," he said in amazement. There in the grass was a chest of some sort. It looked like an old seamans chest. "We've found a pirates gold," he laughed and lifted its lid which came up easily as if it had been regularly opened, but he immediately stopped laughing. And then Mollie looked in. It really did seem to be a pirates chest because all the two of them saw was gold in various forms and diamonds and jewelry of every size and shape.

"Good grief!" Molly exclaimed. "You weren't kidding. There's a fortune here."

"We're rich." Tony said. "Just look at all that."

"You forget, Tony that we're living on what's not much more than a desert island. What are you going to do with it?"

Suddenly behind them came a command. "Up with your hands! Up, up! I'm armed and I'll shoot.!" They both turned and saw standing in back of them a vision pointing two ancient flint lock pistols at their heads. It seemed to be a man of medium height, but he looked taller because of hair that fell to his waist and tied with a red ribbon. From his chin fell a beard that also fell to his waist.

"Are you a pirate?" Mollie asked looking him over.

"Do I look like a pirate?"

"A little bit."

"Oh good."

"Why do you want to look like a pirate?"

"To scare people like you away."

"What kind of people do you think we are.?"

"People that want to steal my gold."

"We don't want to steal your gold."

"Of course you do. Why wouldn't you? Everybody wants riches and here is a fortune. But it's mine. All mine. Do you understand. It's mine and it's going to stay mine—he, he, he", and the old man started laughing insanely. Mollie looked at Tony, back at the man and then back at the chest of gold. "No you don't!" the man screamed, "get away from my gold. I had to kill for that and I'll kill you too if you try to steal it. I'm a good shot. I shoot rabbits with these guns and that's not easy. I could put a bullet right between your eyes. Now step back from that chest. I have to decide what to do with you."

Mollie was studying the man who somehow didn't look like a pirate or someone who could kill.

"You killed for this gold?" she asked him.

"Well, not exactly, but I was with the pirates that did the killing."

"What were you doing with pirates?"

"I was pulled off of one of their victims ships and made their cabin boy. I was ten then and that was fifteen years ago. That was before we were wrecked on the beach where you were looking a few minutes ago."

"Then your only twenty five years old?"

"That's about right." the man said standing up a little straighter.

"You fooled me. You look older."

"It must be the look of toil that I've lived," The man said proudly.

"No," Mollie replied, "it's that filthy beard."

"Oh," the man said sheepishly. "Well you try shaving with a broken piece of glass—but I guess neither of you have to do that yet. Anyway, I don't want to have to kill you—you see I've never killed anyone yet, but there's always a first time. Now I must decide what to do with you otherwise you will surely steal my gold. My name is Henry, by the way—I think. I've forgotten so much. What's yours?"

"I'm Mollie and this is Tony, Mollie explained, "and what do we want with your gold. What would we do with it. Aren't you aware that you're living on no more than a desert island? What could we use this for. A boat's anchor maybe."

"It doesn't matter, It's gold and it's mine. We'll go up to my house now where I can think. You two look dangerous to me. Now march," and the three marched for about an hour before they arrived at what looked like an upturned boat. "I know it looks strange, but I had to build it with what I had. Now, sit down and we'll talk," but they didn't get much said before it turned dark and Henry fell asleep.

He had been pointing his pistols at Mollie and Tony all the time and when he nodded off they were laid on the ground beside him.

Mollie looked at Tony who was closest to them and tilted her head as if to ask whether he could reach one. Tony eased his hand over until he could snatch it up and poke Henry in the ribs with it. Henry woke up with a start and then smiled at Tony.

"You can put that down it's not loaded. I'm low on pouder and didn't want to waste it in another gun. However, this one is loaded" and he raised the one he still had in his hand.

Out of curiosity Tony pointed his pistol away from Henry and pulled the trigger and it only clicked.

"You should believe what I say, Tony, because this one is loaded and I'm a very light sleeper. Now let's get some sleep and in the morning we'll figure out something. I probably won't kill you. You look too innocent. Trusting what Henry said the three of them had a good night's sleep.

The next morning Henry was the first to speak. "Now here's the problem, leant just let you two go now that you know where the treasure is, can I?"

"Why not?" Tony asked.

"Why, you'll steal it of course. Maybe not right now, but one day it would be eating away at you and here you'd come to steal my gold. No, that wouldn't do. You see it's my gold and I intend to keep it."

"Listen, Henry, How many times do we have to tell you. We do not want your gold. For one thing, it may be gold, but on this island it has no value. We have no use for it. And more importantly it doesn't belong to us. It would be stealing."

"Well, what if by mistake you gave away its location and someone else stole it. You'ld still be responsible."

"You're right there," Mollie said and realised Henry was right. "We can rehide it?" Mollie then suggested beginning to form an idea.

"I can't do it all by myself and if you help me you'll still know where it is."

"It won't matter if we hide it where no one can get to it."

"How is that possible. If I can get to it others can too."

"Exactly. Well put it where even you can't get to it."

"What good is it to me then?"

"As good as it is now. You must realise it really has no value here on this island. There is nothing that you can use it for. Everyone here barters for food and necessary items. Other than a trinket a diamond is useless."

"You're trying to trick me. You do want my gold but it's mine and I intend to keep it."

"Think of it this way. If we hide it where no one can ever retrieve it it will still be yours. You can dream about it at night and know that you have gold and silver diamonds and in fact own a fortune. And what's even better no one can ever steal it from you. You'll never have to be frightened of losing it again."

"Tony and I will help you haul your entired fortune out to the end of the reef and rehide it in one thousand feet of ocean. It will be there forever waiting for you. And no one will ever be able to steal it from you. It will be like a safe deposit box."

"What's a safe deposit box?"

"You wouldn't know if I told you. Just think of your fortune as being safe forever."

"That would work wouldn't it? No one could steal it from me then."

"I think my people on the other side of this island would welcome you to be one of them because you would no longer have to shoot at them to protect you gold."

"So you really think so?"

"I know so. Let's get started. This is going to be a big job."

And it was a big job. All day they hauled bars of gold out to the end of the reef to drop them into thousands of feet of water and threw jewelry and loose jewels far out to sea until there was nothing left except three finger rings. A large diamond ring that was for Henry to be a receipt for his fortune that was now safe from vandals residing in the bottom of the ocean, and two small gold bands, one for Tony and one for Mollie to remind them of their great adventure.

The next day the three of them went back over to Mollie's people where Henry was greeted with open arms and a large luau that introduced him into their community and everyone was happy that there was finally peace on their island. And Henry was content to know that his fortune was safe.

Mollie was now feeling restless and felt it was time to move on and wondered if Tony would like to join her.

"Sure," he said. "I would somehow like to eventually go back to where I came from although I don't remember much about it. Sure I'll go. What did you have in mind?"

"Well, I thought we'd take my canoe, although it's a little small, and continue sailing north. There's a large island chain somewhere up there that I'd like to visit."

"What's so interesting about those islands?"

"I don't know. It's just a feeling I have."

So they decided to leave in the morning, but the island chief told them to talk to the islands elder first. He knew things about the islands to the north that might be helpfull.

"So you want to continue your adventure?" the old man said when they had located him living by himself in a grove of coconut trees.

"We thought it might be time to go," Mollie said.

"Mmm." The old said to himself. He seemed to be thinking about something. "Would you consider taking a passenger along?"

"Who would that be?" Tony asked.

"That would be me. I could be of great help to you. I know these waters well and might be able to teach you something about sailing your vessel."

"You're right about teaching us something about sailing this type of canoe. We are certainly novices. However, my canoe is barely large enough for Tony and Myself. I don't think it could came another passenger."

"Oh no, Your canoe won't do. We will have to build another. Something stouter than yours. What do you say?"

"We don't want to put you to the trouble of having to build another canoe, but if you really want to come I guess we must."

"Wonderful! With a little help from you two who seem to be strong I can do most of the work. I was once a master canoe builder. That's when I was younger of course. All right, let's get started. I've been thinking of taking a trip lately myself. It's time you know."

Mollie and Tony didn't know why it was time for the old man to take a trip. Most old people wanted to stay home and rest, but they agreed to take him along.

To build a large seagoing canoe was quite an education for Mollie and Tony, but eventually it was finished and after a christening ceremony it was launched—and they were launched.

The first thing that Mollie and Tony were taught was to keep the canoe upright. How to reduce sail in a storm and how to keep the ama to windward. If they changed course or the wind shifted to far one way or another they were shown how to turn the boat boat around causing the bow to be the stern and the stern the bow with the ama being on the opposite beam of the boat. They did this by tilting the mast in the opposite direction and reversing the sail. These things relative to the boat and other things such as pertaining to navigation, star movements, bird flight, and wave direction and condition. Details needed for navigating the ocean at that time and in that place. The old man seemed to be a wizard at sailing those waters and knew exactly where he wanted to go. Mollie and Tony had no idea of where they should go and so went along with the old man's wishes.

The old man used the steering oar with precision and searched the far horizon with anticipation. The boat was fast and they made good time on the second morning out Mollie awoke to a different motion to the canoe and looked over the side.

"Tony!" look at this she cried and Tony looked over too.

"What's happening?" he said as he watched the surface of the ocean drawing away from the boat. It looked as though they were five hundred feet up in the air and going even higher.

"Look at this!" Mollie called to the old man who seemed unconcerned as he steered the boat as usual with his eye searching the sky in front of them.

"Yes," he said, "were almost there—oh, but you of course don't know. We should be reaching my island in a couple of hours. I see it just over the horizon."

"How can you see if it's over the horizon?" Mollie wanted to know.

"Well, that's my little secrete. You'll see. And soon Mollie and Tone did see something in the distance. But it didn't look like any island that they could recognise. It seemed only a clowd that had the vague outline of land. As they go nearer it did bigger and took on the shape of a vast island that covered the view forward.

The old man carefully guided the canoe into a lagoon and onto a quiet beach where the three of them stepped out onto white sand that was soft and fine as face powder. "Ah," the old man said, "just as I had hoped, I'm home," and he looked about him with an expression of peace and finality.

What Mollie and Tony saw was a land that stretched out as far as they could see or at least what could be land because it wasn't exactly solid or didn't seem solid. It was a vision that was almost transparent as if made of colored crystal. There was nothing vague about it however. The green of the lagoon was vivid and the trees of the forest that met them at the beach were as green as any tree might be, in fact if anything greener. But at the same time it seemed that they were looking at something unreal.

"Where are we? and what place is this," Mollie wondered aloud.

"This is my home," the old man said. The one I've been looking for all my life."

"How long are we going to stay here?" Tony asked looking around in amazement at what he saw.

"You two will not stay long," the old man said referring to Mollie and Tony. "In fact you will be leaving first thing in the morning. You see you can't stay. Not yet. You have a long journey ahead of you. I've taught you everything I know and you're now capable sailors. I have now dought that you will accomplish whatever you set out to do. In fact you had better get back in your boat. You'll need a good night's rest. It will be a long morning. Now a little advice. Don't stay long in one place. There may be times and places when you think you've arrived, but don't be fooled by false promises. You have a long way to go to reach the place that's meant for you. It will be a long and dangerous journey, but in the end it will be worth it. It's getting late now so go and get a good night's sleep."

And sure enough the following morning they awoke to an exaggerated rhythm of the sea and there was no land in sight. The vision of the previous day was gone.

"Tony," Mollie said, "wake up I think we're in for a little weather."

After Tony had observed the situation he agreed. "We'd better put up the smallest storm sail. This could be a rough day."

And it proved to be just that. At first the sea was flat and almost oily looking and then a few tiny williwas spun across the surface just before their whole world tuned upside down. Or almost, before they were completely turned turtle they were soon able to remove the storm sail that was even too much to carry and secure the mast in its downward position. Now with the storm anchor over the stern the boat ran before the wind. Down into a trough it would go when everything seemed relatively calm and peaceful and then back up into the wind and waves where it was tossed like a cork in an opened bottle of soda.

All day and that night the two huddled under the boat cover wondering when it would end.

But all storms eventually pass and when the sun came up the sea was calm, the sky again blue, and they found themselves just offshore from a bare bit of ground. On closer examination they realized it had one bean beautiful, but that now was not much more than a desert island having been ravaged recently by a severe storm. The trees were almost all torn up and destroyed and only devastation remained. It had probably been caused by the same storm that Mollie and Tony had just experienced.

Finally deciding that there would be no advantage to land there they started to raise sail intending to go on. On one last look back Tony saw something moving. "What do you think that is?" he asked Mollie who now studied where he was pointing. There was only one neatly trimmed tree still standing and something was clinging to where its top had been cut off.

"It's someone waving to us." Mollie finally said, "Quick put into that small bay!"

There was a small bay all right, but it was almost total clogged with old trees and debri. They were only half way in when a woman, the one at the top of the tree, jumped into the water and fought her way out to the canoe holding a small child. She handed the child up to Mollie and then deftly pulled herself aboard.

"Oh thank God! Thank the good lord! I thought I was doomed. They're all gone you see. Everyone was washed away. I only barely had time to cut the top of my tree off before the storm hit. Everyone's gone. They're all gone," and she began crying and rocking her baby that she now held close to her.

"I'm sorry to hear all that." Mollie said trying to comfort her. "but you're welcome to come with us. We have plenty of room and enough food and water for several days. Maybe you know of somewhere we can take you."

"Are you familiar with this area?"

"No, never been here before."

"Then we are both fortunate. You've saved my life and I may be able to save yours. There's only one island chain to the north it's where my family came from. Four years ago my family and one other set out to establish a new land here. It was beautiful then, but as you see there's nothing left of it now. Our dream has been washed away. Anyway, these islands to the north are my old home islands and I can show you how to get there. They're not easy to find and if you miss them there is no more land for many weeks of sailing. You'ld never make it."

"So let's go then," Tony said getting impatient.

"All right. I'll steer and you two get some rest. You must have come a long way."

"You have no idea how far," Tony replied.

The lady, who's name was Midwi, sailed competently out of the bay and set sail on a course that she seem to know to the north west. Three days later they sailed into a lagoon to a crowd of islanders that were cheering and waving that had come out to greet them. It seems that many of Midwi's people had been found floating on what they could find left from the typhoon by fishermen from these islander and there was much rejoicing.

Mollie and Tony stayed with these people for two days getting to know them and enjoying the good life that they seem to be living until Mollie said it was time to go.

"This is a beautiful spot with beautiful people, maybe we should just stay here. This may be where we are meant to be."

"Remember what the old man said, Tony," reminded Mollie. "Be wary of temptations. There would be times when we we would want to end our journey, but that we should go on. He said it would take a long time. It's only been, what? five days total. We must go on."

When they told the chief of the island what they had decided he was disappointed.

"Oh, I'm sorry to hear that. You are welcome, you know, by all of us to stay as long as you like, but if you must go I have a request of you to make. There is an orphan girl about six yeas old that begs to go with you. Would that be possible?"

"Well, we have plenty of room, but why would she want to go with us and leave all you good people?"

"She's had a difficult life ever since her mother died two years ago. If you take her along you may find her a difficult child, but I don't think she's really bad. It's just her history."

"What history?" Mollie wanted to know.

"Well, her mother was thought to be a witch and was never accepted into the community and, right or wrong, it's rubbed off on to the girl—and you'll see that she is a little different."

"Well, she's welcome to come along." Mollie said as Tony was very slightly shaking his head no.

And so they set sail with Miri the little girl. She was no trouble at first keeping to herself in the bow of the boat if anything seeming to be a little distrustfull of the others. Soon there was a pod of dolphins sailing beside the boat that moved toward the bow seeming to be interested on the girl who was attentive to them as she was talking to herself.

"That's so sad," Mollie commented to Tony. "Miri feels that she has only herself to talk to. We should try to talk to her." and she called to Miri. "Miri, we would very much like to hear what you have to say. Wouldn't it be more fun to talk to us than to talk to yourself?"

"I'm not talking to myself," Miri replied and went on with her own conversation.

"She thinks she's actually talking to someone," Mollie mused. "Who is it you're talking to, Miri?" she asked.

"The dolphins, Of course," Miri said nonchalantly.

"The dolphins?" Mollie asked.

"Do they speak back," Tony said derisively.

"You don't believe me, do you?" Miri said resignedly. "Nobody on the island does either. I thought you'd be different."

Mollie looked severely at Tony. "We are different, Miri. We believe you, but you must tell us all about yourself. Then we can tell you our story."

"Do you really want to listen to me?" Miri asked in wonder as if no one had ever given her a thought.

"Of course," Mollie said sincerely.

"Well then, I had better tell you what the dolphins have just told me. They say that there is a new great rock coming out of the water to our north throwing rocks and sand into the air and that we had better steer clear of it. It could be dangerous. In other words a new island is in the making."

"Come back here with us for a while," Mollie said patting the seat beside her. We want to hear all about this. Where did you learn to speak to dolphins?"

"Oh, not just dolphins. I can speak to all the animals, fish and birds too," Miri said as she worked her way back to the stern and sitting down beside Mollie.

"When did you know you could do this?"

"I've always been able to. My mother said is was nothing special. Many in her family were so blessed—excuse me a minute," she said as she looked over the side of the. "They're going on ahead. They'll keep a lookout for the big rock," and Mollie watched as the dolphins sped up and raced far ahead of the boat.

"None of the islanders believed you?"

"No, they think me crazy like my mother."

"Well, we believe you," Mollie said emphatically with a severe look to Tony.

"We sure do, Miri," Tony said. "You're going to be a great help on this trip," a if to say, 'How's that, Mollie?'

"Oh, I hope so. Then you'll like me?" Miri sad hopefully.

"We like you, anyway, Miri. Where did you get the idea that we didn't like you?"

"Nobody on the island does."

"That's not true, Miri. They just don't understand you. You probably don't understand them."

"Boy, that's sure true."

"Well, that's settled then. Everybody on this boat likes everybody. Agreed?"

"O.K."

"O.K."

"O.K."

That night they saw great flashes of fire and had to stop the boat to let sand and rock fall into the water just to the north of them and to quickly scoop up a small hot pebble that had fallen into the boat. Just as suddenly as the island had erupted it quieted down. Miri was again at the bow where she preferred to be and was talking to dolphins shining in the phosphorescent light of the sea.

"This is Quik Quik," Miri said turning around to face Mollie and Tony and pointing to one of the Dolphins. "He's going to lead us around the eruption so watch me and I'll signal you where to go." The dolphin was as good as his word and the three in the boat soon were sailing again in smooth waters.

By then it was morning and Miri was informed that the dolphins had regretfully to leave them. They were on a yearly migration and had to sail west now across a great ocean and wouldn't be back for a long time. But it would be all right because their friend the pellican would be available in an emergency.

"Do you believe in miracles, Miri?" asked Mollie. "I ask everyone I know if they believe in miracles."

"Why?"

"It's just something I'm curious about."

"What do you mean exactly by miracles?" Miri wanted clarification.

"When something vey unusual happens to save a situation from disaster.

Something almost impossible."

"Yes I do. My grandmother used to tell me stories that would fit that idea. Would you like to hear one?"

"Very much so," Mollie said looking at Tony who was shaking his head. "Wouldn't you, Tony?"

"Oh yes, of course," he said nodding vigorously.

"Well this one I like best of all because it really happened to my grandmother when she was about as old as I am now. She was night fishing alone in her canoe with a flare made of bush material tied to the bow of her boat to attract fish and she wasn't having much luck. The fish just weren't coming to the surface and so she started to arrange her things to go home. Suddenly a shadow broke the surface of the water and then it disappeared. When it returned my grandmother saw that it was a rather large fish a little bigger than the ones she usually caught and it seemed to be looking at her. She slipped her hand into the water and quickly grabbed it around the middle and lifted it aboard. This is the way she always fished. She was very good at hand fishing. Anyway she had the fish in the boat and said to herself, but out loud, "Well, you'll fit nicely in my pan"—and then was startled to hear the fish speak back to her.

"What are you going to do with me," it asked.

"Probably eat you. You look tasty."

"I don't feel tasty and I would rather not end up in your pan if you please. If you put me back in the water I will give you magic and you won't regret it," said the fish who was gasping for water.

Magic was something my grandmother cared little about at that time, but she felt sorry for the fish. It looked so sad as it flopped in the bottom of the boat. "All right," Mollie said. "You win. I'll put you back. You're too big for my pan anyway," and she heaved the fish up and over the side.

In an instant it was gone and Mollie thought to herself, 'There goes my magic what ever that is," and she again started to put her things away in preparation of her return home. And then there again was the fish with a splash next to her boat.

"Sorry about that, I had to get a big gulp of water. You almost drowned me in all that air."

"Oh, it's nice to see you again," my grandmother said. "I thought you had forgot about my magic."

"I never forget promises. You won't receive it immediately, but don't be discouraged. You will one day have it for sure. You must gain a little more wisdom first. But I must be going. I have other business you see. Now I'll swim around your boat three times and spit in the air and that will insure your magic. Good by," and the fish did just as he said he would—one—two—three—spit—and he was gone with a flip of his tail.

"Is that the end?" Tony said beginning to get interested in the story.

"Do you want me to finish or not?" Miri said a little perturbed.

"Oh finish it by all means," Mollie said looking sternly at Tony. "Tony's just a little impatient to hear the rest of it."

"All right, but my grandmother always said that impatience leads to no patience," Miri said, satisfied. "Well it wasn't until my grandmother was older, about your ages, that she first knew anything about magic. It was just such another night when the fish weren't cooperating that it happened. She had taken a little nap when something awakened her. At first she wasn't aware of what it was and then realised something strange was going on. The stars that had been particularly bright that night were getting bigger. They were getting huge and even brighter and she looked over the side of her canoe and saw the entire earth as a blue ball getting smaller as the stars were getting larger. She was rising into the sky!

Soon there were stars of all sizes passing by her. They all seemed to be moving in an orderly manner and she watched fascinated as they coasted by far enough away to be safe. Off in the distance it was another story. At the edge of her vision occasionally two would collide and if it was a direct hit they would explode into millions of bits of light. On the other hand if they just brushed each other they would only scatter small amounts of the same matter and continue on in a little different course.

My grandmother was sure she was not in danger until she noticed a star directly ahead that seemed to be heading right for her. She tried to paddle her way to one side or the other with no effect. Her paddle just waved around in the clear air. And then she closed her eyes and made ready to die, but instead she just bumped whatever it was and bounced off it as though it were a huge balloon and then she flew away in a slightly different direction.

For a while she had clear sailing, but again there appeared dead ahead another huge sphere and this time she made no attempt to avoid it, but just waited to see what would happen. As she approached it it grew larger and larger until it filled the whole sky and then without even a tiny bump she sailed into it, right through its edge into its interior. And now she was in another world. Instead of being on the outside walking a hard surface as she did on earth she was now on the inside free to move in any direction to dive and soar and do loops, but she was more interested in investigating this new country and flew on until she was brought circling down onto a broad bay similar to the one she had recently left. Afraid to leave her canoe in case it took off again and left her behind she stayed put as it drifted up onto a sandy beach where it stopped.

Out of a forest that lined the beach stepped a man that walked over to sit on a large rock next to my grandmother's boat.

"Ah, I see you've made it. I've been watching you since you left your blue pebble. Only once did you get slightly off course when I had to nudge you back."

"Then that was your star that pushed me over here?"

"Yes indeed. How do you feel?"

"I feel wonderful. It must be the air up here. By the way where am I?"

"Well, you're here of course. Where else could you be?"

"Everything looks so familiar. You look a lot like those I know back home."

"Well, that's how it should be."

"What do you mean?"

"I am who I am because you are who you are. If you were someone else, I would be someone else. I am who I am because that is what you expected."

My grandmother wasn't sure she wanted to carry on this conversation so she changed the subject. "Did you bring me up here?"

"Yes I did, but you mustn't say 'up' here. There is no up or down here. You might as well say we are down from your pebble."

"Why did you bring me here at all?"

"Well, occasionally we here have been curious about your little blue rock, but not enough to investigate. It was only recently that I discovered I could make contact with you. It was very unusual. Do you know why that could be?"

"Not at all—unless it is my new magic."

"Magic?"

"Some time ago a fish promised to give me magic. Maybe that's it."

"No doubt. And so you feel well here?"

"Very well, thank you. Why did you bring me here?"

"Because your blue pebble seems to be a very strange place and I wonder why."

"What do you mean strange?"

"You don't seem to be at peace with yourselves or one another."

"Is that so important?"

"It's just that you are so different from us. You are so active. You don't seem to be able to sit still. You're all rushing about in different directions and when someone gets in your way you get upset and go to war. We here are wondering if we're missing out on something. Are you a happy people?"

"You are at peace here, always?"

"Oh yes. For ever. That may be why it feels natural. Does that seem dull to you?"

"No, not exactly. I would say that you should carry on as you are. Don't worry about us."

"Oh, we don't worry about you. You will ether become a star as we are or not. It's up to you. But I'm afraid you can't stay here any longer. You must now return to your little blue pebble. Maybe one day we will meet again. Good By."

"Did your grandmother get back home safely," Mollie asked.

"Yes she did, but as she was leaving she turned in time to see the man she had been talking to melt into a small shimmering round object and the familiar island disappeared in a vast cloud.

"That's quite a story," Tony said, impressed.

"Do you believe it?" Miri asked hopefully.

"Oh, yes," Mollie said. "It's true isn't it?"

"My grandmother said it was. Does that fit your definition of miracle?"

"Not exactly, but close enough." Miri then went forward to the bow where she settled herself as a look out for the boat.

For two days they sailed north without incident just before sunset on the second day a dense fog or cloud settled in ahead of them and they reduced sail.

"Better go slow until it clears," Mollie said and they coasted slowly through the night. As the sun came up they saw land dead ahead and soon perceived it to be a large island and they coasted onto a soft sand beach where some natives welcomed them. At first they seemed friendly enough, but at the end of the day Mollie became suspicious of their interest in Miri.

"Keep an eye on Miri, will you Tom?" Mollie said. "I don't like the way the chief has taken an interest in her."

"I've noticed the same thing," Tom agreed. The three of them were invited to spend the night in the chief's shelter and so they did thinking that was the safest place to be.

The next morning Miri was missing and after searching around the compound Mollie asked The chief if he'd seen her.

"Yes, I haven't had time to talk to you about that. I've noticed that she's quite different from you two. What do you know about her?"

"Not very much. We found her on the last island that we last visited and agreed to look after her as she had just been orphaned."

"Ah, I see. Then you won't mind if we keep her here?"

"No we couldn't do that. We are responsible for her and anyway she wouldn't want to do that."

"Well, we'll see." said the chief who then strode off.

"I don't like this," said Tony. That man doesn't look good to me.

"No, I'm afraid your right. Let's see if we can find her."

It only took a few minutes for them to do that. She was sitting in a kind of throne surrounded by natives who were bowing to her and mumbling incoherently.

"What's going on, Miri," Mollie called out, but before she could say anything the chief who stood next to Miri shouted her down.

"No questions, little one. You are not to speak to our new god. No one is allowed to speak to her."

Mollie and Tony were stunned into silence for a moment and then they were forcibly escorted from the clearing where Miri sat immobile.

"What's going on Mollie?" whispered to an older woman walking next to her.

"You should be very proud," the woman said not very encouragingly. Your friend must be very powerful because our chief has made her a god. I don't see it, but he is sure she has special powers."

"It looks to me more like she's under guard. Why would that be?"

"Your friend it seems didn't like the idea. I wouldn't either. She's now no more than his slave."

"You don't very much like the chief do you, why is that?"

"No, not very much. Maybe one day I'll tell you why, but not now. For now I'm going to give you some advice. Never go swimming in the Chief's bath—in fact don't even go near it. He is the only one allowed to swim their and any one else found to have bathed in it is instantly put to death. The chief is just waiting for the opportunity to do you harm. One other thing. There's a secret cave that only I know of that might be of use to you. It's under the large tree that was blown over many years ago on the edge of the beach. If you ever get in trouble—and you probably will because the chief doesn't trust you—its large enough to hide in."

"Thank you so much," Mollie said. "You've been very kind."

"Well, you look like good people and I don't want you to get hurt, or maybe killed."

Later Mollie and Tony slipped away into the jungle where they could be in private. "Well now we've done it," Tony said sitting down on a rock.

"It's not our fault, Tony," Mollie said a little peeved, "Except that we seem to have landed on a bad island. Anyway we've got to make a plan."

"What do you have in mind?"

"I have no idea, but maybe you could help me with one.

"Of course, but we're a little outnumbered."

"I know, so I think we should first get the peoples trust and in the meantime we'll figure out an escape for Miri."

It took about a week to become one of the people although the chief didn't trust them for a minute. Miri was paraded in front of the people daily at which time the chief would tell the people what their new god was supposed to be thinking and it was usually that they weren't working had enough and then she was escorted back into her shelter that was no more than a jail cell. Two weeks of this and Mollie had a plan which she conveyed to Tony one night.

"O.k., Tony times running out. It's time to move."

"I don't know," Tony said sceptically. They've got guards around her day and night. What have you in mind?"

"You remember that we were told never to swim in the chief's bath? that it would bring instant execution if we did?"

"Yes I remember. It's strictly taboo. No one but the king."

"And now Miri has been given permission."

"That's true. I had forgotten. You plan something around the bath?"

"You have it. Miri is allowed to bath whenever she wants as long as she is accompanied by to women guards."

"You think we can overpower the women?" Tony said sceptically.

"Oh, no, not that. They're tougher than the men. No, what we have to do is distract the women some way and I think I know how. While Miri's in the pool I'll jump in beside her. One of the women will be immediately dispatched to the village to warn the chief that I've gotten into his pool. I'll grab Miri and head for the opposite side of the pool as if I'm going to escape with her which would be a death sentence for the guard. She isn't allowed in the pool so she will have to run around it to where it looks as if I will pull her out. It's a long way around and so I'll have plenty of time to swim back across the pool and join you on the other side. Hopefully we can get away before the guards from the village arrive."

"Hopefully," Tony said sceptically.

"I think their's a good chance."

"That's the crasiest plan I ever heard of. If we're caught we'll both be killed immediately for messing with the chiefs silly pool. And what's more, where do we run to. They'd have us in no time."

"We'll head for the beach and hide in that cave that we were told about."

"I think we'd better go down and look at the pool layout then to see if your plan will work."

"You're probably right so let's get started."

They soon found the pool and Tony sat down at its edge. You think any ones around?"

I don't know, but we'd better not be found here." at which Tony stuck his foot in the water. "What did you do that for, are you crazy?"

"Just testing it—Oh, Oh!" Tony said jumping up. There must have been guards hiding in the trees because the minute Tony put his foot in the water they leaped up and started running towards Mollie and Tony as fast they could run.

"Let's go!" Tony cried and grabbed Mollie by the hand and they headed for the beach not looking back. "The cave! We've go to find the cave."

Desperation helped them momentarily outrun their pursuers until they spotted the dead tree and dove to the ground. At first they saw nothing but some brush, but they cleared that away to expose the entrance to a small cave and they crawled in pulling the brush in behind them.

"That wasn't too smart," Mollie whispered after she get her breath.

"What wasn't?" Tony wanted to know.

"Putting your feet in the water. We were all right until you did that."

"How did I know there were spies. Anyway it's done.

"Well, I guess we'd better stay put for awhile now, Mollie suggested and they needed the rest anyway.

They were lying in a tunnel only about three feet in diameter only large enough to crawl in and they lay still until they thought their pursuers had gone. Just as Mollie started to back out she felt something cold on her feet and turned her head around to see water entering their tunnel and then more.

"Quick?" she said to Tony. "Move in further the tide must have come in and I'm getting soaked."

Fortunately the tunnel was sloping upwards and so they were just able to move their heads into air as the water pushed them further into the cave.

"Hurry! Keep moving," Mollie cried as the water continued to rise around her. But soon the whole tunnel was filled and they were swimming under water. Just as Mollie's lungs were about to burst her head broke the surface and she began to breath again.

As the tunnel turned a corner the cave opened up and a light shown down from above and they could see quite clearly. They had entered a large open space still underground with a hole in the the ceiling that was letting in light.

"Better continue on," Mollie said, "We can't go back the way we came, at least for now. Maybe there's another way out."

They had only gone a short distance when the ground opened up beside the path they were on and revealed a huge whole in the ground. It was directly under the hole in the ceiling where the light was coming in. At that moment a roar from some giant animal filled the cavern and they both jumped back against the wall.

"What was that?" Tony said shaking all over.

"Something's down in that hole," Mollie suggested. "I hope it can't get out."

"How did it get down there I wonder?"

"I'll bet it somehow fell through that opening in the roof. In fact it may have caused that hole when it fell. The earth probably collapsed down here weakening the ground until it finally fell away."

"Well," Tony said, "There's not much path left around the edge of that hole. How are we to get around it?"

"There's still a little ground left. You go first and I'll follow. We should be able to make it."

Tony went first clinging to the the rock wall while tiptoeing along a two inch path until he successfully was passed the large hole. Then Mollie followed inch by inch. The path was probably weakened slightly by Tony's passing as it suddenly gave way just as Mollie was reaching the other side. Down she went clutching at the wall slowing her up just enough for Tony to grab her arm as she went down.

"Hang on!" he yelled. "I've got you," which advice Mollie didn't need as she dug into Tony's arm with fierce abandon. With both pulling with all their might Mollie was slowly dragged back to safe ground.

"What will we do if we have to go back," Tony wondered.

"We'll just pray there's another way out," Mollie offered.

"Well, let's hope so and they continued on as the roaring of what ever it was died away.

Soon they saw a tiny light at the end of the tunnel and they came to what appeared to be it's end, but there was a huge log blocking their exit. In a few minutes however they had it removed and walked out into the sunlight of a small beach. They also quickly saw that there was no escape to the left as tall vertical cliffs rose up to the sky continuing out into deep water. So they started hiking along the beach to the right, but hadn't gone far when they had to dart back into some trees that edged the shore. There was a village that didn't look very friendly. There were boats pulled up on the beach and the islanders were having a party of some sort. A huge fire was blazing and they were all dancing around a man tied to a tree. It seemed an inopportune time for Mollie and Tony to join in on their festivities.

"Back to the cave for now I think," said Mollie and they retraced their steps replacing the log again where they had found it that fortunately for them hid the cave from outsiders.

"It's just as well," Mollie said as they were safe inside.

"What do you mean 'just as well' "Tony asked a little perturbed. "I suppose you have another idea in mind."

"No, the same one I had before."

"You're not making any sense, Mollie" Tony said sitting down on a flat rock.

"We have to go back," Mollie said matter of factly and there was complete silence from Tony for several seconds.

"I know you're not serious," Tony finally said leaning back comfortably against the wall of the cave, "but if that is supposed to be a joke it is not funny, not funny at all."

"I'm not joking. We have to go back for Miri."

Tony then sat up with a jerk. "If you're serious then you really are out of your mind— as I've often suspected by the way—because it can't be done. Even if we wanted to we can't get back across that hole. We might not even be able to get through the water. We might have entered the cave at some freak low tide. It may normally be always flooded, now let's not hear any more about that, we need to to plan an escape from here."

"We have to go back. We are responsible for Miri. I won't leave her and I can use your help, but any way I'm going back. Tomorrow. Sleep on it," and Mollie made herself comfortable for the night. Tony was in no mood to talk about this, her most fantastic idea yet, and turned in too.

The next day having realised that Mollie was right Tony agreed to go back for Miri and they made their plans. The small tree that was covering the entrance to that end of the tunnel they realised might just work to bridge the gap in their path where the hole was and they dragged it over to it. With just a little effort they were able to maneuver it over to the other side and they successfully slid across it with the wild animal roaring below them.

"I hope that thing can't jump," Tony said.

"It probably can't or it would have by now, come on let's go."

At the other end of the tunnel the seawater was coming in, but not enough to completely fill the entrance and they crawled out coughing and sitting.

"If your plan works how are we to be sure we can get back in there," Tony said pointing at the hole in the ground that was now slowly filling with water.

"We'll just have to take our chances, I guess," Mollie replied looking where Tony was pointing.

"So, now what do we do?"

"I'm going to find Mandy, that's the lady I've befriended." For some reason she doesn't seem to like the chief and I think she will help us out."

"How is she going to do that?"

"I'm going to give her a note to take to Miri. She has a lot of freedom around here and I think she'll be able to manage it. I'll instruct Miri to come for a swim as soon as possible and then we'll carry out our plan."

Tony just rolled his eyes in disbelief and finally said, "O.k., carry on."

Mollie soon found Mandy who was amenable to the idea and while she left to deliver the note Mollie and Tony made themselves comfortable far enough away from the ponds as not to be seen and yet where they could keep an eye on any activity there.

After an hour went by and nothing had happened Tony was beginning to get worried. "You think we'd better check on things?" he suggested.

"No not yet. If we're seen it will be all over." And it was good that they waited because in only a few minutes more they spotted Miri accompanied by two large female guards come in sight. The two guards seemed a little tired and sat down on the grass beside the pool and started to drink something out of a large goard.

"I hope that's some of their fermented juice," Mollie whispered. "If so, it will slow them down some."

Miri then stepped into the water looking around her as

if she were looking for someone and Mollie and Tony stole down to the edge of the pool.

"She must have gotten the note," Mollie whispered to Tony. "I think she's looking for us. O.K., here I go," and she stepped out into the water took Miri by the arm and started swimming across the lake.

The guards for a moment may have been inattentive, but in an emergency they knew what to do. One yelled to the other who took off running as fast as she could back for the village while the first one started around the lake, it was going to be a long run because the lake was long and narrow and the guard had to run five hundred yards to the north end and then back another five hundred to get to where Mollie and Miri were approaching the shore.

Mollie was taking her time allowing the guard time to get around the pool before she and Miri jumped back in the water and swam back to where Tony was keeping a look out for any more intruders.

It worked like a charm. The guard didn't dare get into the pool because she wasn't allowed to and had to run all the way back around the the pool and that time the three outlaws were well on their way to the tunnel. The tide was just beginning flood which gave them room to dive under the log and quickly get into the tunnel. Crawling frantically forward they were just able to get into the high ground before the entrance was filled with water.

"That was good timing, how did you do that?" Miri wondered.

"Just luck I'm afraid," Mollie said.

"I hope we'll still be in luck when we reach the log,"

Tony added, but when they reached the hole in the ground the log was still in place and the three quickly crossed it to the tune of the wild animal's roaring. They continued on when Mollie noticed that Miri was no longer with them. "Miri! Where are you?" she called.

"I'm here with Montro," Miri called and Mollie and Tony had to turn around and go back to find Miri.

"Come along Miri," Mollie said impatiently. We have to move along—what are you doing?"

"This is Montro, Mollie," Miri said pointing down at the beast that was making all the noise. "He want's out of here."

"What are you talking about?" cried Tony. 'That's a dangerous wild animal. Now come along."

"No, he's not dangerous and if he doesn't get out of this hole he'll die. Can we help him?"

"How do you know he's not dangerous Miri?" Mollie asked sitting down on the log.

"He told me. He told me his name is Montro and he just wants to get out of here. He says he's been hoping you would help, but you just ignored him, is that true?"

"Well we don't speak his language, as it seems you do, so we didn't understand. Is he really friendly?"

"Oh, yes. Very friendly. He says if he can get out of here he may be able to help us too."

"All right Miri we'll help if we can although I don't know how."

"Are you crazy?" Tony whispered to Mollie. "That monster will eat us alive the minute he see's daylight."

"I think we should listen to Miri," Mollie said, "she's usually right."

"Montro thinks that if you can slip that tree you're using for a bridge down to him he can crawl out on it."

So they maneuvered the tree around until they could slip it down into the great hole and watched a huge furry animal with giant tusks crawl up and join them.

"I guess you know we just burnt our bridges," Tony said to Mollie pointing back to where the tree had been giving them an escape back out from where they had originally come in from. "We can never get that tree back up there."

"You're right, I hadn't thought of that. Well, we'll just have to move on."

And so they headed for the exit where they had seen the violent natives.

"Montro wants to know if you've seen the natives up the beach?" Miri offered as they carefully exited the tunnel.

"Yes we have," Mollie replied, "Does he know anything about them? Are they friendly?"

Miri talked to Montro for a few minutes and then turned to Mollie. "Not at all friendly. They are murderers and torturers. This is what he meant when he said he might be able to help us."

"How can he do that?"

"It's great sport for him. He chases them until they turn on him and then he runs away. He's much faster than they are. They kill his people if they can find one injured or old, but otherwise he has nothing to worry about."

"What does he have in mind then."

"They'll probably be just sitting down for dinner so he'll run through their camp scattering their fire and food all over them and run out the other side while we make off with one of their canoe's, but we mustn't be seen. It's got to appear as though he's the only one around."

"Sounds dangerous to me." Tony observes.

"He wants to help us out because we saved his life."

"O.k. he'd better go then it's starting to get dark."

"He wants to know if we are all ready then?"

"Yup, let's go."

So off Montro went running like a deer right through the natives camp scattering embers from their fire all over them and dancing about before taking off and out the other end of their camp. Screaming in rage the entire group leaped to their feet as soon as they realised what had happened and streaked off after Montro waving spears and shooting arrows wildly into the brush.

Mollie and the others took a quick look around to make sure there weren't any others left behind and then darted for the beach where the canoes were pulled up on the beach. The first one was to small for extended voyages, but the second seemed about the right size although a little large and they tried to push it into the water with no luck. It was too big and too far up on the beach to move. Just then they heard a weak call from behind them.

It was the man that was still tied to the tree calling for help. Tony immediately ran over and cut him loose thinking that he'd quickly disappear into the forest, but instead for a moment he just watched Mollie and the others trying to get the boat off the beach and then trotted over to them.

"You'll never do it that way, you'ld better let me help," and he ran over to where some log rollers were stacked and brought several back to the boat. "Here get these under the keel and it will roll easily."

The man was pretty week from having been tied to the tree for probably days, but with all of them pushing they quickly got the canoe into the water. Soon they were offshore and making good time using the paddles that had been on board. Unnoticed the native that had helped them get off the beach had climbed aboard too and now to the others surprise he spoke up.

"Keep in to the shore as close as possible. We'll be hidden by the trees that way."

"We can't do that," Mollie said. "We have to let our friend be able to see that we've got away. Then he can go join his friends."

"Yes you're right," the man said. "That is the right thing to do," and so they stayed offshore until they could see their friend safely away from his pursuers.

"How did you get aboard?" Tony said amazed.

"I stepped aboard with the rest of you. By the way where are you headed?"

"We're on a long voyage and I'm not sure you want to come along."

"No I don't," the man said. "If you'll just drop me off around this point I can swim ashore. I have business with my people on the other side of this island."

"You belong to the Heron group?" Mollie said surprised.

"You might say they belong to me. I am their chief."

"I thought Gondo was their chief."

"Gondo wants to be chief. That's why he had me captured and sent to the Amons. He's my brother. My name is Hercule, by the way. What do you know about the Herons?"

We were living with them until we fell into the chiefs disfavor. We had to escape to the other side. To the Amon's side."

"Ha, ha, ha," the man Hercule roared. "Gondo sent you away and you now bring me back to unseet him. Ha, ha, ha, that is a great laugh—a great joke on him. Well, in that case you must stay awhile with me. You have saved me and restored me to my rightfull plition. We'll have a great celebration!"

"You sound pretty confident you can depose your brother," Tony said questionably.

"Oh that's no problem, I'll be welcomed back. I am well loved here and my brother is despised. That's why he tried to kill me."

"You have a strange kind of brother."

"He's just a little intemperate. I'll have him under control in no time. Pull in here under these trees until it's safe to come out. That will be when I come back for you. It's getting dark now so it's a perfect time for me to slip through Gondo's guards. I'll have everything under control by morning and that's when I'll come for you," and he jumped off the boat as it slid up onto the sand and disappeared into the trees.

"He seems pretty sure of himself," Tony said sceptically.

"Well we'll wait and see. If his plan falls apart we can quickly get away from this position."

After a night's rest as the sun came up a joyous procession came singing down the beach. Hercule was in a kind of throne being carried by Gondo and some of his guards and Mollie wasn't sure if he was in charge or if Gondo was, but soon it was dear. Hercule was in charge having put to work his old enemy.

"It's all right now!" Hercule called. "Come along now, we are about to have a big luau and you are invited.

Almost the whole village had followed their new-old chief and were cheering and singing as they danced along. Mollie's old woman friend was there and Mollie walked up to her. "It looks like you're feeling better —" she said smiling.

"I should say so," the woman said triumphantly. "You see this is my husband," she said pointing to Hercule. "I thought he'd been killed by Gondo."

"I see now why Gondo was not your best friend."

"You see right. Come on, we will have a wonderful time." and they did.

It took two days just to recuperate from the party before Mollie and the others could think about moving on and when they did Hercule and his village piled their canoe full of food and water to last them about a month at sea and with garlands of flowers set them off.

"That is sort of funny how Gondo's actions caused his own downfall," Mollie said making conversation.

"Is that one of your miracles," Miri wanted to know.

"Not exactly, but close I guess.

"Enough of that," Tony said impatiently, "Let's plan our trip."

"Not much to plan," Mollie replied, "just follow this course and hope we get to where we're going."

"We'll get to where we're going all right. I hope its where we will want to be."

"True, and while we're at it we had better steer clear of any more islands. They seem to bring us bad luck."

"I'll second that motion," Tony said with satisfaction.

The next week they sailed in ideal weather avoiding anything that looked like an island when they ran into a squall that turned into a full force storm. For two days they were thrown about like snowflakes in a blizzard until they thought their canoe would tear apart. When it was over they realized that their boat was in need of serious repair and began looking for some hideaway where they could work.

To their left was a cloud under which was probably an island and they cautiously approached it. Keeping well off they examined it the best they could going around it twice. It was small and appeared to be uninhabited and so they landed their boat in a small cove and went to work.

The lashings that held the frame of the ama together were coming loose and they went into the forest in search of the correct vines to make new lashings with. Soon they found what they were looking for and began gathering together enough to finish the job when a vice from out of the bush startled them. "Well, well, what have we here? A vision, a hallucination? Maye I've eased something that hasn't agreed with me. You are not real, are you?"

Mollie had turned around and was now looking at a tall elderly man sturdy and fairly well shaven wearing clothes made of what looked like palm fronds. "We are real all right, but are you?" she asked in amazement at this sight. "We had no idea there was anyone on this island. How many of you are they?"

"Just me I'm happy to report. Where did you come from, I've seen no ship."

"We've come by canoe that's in need of repair," Mollie said. "Well be off just as soon as we're finished." She didn't want him to think other wise. There might be others to avoid.

"Oh, well, feel in no hurry. Stay as long as you like. I've had no company in—oh—thirty years I guess."

"Thirty years?" blurted Tony. "What are you talking about?" He was beginning to doubt everything this man was saying.

"Well that was the last time I talked to anyone. It was to the captain of the bad ship Rover. That was just before he had me put ashore here. To my great good fortune I might ad."

"You're telling us you've been on this island for thirty years."

"That's about it.

"Why were you set ashore? Did you mutiny?"

"You might say that. I did try to take over the ship for is own good. You see I was the first mate on the the pirate ship Rover, and the captain objected. I would have been keel hauled, but I had many friends on board and the captain thought this was a better idea."

A pirate ship you say?" Are you a pirate?"

"Was. Was a pirate. I am now a country gentleman."

"On your private Island" Tony said sarcastly.

"Exactly," the man said excitedly. "On my own island."

"You must be anxious to get off of you private island." Mollie said thinking he might want their canoe for himself.

"Not on your life," the man said emphatically. The only way I would leave is in a box. I've made a pact with my god and I intend to keep it."

"Why do you want to stay on this bit of rock for heavens sake?" Tony asked wondering why anyone would want to do that.

"You have said it. 'For heavens sake' is the reason. I had better explain. My name is John, by the way. They called me Big John on the Rover. You are looking at an evil man. A man capable of horrendous acts. I've killed many aman in my bad days. I wasn't always bad though. I grew up in a God fearing family until my mother and father died and I was left to fend for myself. That's when everything went wrong. I shipped out on what I thought was a whaler, but turned out to be the Rover, a well feared pirate ship. On that ship you did as you were told or you went over the side. Well, I learned and worked hard at murder and soon became her first mate. I was well liked by the crew and that's why I tried to take over the ship. I thought the crew wood be with me. I had had enough of that ship, but as often happens the captain got wind of my plans and tipped over my cart. And so here I am. That's why I've worked out something with my God. I will spend my life here by myself in Hadies and he will see what he can do to pardon my sins."

"Would you leave if you could? For instance on our boat?" Mollie wanted to be sure that he didn't have designs on stealing their boat.

"Your making me an offer?"

"Then you might?"

"As I said before, not on your life. I would burn the minute I stepped off this island."

They were then invited up to his 'Estate' atop his mountain which turned out to be several grass huts adorned with shells and wood carvings.

"Did you do these carvings?" Mollie said amazed at their beauty. John got up from where he was sitting, went to the door looked first to the left and then to the right and returned to his seat. "I must have. I don't see anyone else around do you?" and Mollie realized what a silly question she had raised.

"No, I guess not, but they're so beautiful."

"And you didn't think an old pirate could have accomplished that. I've had time to practice."

"Wait a minute," Tony said jumping up. You said your ship was the 'Rover?'"

"That's right why do you ask?"

"Does the name 'Henry' mean anything to you?"

"Sure, that was the name of our cabin boy. A good boy. I've often wondered what happened to him—say, why do you mention him?"

"Well, well, what a coincidence. We happen to know your Henry. We met him on the island where the Rover was wrecked. Your Rover I presume."

"The Rover wrecked? You're sure?"

"Oh yes. All the crew eventually killed themselves over the gold and Henry was the only one left."

"That's wonderful news!" John said. "The best I've had in—thirty years. What happened to Henry?"

"Oh, he's fine. He's found a home with some natives."

"Good. I'm glad to hear it."

They stayed the night with john and the next morning were back at work on their canoe. John was helping them and Miri did what she could and spent the rest of the time sitting on a rock overlooking the tide pools.

"I see you like my fish", John said walking up to see what Miri found so fascinating."

"They're so beautiful. I've never seen so many kinds."

"Every color of the rainbow. They live in the coral. I used to sit as you are doing and watch them by the hour. They have a world of their own."

That evening Miri seemed to be seriously thinking about something and not joining in the general conversation.

"What are you thinking about, Miri," Mollie finally asked her. "You haven't said a word for a long time."

"No, I've had a lot on my mind."

"And what might that be?" Mollie said smiling to herself as to what could be so important to a little girl.

"Well, I guess I'd better tell you," Miri said looking up and facing Mollie directly. "I don't think I'll be continuing on with you both. I'm going to stay here on this island for a little while."

"What do you mean by that?" Mollie said startled. You don't want to continue on with us. Is it something we've done?"

"No, "Miri said finally. It has nothing to do with you. And it's nothing I want or don't want. I believe it's what I must do."

"I think we had better talk about it, don't you?"

"If you want to, but it won't change things."

"Tell us what you are talking about Miri. We don't understand."

"I don't either, exactly. I just know that I'm not going to leave this island." Miri was sitting back slightly in shadow, but she seemed to be emitting a fain glow. An aurora. "I don't feel sad about it—except that I won't see you two for awhile. I feel a peace that I'm not familiar with."

"What do you mean you won't see us for awhile. If you stay here you won't ever see us again."

"I'm not so sure about that. Anyway I must stay here. For awhile anyway."

After that they went to bed. Just as Mollie was finally dosing off after thinking a long time about what Nollie had told them she jumped up at the sound of Mollie crying out in what sounded like joy.

"Gramma!" she cried "It's so beautiful. I know. I'm coming." And then she dropped her arms that had been outstretched and and she was quiet. John who had heard the commotion got up, walked over to Miri and closed her eyes that were still staring at the ceiling. "She's at piece now," he said crossing her arms in front of her.

"What do you mean?" Mollie wanted to know.

"She's gone to heaven." That must be what she meant when she said she couldn't be with you anymore. She somehow knew she was dying."

"But she hasn't been sick."

"No. I think God was aware that Miri, as young as she is, knew what she had to know and there was no need for her to spend any more time in this dreadful place. It's ironic isn't it. Here I am eighty years old and I still have much to learn. She has beaten me to heaven by seventy years.

"What are you talking about?" Tony asked thinking John had probably spent too much time in the hot sun.

"Don't you know, then I'll tell you. Miri is not the only one that will live forever. We all live forever—

"You're going to die soon john, you said so yourself."

—we all live forever," John continued ignoring Tony's interruption. It's simply a question where that will be. Miri already knew what was needed to know and was ready to move on. It usually takes us a lifetime to find the answer. It's a miracle."

"What's this thing that we 'all' have to know?" Tony asked derisively.

"Oh, that's for you to find out. That's why it takes so long. It's an individual thing, you see. The ultimate goal is universal, but how we get there is personal. For instance I am a murderer and an evil man. My trip must be far different than yours for me get to the same final spot. Some of us never figure it out and keep coming back to this godforsaken place."

"You don't like it here?"

"You children have much to learn. You are presumably going to live a long life and have many various experiences in that time. Many of them enjoyable. One day you too will have found the answer."

"What answer?" Tony insisted.

"Whether you move on or come back. But it's time for us now to do our duty. I am in possession of a fine rosewood box that I had been saving for my own exit, but now know will be perfect for Miri's casket. I'll prepare that while you two dig an adequate hole for Miri's last room under that the tallest tree on the island. That was to be my final spot," he said pointing to a tall tree but will be much more appropriate for Miri. Now let's get to work."

While Tony and Mollie dug the hole in reasonably soft sand John fitted Mollie's box with satin and gold lace that had presumably come from one of his previous adventures.

Then they lowered Miri into the last place she would ever know on this earth while John said a few words over her.

Before Mollie and Tony were to leave John showed them around his grounds. There were several out buildings that along with the wood carvings held piles of papers.

"What are these?"

"Those are the back issues of my newspaper."

"What do you mean newspaper. I'm sure you don't receive any newspapers here. "No, you're right. I don't receive any newspapers here I print them. 'The One Island News' I call it."

"What kind of news can you dig up here?" Tony wanted to know.

"Oh, you'ld be surprised. Nero, that's the blue fish Mollie was so interested in, gave birth to twins—that's unusual. Horace the senior turtle on the island died. Spike, the shark, broke his own speed record in the lagoon the other day, witnessed by several barracuda that were official timers. You'ld be surprised at all the news that's generated on this island. You just have to be attentive. I discovered how to make paper out of some native plant material and started

my newspaper as an avenue from which to print my poetry.
On this island I'm the poet laureate."

"May I see something?" Mollie asked seriously. She was
a budding poet herself.

"Here's one," John said pulling a sheet of paper out of
the pack.

> So here I sit a castaway
> on this lonely beach
> Hoping ships will pass my way
> but always out of reach
> I see a ship that's sailing on
> a ship far out to sea
> that far ship will soon be gone
> A ship I'll never see
> time for him is flying by
> his ship is running late
> my time here is running out
> and here it's I must wait
> a month goes by a year or two
> it seems I've lost the time.
> it matters little now to me
> (now what will rhyme with time)

"So, you're the poet laureate. Who is your competition?"

"Oh, Shelly, Wordsworth, —. You see I carry them with
me," and he pointed to a volume of classic poetry sitting on
top of a sheaf of papers.

"And you're the judge?"

"Why not? someone has to be. Maybe now you can help."

"All right, now let me see—yes, I agree, you are the winner. How's that?"

"Wonderful. I knew you had good sense."

"So this is what you do all day? Carve totems and write poetry?" Tony said looking around the compound.

"And do my serious work."

"And what would that be?" Tony asked a little skeptically. "You're going to have to work awfully hard aren't you to get back into the good graces of your god."

"No, good works don't redeem you. Working to please god is a waste of time. It's more simple than that. You only have to believe."

"That's what my mother says," Mollie joined in. "If you believe, God works everything else out for you and one day you will go to heaven."

"That's about it, little girl. My, you are wise for your size,(wise for your size. Might make a poem) And I've had more than enough time on this rock to know I need help in this world and I am now fully committed. In that way I am free to do my work."

"To please your god." Tony offered.

"Well, yes, in a way. We are all born with qualities and gifts that are unique to each individual. We are all different in that respect. No two of us are exactly alike and it pleases God when we use the gifts that he has given us. It took me a long time to find that out, but I finally came to my senses. Just because I'm on this island by myself doesn't mean I should give up. Simply to lie around and pick fruit is not what is expected of me so I do the best I can with what I've been given."

"And that is?"

"I write stories for children."

"That's what all these piles of paper are. Children's stories?"

"Precisely."

"Well, I don't know whether I should tell you this, but aren't you aware that there are no children here to read them."

"That's not the point. This is the gift I've been given and so this is what I do. You see it doesn't matter what you do or where you do it as long as you know what your gift is and it's pursued. If I were to go back to civilization this is what I would do and so I do it here."

"It seems to me you would be better off to go where children could read your stories."

"Possibly, but that would be another world and I would be another person so who knows what would come of that— say, I've just had a thought. If you two wouldn't mind, I will give you four of my stories to take with you. You will undoubtedly find children in your travels that would enjoy them. Maybe they will be published and then I will become famous. Just think of that. Someone might write a story about me, the mysterious hermit of hermit island. What do you say, will you do it?"

"Of course, but you must have hundreds of stories here. We can't take them all."

"No, just four. Sometime in the future you can send someone for the others. I of course won't be here. It will be a miracle if I last out the week, but I'll pack the stories up carefully and they will be here."

T wo days later Mollie and Tony were sailing out of the strange man's lagoon and as they turned they saw him at the top of his hill waving and they waved back and then they waved to the tall tree under which their friend Miri was now at piece.

"I suppose you knew, Mollie, that at first I didn't want to take Miri along with us. I didn't want to have to take care of her. Didn't want the responsibility. It turned out that she took care of us, didn't she?"

"Yes she did. It's kind of lonely without her."

"I know. I miss her not here talking to the fish."

"Well she's in a better lace now, you have to believe that."

For two days they sailed in a calm sea without much to talk and then to break the silence Mollie asked Tony what he was thinking about.

"Oh, I was just going over in my head what the old man said. That we all have a gift. Something that we are supposed to do with our lives. I guess we'll find out sometime what it is. I sure don't know now."

"Is there anything that interests you?"

"What you two were talking about. All that about God, heaven and Hades. I think I'd like to know more about it."

"I would too. Why don't we make a pact to work together on it when we reach someplace to live. If we find a place.?"

"O.k. It's a deal. Here, shake on it," and they did.

In a week their food ran out and they lived on what fish they could catch and in another week their water was running out there having been no rain and they began to worry.

"I think I've lost ten pounds," said Tony one morning, "If we don't find some land pretty soon we're goner's."

"Don't think about food. Think about the bountiful island that lies just over the horizon because there has to be one soon."

So they sailed on until they were hardly able to tend the sail, and then with little warning a whirlwind came spinning across the surface of the sea where they were drifting and before they knew what was happening it lifted the alma out of the water and almost turned them over before settling back down. During those moments of terror Mollie fell out of the canoe and into the water. As she surfaced she saw the boat only a few feet away and she wasn't worried because she'd fallen out before and tony had always helped her back in. But this time as she began swimming back to the boat Tony seemed unaware of her plight and kept sailing on with the canoe moving away faster than she could catch it. Stopping for a moment to catch her breath she noticed that there were two people in the boat that was now out of her reach. With her mouth open in amazement, which is not the thing to do in salt water she recognized herself still sitting in the stern where she always sat as the boat slowly sailed away.

Confused, Mollie didn't know exactly what was happening, but noticed that she was exhausted. There was a palm log with some fronds still attached nearby and she was able to crawl up on it where she closed he eyes wondering if this was to finally be her end. After just a few minutes on her raft she felt herself being jerked up into the air and onto the deck of a large boat.

"She's alive! She's alive! It's a miracle," someone was shouting and soon Mollie's father was bending over her. "Are you all right, Mollie? Are you really all right? This truly is a miracle. We had just turned around to head home when we spotted something in the water. I just can't believe it," and then he turned to some men that were nearby. "All right boys," he said, "let's get her below. She needs some rest." As they raised he up to carry her off she looked out over the stern of the fishing that had picked her up just in time to see an outrigger canoe heading for a large mountainous island that Mollie recognized as the big island of Hawaii. And then both the canoe and the island disappear into a bank of fog.

Mollie was only half conscious when they carried her off the fishing boat and back onto her island and it was another day of rest before she felt like talking to any one. When she was finally recuperated she approached her father who had knocked on her door and come into her room.

"What day is it to day," she asked him, "and what made you look for me so far north?"

"It's the fifth. You've been lost for two days," her father said, "and it wasn't all that far north. It was only a mile or two from where we had originally been searching for you."

"But I guess then you must have been originally looking for me almost to Hawaii."

"No, no. Of course not. We've never been more that ten miles away from this island. We knew that wave couldn't have swept you away any further that. You've probably been dreaming. Come into the living room now I have something to talk to you about."

'Dreaming?' Mollie wondered. 'Could I have been dreaming?' and she looked down at her finger where the gold ring still rested that she had retrieved from the gold hoard and she realized that it had not been a dream. 'I think not' she said to herself. 'I believe I've had some kind of an adventure.'

In the living room Mollie's father opened the conversation. "Mollie, I've got to fly back to the states on some business. You and your mother will stay here and I'll be back in about two weeks.

"When are you leaving?"

"In a couple of days."

Mollie went outside to get a little sunshine and sitting under a baryon tree she began to think and after about two hours she had decided on a plan. That is if her father agreed and she went back into the house.

"Father," she approached him. "Will you be making a stop in Hawaii?"

"Yes I'll have to stop there for just a few minutes. Why do you ask?"

"I wonder if I could go with you, as far as Hawaii. You could leave me there and I could stay with your friends until you picked me up on the way back."

"Oh no, I don't believe that's a good idea especially after what you've just been through."

"Oh, Please! This is really important to me and I may never have this opportunity again. At least think about it. I really want to do this."

"Well, I'll think about it, but don't get your hopes up."

The upshot of the matter was that after her her mother had talked it over with her father she was allowed to accompany him as far as Hawaii.

After settling in with the family friends of her fathers she set off for the museum where she had been earlier. The curator was not well aquatinted with the Wolmsly history but did find two historical volumes about the family.

"I don't know much about them myself," he said "except that they were well respected and liked by the locals. This volume" he said, handing Mollie a large book, "is an autobiography following much of their lives, and this," he said handing them a small pamphlet. "This was written by a news reporter soon after they had arrived. The missionaries had just set up a small newspaper on the island and it seems to have been an unusual incident. Have fun—oh and here is a volume that Tony Wolmsly wrote some time later, He swore it related their trip in reaching the islands, but seems too far fetched for it to be real. It seems to be some kind of children's adventure story."

Mollie first tackled the larger of the two books and was soon absorbed. It seemed that the children were adopted by some locals named Wolmsly and grew up officially using that name. Not being related by blood they eventually married each other and lived out their lives ministering to the natives and traveling among the islands.

This was all very interesting to Mollie, but she wanted to know more and turned to the small volume.

"Ah," she said to herself, "this is more like it." She was now into the original arrival of the two children. It seemed to be quite an event. When the canoe was discovered, there were two half starved children in it thought to be dead, but soon found to be alive. They were taken under the care of the Wolmsly's and later adopted by them. Nothing could be discovered as to how they were found to be on the island. They had obviously fallen off a ship at one time which they continued to deny relating instead some incredulous story of a long sea journey that included battles and adventure. First related by the boy it was then backed up by the girl that, but was assumed by the locals to be imagination caused by too much sun.

"Well, well," Mollie thought as she read the account. So it really had happened.

"If you are through with these I'll put them away now," the curator said when Mollie had put down the books.

"Yes, I've found what I wanted. Were there any other artifacts of their trip saved. Anything at all?"

"Well, their boat was beyond salvage, but there were a few things I believe that were retrieved. Let me see if I can find them. Ah, here they are," he said looking through some cabinets. "I remember now that these became a mystery. These carvings were obviously not carved by the children. The work is highly advanced. And these books, were of course not written by the children. Only a well educated person could have written them."

"Did the children have an explanation?"

"They referred back to their imagined adventure and no one could get anything else out of them."

"Are these all the books there are?"

"The children said there were hundreds more on some desert island with the writer. Nonsense of course. No more were ever found."

There were only three of the ancient books in the cabinet withering away and when the curator left the room for a moment Mollie found the cabinet door unlocked and she stealthily opened the door and place the fourth book on the shelf with the others. It looked a little out of place being in better condition. That was because it had been in Mollie's pocket since she had been rescued. She then slipped out of the museum and went home to where she was staying with her friends.

She was wondering why in the world she had been on that adventure in the first place and decided that the only answer was that she was there to help these people reach Hawaii safely. For a brief span of time she took the place of her own grandparent.

When Mollie's father came to pick her up for the flight home he asked her if she had found anything interesting about the Wolmsly's.

"Oh, yes. They were very interesting people. I'll tell you all about it on the way home. One thing I'll tell you now. We'll never be able to trace our history further back on that side of the family."

"Why is that?"

"Because our great grandparents were adopted. They came to this island as children and were adopted by a family named Wolmsly. If they ever knew their real names that information was eventually lost and they were known only as the Wolmly's. It's complicated and I'll tell you all about it on the plane."

"Oh, good, I want to hear all about it."

On the way home Mollie told her father all that she'd found out about their ancestors—all except of course her role in their early days. It was a little confusing. If she was for a time her own grandmother she would have had a traceable Maiden name, but then again if the Wolmslys were really her grandparents—Mollie finally gave it up.

"You say Tony later wrote a book for children about a fantastic journey by canoe across the pacific and that he always swore it as his own trip?" Mollie's father asked after he'd listened to Mollie's story.

"Yes that's right."

"Could that have possibly been true do you think?"

Mollie smiled to herself. "Theirs nothing that's impossible." she said noncommittally.

Mollie and her parents stayed another five years on the island and then moved back to the mainland United States where after college Mollie married a man that resembled her old friend Tony. As he was interested in the same things that Mollie cared about they spent the rest of their lives touring the world and writing travel books.

THE END

Printed in the United States
by Baker & Taylor Publisher Services